VANISHING POINT

By the same author

Cross Cut

Out of Time

Wake Us Tomorrow

Rivenland

VANISHING POINT

Lee Ellis

Time Link

First published 2012 by Time Link Publications
12 Warneford Gardens, Exmouth. EX8 4EN
timelink@btinternet.com

ISBN 978-0-9557928-5-4

A CIP catalogue record for this book is available from the British Library.

Cover design based on an original painting by Carole Ellis

Prepared and printed by:
York Publishing Services Ltd
64 Hallfield Road
Layerthorpe
York YO31 7ZQ

Tel: 01904 431213

Website: www.yps-publishing.co.uk

1

IF it hadn't been for the freak storm in September the body may have lain undiscovered for six months. It's unusual to shift the sand so far up the beach so early, but the wind has pushed it high against the rocks and wall, blowing it into deep piles, making the road impassable. A team has been assigned by the Council to clear the road, dig out the sand from the inlet with JCBs and deposit it further up the beach. They've been working for a couple of hours, gradually reaching the original beach level and have stopped for a break.

Jose sees it first. She was here early to catch the light on such a clear, bright morning, when there are fewer people about. She's been sketching up on the ridge, close to the beach huts and has a good view across the estuary and out to sea. Up to now she's not taken much notice of the men clearing the sand. It's been a wild couple of nights, the wind battering the sea wall and sending huge sprays of water high and wide. Then it whipped up the sand. It usually takes a couple of months of autumn wind lashing to gradually cover the far end of the promenade and the men set to work clearing it in November. This end usually escapes the worst, needing only a few shovelfuls re-deposited on the beach, but two stormy nights have done more than two months work. With cars ploughing through the sand mired road as if they were on safari and the beach carved with mounds and drifts, they'll be busy for a few days.

They've already cleared most of the road and have been levelling the beach, undoing nature's frantic sculpturing. The sudden, unaccustomed silence as they stop work jerks Jose's attention from the sea to the beach. She's almost finished her sketch of the rocks. Perhaps the JCB, its bucket half buried in the sand will make an unusual picture. She'll have to be quick, after the break the men will turn it around. She flicks over her pad and starts to draw. The men are sitting on the wall, munching on sandwiches and chattering. She'll take a little artistic licence and bring them in closer, contrasting with the machine. She sketches them rapidly and then looks back to the JCB, marking out its outlines with a few strokes. Her artist's eyes, vigilant for the slightest change of colour hover where something is lodged at the front end of the blade. The wind tossed sand is pristine in its yellow beige uniformity, but there's the hint of a darker hue – light orange, no – more pinky, even slightly brown, almost as if tanned. She screws her eyes. It could be the light of the rising sun, caught by the clouds. She peers again. No, definitely not sand, perhaps the shadow of the metal played at the edge, but the wrong shape for the outline is too irregular, like splayed, thin projections that could almost be...fingers. She gets up, drops her pad and runs to the road.

The men are returning to the JCB. She crosses the road, then stops at the beach wall. She looks again. Not just fingers, but an arm. A body right under the front of the JCB.

"Stop!" she shouts.

The men stare at her in bewilderment. She gets over the wall and runs awkwardly towards them. The sand is deep and soft and she sinks up to her ankles. She struggles to clamber along, thrusting out her arms as her unsteadiness increases and almost loses her balance. The men watch, mystified as she finds firmer ground and makes better progress.

"Don't start up again," she says breathlessly as she nears them.

"What's up?" says one man.

As she nears the JCB she sees more, a cuff and then, alarmingly, an arm. As she gazed across the beach from the ridge the wind blasted smoothness of the sand was the epitome of peace, albeit a transient one – the true calm after the storm. Now it's a granular shroud hiding violent reality beneath. She and the men reach the front of the JCB together. For a moment they all stand motionless, staring at the exposed fingers, the slightly tanned hand and the red sleeve. Then one man bends down, about to scrabble the loose sand away.

"No!" Jose barks, "Leave it alone. We must get the police."

The man instantly steps back as if the arm might suddenly jerk out and grab him. But Jose is just as nervous, her hand shaking as she fumbles in her bag for the phone and then stabbing the three numbers. The men stand transfixed as they wait for the police.

"Good job we took a break," one says, "Otherwise, might have..."

"Shut up," says another, "don't want to think about it."

Yet Jose is surprisingly calm. Her hand no longer shakes and several times reassures the men to 'be patient.' She stares at the protruding arm, artificially separated from its torso by the pervasive sand. It could be a bizarre holiday creation, a disembodied sand arm rather than a sandcastle. The feeling doesn't last, her nervousness returning when the police patrol car arrives. The sand is carefully removed to reveal the body of a young woman. By this time the shock of the discovery begins to take hold and she shivers though it's not unduly cold. She doesn't want to look at the body and her reluctance increases as the men recoil from it.

"Her face," one says, "Her face, it's..."

"What is it?" Jose says, making no move to get nearer.

"We didn't do that, did we?" the man says to his companion, "not with the JCB..."

"No," says the other and then, turning to the policeman, "that's not our doing."

The policemen pull them back and call for more senior back up.

"Best not look," the second man says, coming over to Jose," not very pretty."

The area is sealed off. Jose and the men sit on the beach wall. Jose wants to leave, but the policemen make them stay until the detectives arrive. They all make short statements. There's little to say. Her shivering increases and she's anxious to be away.

"Do you know her?" she asks the men.

All shake their heads, except one.

"Something familiar about her, but then...with the face... like that...can't really tell."

Two more cars appear. A youngish detective talks to the policemen. The JCB is carefully reversed. Then he looks at the body before conferring with his colleagues again. He looks across to Jose, then shakes his head. One of the policemen comes across and double checks her statement. She can go. They may wish to speak to her later, though it's unlikely. She pulls up her collar and returns to the ridge. She crosses the road almost in a stupor and retrieves her stool and materials.

She strides along the promenade quickly, glancing back only once to the grim scene on the beach, her legs pounding, her arms swinging, her eyes set on the clear outlines of the far side of the estuary, her mind numbed into emptiness. A few children play on the sand dunes, rolling towards the beach wall or sliding on boards as if they sledge on smooth winter snow rather than sand. The man at the ice cream kiosk is just opening up. Jose knows him well. He speaks to her. Something about the cool breeze from the river, glad to be rid of the storm, but a warm day it seems. She doesn't answer. He speaks again. She turns. What? Oh yes, so it is. He shrugs, carries on taking down his shutters. She walks on.

Eleven o'clock. There are more people near the inshore lifeboat station and the coastguard tower. A small queue is forming for the boat trip along the coast. They are still serving breakfast in the Estuary Café. The walk has done her good. She feels a little warmer. The smell from the café is inviting. She slows down, wondering whether to go in, but then reconsiders. Her stomach is not yet fully recovered. Besides it's a drink rather than food she needs. And company. She needs somebody sympathetic to listen to her. She rings Tanya.

"Will you be finishing at twelve?"

"Yes, should be, I was..."
"Can you meet me for lunch in the Warren?"
"I suppose so, but..."
"Good, see you there."
She rings off before Tanya thinks of an alternative. Tanya will come. She won't let her down.
She hovers at the loosely fenced eyesore on the opposite side of the road to the Plaza leisure centre. The area is intended as a new water sports centre, but it's been derelict for months. Demolition has been curiously retarded. Wind, rain and sporadic vandalism have made the building unsafe, while the mounds of old bricks and mortar litter the site. She crosses the road and skirts the green opposite the Plaza. It's a large, imposing building, always busy with a variety of events. More than usual cars are parked outside. She wonders about this for a moment, then walks further along the front, towards the clock tower and 'The Warren' pub.

If Jose had been in less shock she might have noticed the television company's vans parked at the back of the Plaza. Inside, bemused consternation is the prevailing mood and Jeremy Charlton, director of 'My Town. Your Town' is becoming more and more impatient. Several times the crew has assembled, disassembled and then reassembled equipment. Support participants have been getting distinctly tetchy.
"Should have started hours ago," his assistant keeps saying, irritatingly stating the obvious.
The bill for bacon butties, delivered almost continuously from the adjacent café keeps going up, not to mention beverages, some of which are starting to look distinctly alcoholic. Make up and costume and technicians exchange unhelpful ribaldries.
"Can't start without Punch."
"Or Judy more like."
Carina has not shown up. Frantic phone calls to every conceivable location and contacts have drawn a blank. In any case most have already arrived, which Jeremy finds additionally irritating. Her agent might be excusable, but

what possible reason is there for her accountant and latest male 'friend' to be here? He'll talk to Wendy. She should know Carina's whereabouts.

Wendy Arbon sits beside the open side door where she can chain smoke without causing undue pollution. Perched at her feet is a large glass ashtray, which she is steadily filling with dog ends.

"You shouldn't be doing that," he says.

"Technically, I'm outside," she replies, scraping her shoe along an imaginary boundary line.

"Should have been here by eight at the latest," he says. "She's never been late before."

"How do you know, do you follow her everywhere?"

"I *know* these things."

"When did you last see her?"

"A month ago."

"A month?"

"I'm her agent, not her bloody nursemaid."

"Might be better if you were. What are you doing here anyway?"

"I always like to see how the first of a new series is going."

"I didn't know that."

"That's because you're new. Reginald was directing last year. He was wonderful with Carina. *He* understood her."

"I can hardly understand her if she isn't here. Besides I've done a previous series with her."

"Yes, I'm aware of that," she says with a hint of disapproval.

Jeremy leaves her and mooches around, trying to ignore the mounting costs of so many staff hanging around unproductively. A self absorbed, slightly stooping man, around forty, approaches from the opposite direction. They almost bump into each other. Jeremy is intent on studied avoidance, but Harry Willard is troubled by a profound gloom.

"Watch where you're going, Harry," Jeremy bellows.

Harry blurts out a pathetic apology, though it's no more his fault than Jeremy's and grabs his glasses, which have slipped to the edge of his nose.

"Don't suppose you have any idea where Carina's got to?" Jeremy says aggressively.

Harry mumbles incoherently before sitting down to steady himself and retrieve his glasses, which have finally dropped to the floor. Jeremy sits beside him and stares expectantly. Harry cleans his glasses nervously and takes his time adjusting them back on his face. Jeremy continues to stare intimidatingly, his large, searching eyes, demanding the explanation Harry is incapable of providing.

"No, no, I can't...I haven't a clue...I need to talk to her...I was hoping maybe you could..."

"No good asking me, how should I know, I'm only the bloody director."

"Yes, of course, I see, yes."

"What are you here for anyway?"

"Papers," Harry says, fumbling in his briefcase, "Things I need to show her."

"Couldn't you do that in London?"

"Haven't seen her."

"Join the sodding club, Harry. Only when she does finally arrive, just give me the odd hour or so to get this programme recorded, it's all I ask, it's not unreasonable."

"Yes, yes, of course, I fully understand. It's just you see, this particular..."

Harry hunts in the case, his face pressed down almost into it as he rummages noisily. He surfaces with a paper, which he shakes nervously as if Jeremy should take it.

"Put it away, nothing to do with me," Jeremy says.

He pushes Harry's hand back into the case and gets up. He's seen someone more likely to know what's become of Carina. Dominic Mathers is unmistakable in his green jacket. At around thirty he's a little younger than Carina and a good ten years junior to Jeremy. He seems even younger still and to Jeremy is a boy inside a man's body, though he's unsure what part of a boy. Not his mind, he's too bright and streetwise and he speaks with apparent ease and a kind of rough charm that clearly appeals to Carina. He can't see what else attracts her, other than perhaps an obvious animal vigour. To Jeremy he's like a pet jackal, if such a thing is possible. That's it perhaps, that slouching condescension, it's really quite schoolboyish. He has all the arrogance of youth and moves like the snotty sneak in the playground.

Dominic arrived very early and introduced himself to Jeremy as Carina's 'very close friend.' They've not met before, though Jeremy has heard a great deal about Dominic and has seen him from afar. Several times in the morning, he's tried to speak, but Jeremy has successfully avoided him. Now Dominic stands by the door nearest to the bar, ever ready to put in his order as he leers over a couple of young women. Would he be doing that if Carina was around? Seeing Jeremy approach he quickly extricates himself and marches across with a jaunty air and a cheeky grin.

"Found her yet?" he says breezily.

"Does it look like it?" Jeremy scowls, "or maybe you've got her hidden somewhere."

"It's not me got things hidden away," Dominic replies sharply.

"What do you mean by that?"

"I've come looking, not hiding."

"Is that why you're here?"

"Could be."

"So you've not seen her?"

"Not for some time," Dominic says quietly, almost plaintively.

"Trouble between you?"

"We had a row, she stormed off."

"I see," Jeremy says, thinking Carina may have seen the light and come to her senses.

"No you don't. None of you do. It wasn't all me. She's not what she seems, you know."

"And what's that?"

"The nice presenter of 'My Town, Your Town,' all sugar and ribbons."

"Well, at the moment, nice or otherwise the programme hasn't got a presenter at all. She's disappeared."

Detective Chief Inspector Chris Stover watches Tom Allenby, the pathologist making his preliminary examination of the body. In his time Stover has seen many unpleasant deaths, but this is by far the worst.

"God, Chris, somebody really didn't like her. I'd say they've used a spade or some narrow, but heavy instrument on the face."

A young woman, about thirty five. Stoved in like badly butchered meat, the features are virtually unrecognisable beneath the layer of gore and congealed blood. The surrounding sand is heavily stained into a dark crimson. Her clothes are torn, in places seemingly deliberately ripped. These and the injuries to her face are not consistent with any accidental damage caused by the JCB. It seems someone was as anxious to mutilate her clothes as much as her face. If so, it's not entirely successful. Despite being ragged and grotesquely soiled, it's a good quality suit. The shoes too are very stylish and look correspondingly expensive. This is no ordinary wanderer on the beach.

"Was that how she was killed?" Stover says.

"No, this has been done after death, though not long after. Why ever it was done it wasn't necessary to..."

"So how was she killed?"

"I'll know for sure later, but my guess is a heavy blow to the back of the head. See, here..."

The pathologist points to a dull contusion in the skull.

"Are they always as welcoming in Darrasea?" he says.

"Can be a lively place on a Saturday night, but never seen anything like this. What sort of blunt instrument, not the spade?"

"A hammer, a metal bar..."

Stover scans the beach and the pebbles.

"A large stone or rock?"

"We'll know later when I've done a thorough examination, but it could be."

"And how long has she been dead?"

Allenby puckers his lips and grimaces.

"That too I can be more precise about later, but at this stage...maybe a couple of weeks."

"And she's not been moved?"

"Hard to say. I'll check for traces of anything unusual. Some sort of terrible argument that went wrong, I suppose."

"Why do you say that?"

Allenby spreads out his arms, gesturing widely around. "Such an open place, it was bound to be found quickly."

"It's taken two weeks and buried in quite deep sand."

"Not so deep two weeks ago."

"Yes, buried deeper by the storm, but at this time of the year the wind whips it up."

"Meaning it would lie undisturbed...?"

"At least until the Council come to shift the sand, which they wouldn't normally have done for another month. So this place isn't necessarily so open."

"If you know the area."

"Precisely."

"Well I'm all done for now. If you've everything you need, we'll take her away."

Stover turns to the sergeant, Amanda Barrow.

"Find anything?"

"Not yet, no sign of the murder weapon."

"Keep looking. What about documents?"

Amanda hands him a plastic wallet containing various items.

"Yes, we've got enough. We know who she is."

Jose descends the steps near the clock tower and walks along the beach, kicking the sand and pebbles. She soon reaches where the sand gives way to the new sea wall close to the slipway. It's as far as she can go, the western extremity of the sand, two miles from the rocks. She gazes across the estuary. Here the river Darra can be treacherous, the whirling, eddying water indicating the shallow channel and concealed sandbanks. The wide mouth of the river glistens in the sun, disturbed only by the ferry boat in mid channel. She watches it for a few minutes until it merges with the distant houses of Sumston on the far side. She can just discern a train, distantly miniscule against the hills as it runs up river, along the bank. Then she turns back towards the sea and the spindly grass knolls of Denzer, its empty jutting sandbar the haunt only of birds. The clouds hang like menacing drapes. The sun and slivers of blue sky peek between them, but there's a developing greyness. The relics of the storm might still bring rain and her agitation returns.

She takes the steps and returns to the promenade, pausing to stare again across the estuary, watching the gathering clouds, almost willing them to burst. The feeling passes, as does the threatened rain. But others too have noticed the deteriorating weather and have determined to take counter measures. A small boat, dissonantly called 'Monterey' is being steered towards a trailer, perched behind a four by four on the slipway. At first the inexperienced driver reverses too far, immersing the rear wheels and finds it difficult to advance on the wet and steep roadway. His friend, steering the boat, is as equally unsure, manoeuvring too far in one direction to line up correctly with the trailer. He turns back to reposition only to be loudly reminded by the returning ferry not to get too close. There's an exchange of waves. Grinning and good natured by the mini admiral piloting the little boat, rather more irritated from the captain of the ferry.

The man on the slipway pulls forward. On the edge of the trailer and partly immersed a shoeless third man calls and gesticulates to the boat with directions for a more accurate advance. A second time the boat comes in too tight and has to reverse again. Now he circles right round and comes in slower, making more careful, less fierce adjustments. Will he make it on his third attempt? The man on the trailer bellows. Jose watches transfixed. She has to wait until they successfully pull it in. This time he succeeds. The boat is attached to the trailer and the vehicle pulls forward on full throttle up the incline, making its way along the front in the direction she's just come. She almost expects them to stop, re-examine the boat and pull some unwholesome attachment from underneath or a grotesque stowaway from inside. Dreadful finds from the sea like the JCB's unwelcome discovery from the sand. She waits and watches until they're out of sight. They don't stop, they don't discover. One discovery today is enough.

'The Warren' is almost empty. Jose acknowledges the greeting of the couple of regulars at the bar, but deliberately takes a corner seat at the large table beside one of the windows. For a few moments she stares disconsolately into the garden before getting a drink. She's a little more communicative than she'd been with the ice cream man and exchanges a few words with the others on the freakishness of the wind and the rain. Then she resumes her position in the corner, nestling her medium white wine between quite severe gulps. Her composure returning, she gets another, though it's consumed less aggressively.

Tanya arrives.

"Have you heard the news?" she says, unfolding her long scarf and throwing it with an ostentatious flourish over another chair.

Jose assumes the scene at the rocks has already got around even faster than the town's usually rapid communications network.

"Your usual?" she says, studiously avoiding Tanya's remark.

"I don't know *anybody* who was expecting it."

Jose goes up to the bar. Tanya follows.

"They're recording her next programme in the Plaza...or well, part of it...I don't suppose it's all about Darrasea. They say..."

"Port and lemon and I'll have..."

"No, I'll have red wine, please."

"There were lots of cars outside the Plaza," Jose says, picking up the drinks and returning to the table, "so what's it all about?"

"Carina Fennell."

"What about her?"

"She's here in Darrasea, in the Plaza, making her programme."

Jose picks up the menu.

"You hungry?"

"You're not yourself, Jose, what did you want to talk about?"

Jose taps her pad and paint box.

"What you might call still life."

She briefly recounts her experience on the beach.

"Do they know who she is?" Tanya says.

"One of the men said she looked familiar, but I don't see how because they said her face wasn't really recognisable."

Tanya shudders.

"Don't suppose you'll want to paint anymore today."

Jose takes out her sketch pad and her one completed water colour. Tanya examines them admiringly. The four men and the JCB are at the corner of one sketch. The composition should pull the viewer to a boat out on the sea, but inevitably Tanya's eye is drawn to the figures. They are intended as minor fill-ins, but with her mind suitably prepared, they are grotesque beach fishermen, trawling the beach. She even peers at the stark lines of the JCB blade, though there's nothing, the sketch made long before the discovery of its grisly 'catch.' Conscious she's overly concentrating on the sketch, Tanya puts it down and picks up the water colour.

"You've got the light," she says reassuringly.

Jose grunts unbelievingly.

"No, you have, I like the greyness on the water and the soft shadows from the cliff."

"It's too dark. Maybe it should be. Perhaps I had a premonition of a dark, dark day," Jose says, lugubriously emphasising the last three words.

She laughs. Then Tanya laughs. The tension loosens.

"You're probably not very hungry," Tanya says, staring at her empty glass, "but I'll get more drinks."

"You must be joking. I'm starving!"

Over lunch Tanya does most of the talking. At thirty five, she's fourteen years younger than Jose. They met at an art class just after Jose moved to Darrasea. She still paints, but unable to devote as much time as Jose hasn't yet achieved the same success. She works part time as a hairdresser and like all good exponents of that profession, is a fount of local information. Each little titbit is prefaced with so and so 'came in today.' Jose listens desultorily, interjecting occasionally with mild interest or a rhetorical 'is that really so.' Her mind keeps lurching back to the beach. Tanya senses her disquiet and switches from her clientele's gossip.

"Isn't this the last day of the art exhibition?"

Jose is wrenched from her languid staring at the Edwardian prints around the room.

"Yes."

"Have you sold any pictures?"

"I don't know, I've not been in since the first day."

The Darrasea Art Society's annual exhibition is held in the first two weeks of September in the Edward Hall, a small public hall used for craft fairs and flea markets. It's only a short walk from the pub, along the front, close to the clock tower. As an exhibitor Jose is required to help for at least two sessions. She arranged these on the first day of the exhibition and hasn't returned since.

"Aren't you curious?" Tanya says, "you usually sell a couple."

"We'll have to go along later."

With its beachside location the exhibition is always well attended and has been a successful venue for Jose's paintings, her atmospheric seascapes and well observed pictures of the town appealing to locals and visitors alike. She could have easily popped in and checked if she'd made any sales, but after the dreadful disclosure at one end of the beach she was anxious to get to the other end as soon as possible. She hurried past the Edward Hall, ignoring the large banner advertising the exhibition.

This year's art society exhibition has been a rush for her. After four years as a member, she should be used to the procedures, but almost missed the deadlines both for submitting her entry form and later for the actual pictures. The one of course followed the other, but the form required titles and prices for sale. No problem normally, assuming she'd already painted the pictures! She was largely a victim of her own success elsewhere. While the date for the exhibition crept up, she'd made other sales and with other things intervening kept putting off getting on with their replacements. By the time the entry form had to be in she'd got no pictures. At least none she thought appropriate. She had pictures, but in previous exhibitions her local views had sold well and now she had none of those.

Panic set in when the deadline was a day away. There was no alternative. She had to submit the form before the pictures were painted! For the prices, she took last year's and added five per cent. That left the tricky issue of titles. They had to be sufficiently vague to allow for flexibility, but close enough for what was likely to be the finished version. She'd agonised for hours, coming up with ideas only to discard them, produce new ones and then dump them too. The clock was ticking. Eventually, she'd just put in four fairly anodyne titles – *Restful Haven, Waiting for the Tide, The Rocks, Sea and Sand*...how that last one resounds, reminding her of the beach and the water. The beach with its chilling discovery, the boat on the slipway, emerging from the water with...nothing...

With the titles done and her application delivered, she was left with a bare ten days to produce her four pictures. Plenty of time with determined application and a following wind...but... inevitably...other things intervened. So came 'presentation day' when the exhibits had to be handed in at the Edward Hall.

"You've always got your pictures through selection," Tanya says.

"Probably more through luck than ability," Jose replies.

"Don't do yourself down, it can't be easy convincing the selection panel of...how many is it...five?"

"Six."

"There you are then. Six people giving their approval, it must mean..."

"I find the whole process quite ridiculous. Five members volunteer to scrutinise the entries."

"What about the sixth?"

"The adjudicator, an outsider from another art society though how they *emerge* is shrouded in the mysterious deliberations of the committee."

"Even so, it means after very careful consideration..."

Jose laughs.

"Perfunctory and superficial. I sat in on the 'panel' last year. Pictures are viewed at lightning speed, literally put up for an instant decision. How they determine the final hangings I've no idea – some esoteric and unfathomable formula for allocating 'points.' It must be really humiliating for those not selected. I find the whole process distasteful."

"It's served you well, always selected."

"Yes, okay," Jose admits grudgingly and then, "but *despite* not because of those old farts that run the society!"

Tanya laughs. Then Jose laughs.

"We'll have another drink."

By its nature water colour painting is not for the ploddingly careful artist. The medium is unforgiving on all but those who can fuse speed with expression. That said, setting out to accomplish four good water colours in a single day is not good planning. Yet that was the objective to which Jose had condemned herself. The second deadline loomed up as suddenly and as threateningly as the first. Diverted by distractions she found herself with only two days before 'presentation.' Allowing for framing (she'd naturally run out of frames of the right size) it effectively left only one day.

Now she wondered whether some of the titles had been wisely chosen. *Waiting for the Tide* and *Sea and Sand* seemed utterly restricting. She might have been better with vague titles like *Sunset* or *Morning Peace* or such like. Of course she could be suitably expansive in her interpretation. *Sea and Sand* could be symbolic. Such idle thoughts had wasted the first hour of the day. Looking back now she shudders at the idea of such 'symbolism' for sand, the beach, can now only mean...

She'd got out around ten and walked up to the church. It was surprisingly busy with visitors coming and going. She started sketching, but soon realised that unless she was going to work into the night there wouldn't be time to both sketch and then paint all four pictures. Working in the evening had never worked. The fading light was not conducive to painting even if it was from a sketch. It could be psychological of course, depressed spirits rather than reduced light, but it really didn't matter. Either way it had never worked. Evening painting had to be ruled out. Even in the summer her best work had always been done before four in the afternoon.

So she'd abandoned the sketch and got to work with her brushes. Many of the visitors were intrigued to find an artist recording the church and, more importantly, themselves for posterity, but Jose hadn't time to give them much attention, let alone idly chat. Ordinarily she welcomed observers and for a day at the front always took a few completed pictures in case someone wanted to buy. Today was different. The only game was 'Beat the Clock.' Yet the picture was enhanced by a few figures at the church door. A few lingered and she could include more detail.

Finished by eleven, she packed her things and went down to the front. You had to work relatively quickly before the paint dried and it was a warm day so better not spend too much time examining the picture. If she wasn't satisfied, there were only two options. Discard it and start again or abandon that title. It wasn't perfect. She wasn't sure the shadow from the tower was quite right and neither was she comfortable with the shade of the leaves on the trees in the car park. But there wasn't time. She decided to keep it. The worst that could happen was rejection by the 'panel.'

"Is that awful woman Mary Stokes still on the committee?" Tanya says.

"Secretary now," Jose says.

"But she doesn't even *paint!*"

"Good God, since when has that been an impediment to running an art society!"

"You've never really fitted with the society people, have you?"

"Well you left."

"Yes, but that was different. I didn't have the time to paint anymore, so I might as well have saved the subscription."

"You ought to start painting again."

"Perhaps, one day, if I could get out of the rat race like you did."

"I always said I'd retire at fifty."

"You managed it a few years early."

"And have never regretted it, which is all the more reason why I can't be bothered wasting my time with the machinations of the society."

"Are the meetings just as tedious?"

"Worse, they're steadily getting more like a Darby and Joan club. I look forward to the day when the average age of members gets below eighty!"

As Jose made her way from the church she tried to work out how best to tackle the next phase of the task. Three pictures to be completed in just over four hours. She walked west to east along the promenade, towards rather than away from the rocks. That meant beginning at 'The Warren.' Then it came to her. One of the titles need not be such an impediment. Many times she'd sat in the pub's garden looking out over the estuary, so its seafront position made it a suitable candidate for *Waiting for the Tide*. With her back to the slipway and the marina, she could capture the sea wall, the sandbanks, the promenade and the pub. It was almost midday. The temptation to join everyone else for an early lunch was almost irresistible, but she hurried on, setting her stool and easel across the road.

The pub was getting busy, many strollers successfully netted by the 'specials' board at the back of the garden. The kitchen's inviting smell wafted across the road, but Jose was determined to resist, turning her face to the water and taking in deep breaths of counterbalancing sea air. Then she got started, promising herself a good lunch as soon as it was finished. That way she'd be quick and focused. A few 'watchers' in the garden gave her rather than the tide their attention, but it didn't matter. They were looking in the right direction and as at the church provided pleasing animation to the picture. Painting in more of them gave the title added impact, but she wondered whether it was getting too cluttered. Too many people could lessen the desired effect, distracting the eye away from the focal point, the distant clock tower. Too late, the sky and the sea worked well and the colours had merged. Too many people or no, it would have to do. If she fiddled it would be ruined. Overall it had worked, all the elements, water and sky, people, the receding road, the bustle of the pub, combined and contrasted. It would be the largest picture, reflected in the stab in the dark price, but it seemed the gamble had paid off. She gathered up her things and trundled across the road to reward herself with a good lunch.

"Was it always your plan to become a painter when you decided to retire?" Tanya says.

Jose laughs.

"It wasn't so much a *decision* as a pious hope! I was lucky to make enough money in those last few years to make it possible...just possible...to settle here and..."

"And sell your paintings."

"Not enough to earn a living, but it helps make life more comfortable."

The pub was crowded, but Jose lingered over an elongated lunch and savoured the atmosphere before venturing out again. Just over two hours remained. Productivity would have to increase if she was to meet the deadline. She walked to the clock tower and sat on the seawall. It's a favoured, popular spot, almost emblematic for the whole town, but oddly she'd never painted it before. The sky had cleared, the sun brilliantly radiating between the soft white clouds, reflected in the sparkled water. The beach was busy especially for September and the promenade thronged with jostling strollers. It had to be the place for *Sea and Sand* and from her perch on the wall she worked quickly, oblivious to the gawping by-passers and curious children. If she'd brought a cache of pictures she might well have done a good trade, but that must be for another, more leisurely day when not furiously splashing on paint and wielding her brush so intensely. A few souls sat on the benches beside the flag poles around the clock tower. Together with the flags fluttering in the gentle breeze their full colours contrasted with the softer tones of sea, sand and sky.

"But you've hit on the right approach," Tanya says, "Your views are so well done, they always sell well."

"What do you mean...*views?*" Jose says.

"Well, you know, when you stick to what you do best. I would always know one of your pictures without being told and they must appeal to other people too."

"Really, in what way?"

"It's the colours, there's a warmth people can bond with."

"Bond?"

"Yes, it's really good...a winning method."

"You make it sound like a recipe, as if I paint to a prescription," Jose says, a little irritated at what she takes to be an implied criticism that she may be too 'formulaic.'

"I didn't mean that," Tanya says, trying to retrieve her inadvertent reproof.

"In any case you've not seen the pictures I put into the exhibition. You could have seen them on the first night, but you didn't come."

"You remember, I had a problem that night, I was a bit rushed."

Jose remembers. Tanya had a minor emergency. She was as rushed as Jose was, finishing the final picture at the front. There was hardly time for the paint to dry, let alone make any last minute adjustments. Packing up this third time was so rapid she felt like the door to door salesman snapping his case on his brushes and moving on to the next pitch. It was a longish walk to the rocks, but it was the one title that gave least opportunity for modification. By now it was three o'clock. Her intention had been to paint the large outcrop, partly covered at high tide, known as the 'Venture Rocks.' A ship of that name had been wrecked out in the Channel in the 1830s. The survivors had been brought ashore near the rocks and from then on the name had attached to them.

She walked onto the dunes, put down her stool and laid out her box on the sand. It was a good position, high enough to capture the broad sweep of the beach and the rocks, but after a few minutes she screwed up the paper with a curt 'rubbish.' The water had run badly, the sky would look more like a draining board of dirty dishwater if she continued, but something else bugged her. Something was missing. There were a few people on the beach, but they were too far from the rocks, including them would distract the eye. Artistic licence could bring them closer, but she remained uneasy and stared for a few moments at the blank paper. She felt uncomfortable. There were several motor caravans parked at this end of the promenade, some of them quite old including one battered, but colourfully painted old VW. It was a remnant from another time, very 1960s, though such vehicles are not uncommon on the Devon coast. There was no one in it, though there were people at the other vehicles, sitting on their chairs, staring out to sea or enjoying the sun. Suddenly she felt uncomfortable. Yet this hadn't bothered her at the clock tower or the pub when there were even more people. She looked back to the beach. There was something else, though she wasn't sure whether it was of something there or something not there. Ten past three. She had to make a decision quickly. Either do it again and not let the water run this time or give up and move on. No, these are the *wrong* rocks. She retrieved her things and returned to the road, scurrying quickly past the vehicles and their occupants.

She walked to the end of the promenade, beyond the dunes to the end of the beach, two miles from the slipway and 'The Warren.' There were few people there. She walked further, stopping at the red streaked cliffs. It was an odd feeling. She saw no one, yet she could hear people behind her and if she turned would see the reassuring expanding yellowness, where the river finally met the Channel, the far hills, the soft scudding clouds, the glinting sea and all the people. The same spot, two directions, two utterly different pictures. If she'd turned she could paint such a magnificent picture. But it couldn't be called *'The Rocks.'*

She didn't turn. It would be pointless. The uneasiness she'd felt on the dunes near the Venture Rocks returned. Again it was the people that concerned her. There they were too close. They could watch her and she'd felt intimidated even though no one approached. Now, with her back to them, they weren't close *enough*. Whatever she painted wouldn't convey the reality of the place. A narrowing end, yet with a turn of the head, a different perspective, vast and open.

She worked quickly, partly because of her impending deadline, but also because of her growing unease. She was lucky. The water didn't run, the tones were excellent, the sand, the rocks, the sky, everything went well. But this would not be a picture to sell. She'd made a mistake. The title had hemmed her in. There were the rocks, accurately depicted in their rugged grandeur, but without the people she'd shunned at the dunes they were empty. They were lifeless. The picture was completed in less than ten minutes. It needed no changes, it was complete, but she was glad to get away. All was done. She'd complied with the deadline with her deadest picture.

"Have you made any sketches in here lately?" Tanya says, "It's quite busy. You could always knock off a few. Start sketching me, someone's bound to be interested."

Jose knows Tanya is only half serious, but she doesn't rebuke her, taking it as genuine commendation.

"Not today," she says, "I'm not in the mood."

"Of course not," Tanya says, suddenly remembering Jose's unfortunate experience on the beach, "You're probably still upset."

"More out of practice, I've not sold a picture in here for months."

In the past Jose has done a lot of sketching in the pub. It's good for business and the landlord encourages her particularly in the summer. But Jose has neglected it lately, concentrating on the same sequence of paintings, which delayed her submissions to the exhibition. Some of the snootier elements in the art society look down on pub sketching, but that doesn't bother Jose. Not all sketches are successful. Not everyone wants to buy, but many do and it's a useful supplement to her income. Tanya's right. She should return to it.

Jose eases up again. The afternoon passes swiftly, enjoyably by, though Tanya's understated chiding she should take more seriously. Perhaps some paintings are too tied to a preconceived formula with an eye on easy sales. Tanya is gently telling her not to abandon her true gifts for ephemeral success, not let her art become an assembly line. The money isn't that good anyway and the most carefully laid plans aren't always the best. What of her four paintings for the exhibition? Impetuously conceived and dashed off hastily, but maybe the better for that. How well have they done. Have they sold?

"I'd like to see your pictures," Tanya says.

"You want to go to the exhibition?"

"Before it closes."

Five thirty. They have an hour and a half.

"I wasn't going to bother until the morning," Jose says, "but..."

"I'm sure you'll have sold them all."

Jose is also curious to know and on an income per time expended basis those four pictures will be the most successful she's ever painted. The exhibition is still busy with many visitors. They make their way past the hanging panels.

"Pictures sold have a red sticker," Jose says as they squeeze through the crush.

Tanya feverishly studies the catalogue while Jose cranes over shoulders to find her own pictures. She's forgotten where they were hung. They scour the first room to no avail.

"They must be in the rear room," Jose says.

"Yes, I have them," Tanya says.

Jose checks the numbers and they go to the second room. It's less crowded and they can move around more freely. Tanya mutters the numbers beside the paintings, then stops.

"81, that's yours," she checks the catalogue, "yes, *Restless Haven*."

She stands back admiringly at Jose's picture of the church, then studies the pictures on either side before checking the catalogue again.

"Number 79 and 80 on this side...104 and 127 that side, but I can't find 82. 83 and 84, that's *The Rocks* and *Sea and Sand*. What does it mean?"

Jose is examining the other pictures beside her own.

"82 is *'Waiting for the Tide'*. I remember it was here. This is a replacement from the reserve. It probably means it's been sold to someone out of the area. It's not encouraged, but if people need to be away they're allowed to take the pictures before the end of the exhibition."

Tanya claps her hands excitedly.

"You see, I said you'd sell."

"Only one," Jose says, a little disappointed.

"There's over an hour yet. You'll sell the other three," Tanya says, refusing to be put down, "What about *Waiting for the Tide*? Can we find out?"

Mary Stokes, the society secretary is sitting at a table in the other room, writing in a large ledger type book. Jose recognises the sales record and goes across.

"Oh, hallo Jose, not seen much of you here," Mary says with undisguised censure.

"I undertook my supervisory duties very early."

"Even so I thought you might have visited us a few times."

"I've been very busy."

Mary makes a noise, somewhere between a sniff and a sneeze and delicately dabs her nose with a handkerchief.

"One of my pictures is not on display," Jose says, "Has it been sold?"

"I shall have to check." Mary sighs noisily.

She flicks over the pages, running her pencil down the columns of the book. She continues, stopping several times and then makes a note.

"Ah," she says, suddenly jerking back in her seat and closing the book, "there's something we were going to tell you..."

Jose waits expectantly. At first Mary says nothing, smoothing her hands on the table and not looking directly at Jose.

"We?" Jose says.

Mary looks up.

"Robert and I."

"Robert Darley, the treasurer?"

"Yes, you see...you're quite right your painting has been sold...which is a wonderful achievement of which you should be rightly proud, but...Robert was going to explain...later on...but I suppose now you're here...I could..."

"What's happened?"

"As you know if a purchaser is out of the area they can take their paintings before the end of the exhibition. It's not all that common, often people are still around and can wait, but there are occasions...anyway in this case the purchaser was out of the area. I have to say it was a very respectable person, there was no reason to be in any doubt...it's never happened before..."

Mary stops and looks down, reluctant to go on. She checks the notes she made from the book.

"I'm afraid there's a problem with the picture...er (she looks at her notes again)...*Waiting for the Tide*...it's...the cheque's bounced."

For a few seconds Jose is silent. Mary looks blankly, desperately trying to find something more to say, but nothing remotely positive enters her mind and she too is silent. Then, the initial shock partially digested, Jose explodes.

"You've allowed one of my pictures to be taken away to a complete stranger...no, I correct myself, to a fraudster..."

"We weren't to know," Mary says meekly.

"Oh yes, you did. I've consistently been telling you this procedure is unsound. Why didn't you insist on cash?"

"It would be rather a lot of money for somebody to be carrying around."

"That's their problem. Cash or no picture, haven't I said that before?"

"It is the normal procedure."

"Your procedure, not mine!"

"When you submit your pictures, you do accept..."

"I accept nothing...except what you will be paying me."

"I don't understand."

"You will of course, be making full payment to me, the society will be absorbing the loss."

"Well, that's what we need to discuss. The treasurer will..."

"There's nothing to discuss!"

By now several people have gathered close to the table and are standing rather embarrassedly listening to the developing scene while trying to appear as though they're not. Things are getting out of hand. Mary knows other members of the 'committee' are in the building and looks round anxiously for reinforcements.

"So get the treasurer and I'll have my cheque," Jose says.

"Can we talk about this later," Mary says.

"No, we can't."

Then Mary sees Robert Darley, the society treasurer and beckons him across. He sees Jose in high dudgeon and to Mary's discomfort, moves alarmingly slowly.

Staying in the other room, Tanya has been watching from a distance. As it unfolds more people are diverted from the pictures to the confrontation. As Darley arrives, with his broad, insincere smile, almost all eyes are focused on the drama around the table. Tanya finds those watching, with their raised eyebrows, open mouths and mischievous smirks as interesting as the main participants, but then sees one person still studying Jose's picture. If the 'old farts' of the society had described what they imagined to be the least likely visitor to their exhibition, it is she. A young woman, about twenty, quite tall, slim with dark hair, badly or eccentrically cut, depending on your point of view, fairly long, clean, but untidy. Her large, round eyes, apparently unfocused as they gyrate slowly, though really moving more in a searching motion. Her lips full, the lower one extended a little beyond the upper, creating a petulant expression. Her mouth seems to be never quite shut. She has a small stud in each side of her nose. She's dressed in a long purple jumper, extending over her buttocks, giving her a distinctly unfeminine shapelessness.

She continues to stare intently at *Restful Haven* and cocks her head slightly as if to catch the light or study some detail more carefully. She gets closer, her lips almost touching the picture and then draws back, blinks a couple of times as if refocusing and absorbing the whole picture. Then she steps back and points at the picture with her outstretched, quivering right arm. As if she knows instinctively something unpleasant might soon happen, Tanya steps closer. Seeing her, the woman turns to her.

"She's there, can you see her?"

Tanya glances at the picture. There are a few figures outside the church, but they are indistinct, included to enhance the composition rather than portray any specific individual.

"She's moving!" the woman shouts, attracting the attention of several other people.

"Who?" Tanya says, "who do you see?"

"She's stopped now, not moving, but she's still there. What's she doing here?"

She grabs the edge of the picture. Tanya pulls her hand away and she steps back slightly, but then turns to the picture again.

"There, she's moving again, it is her!"

She shouts so loudly the group at the table turn, many drawn back into the room. Seeing her touch the picture Jose also comes across. Mary Stokes, Robert Darley and other committee members follow, concerned some awful vandalism is about to take place. The woman shouts again.

“There she is, Carina Fennell, right there at the church!”

Several dozen people stand mystified and alarmed. Many, including the artist, stare unbelievingly at the picture, but none see what she sees. She looks around the room as they get closer.

“Don’t you see...there...she’s going away now...but it is her...Carina...it is Carina Fennell...can’t you see her?”

She stares into the bemused, incredulous faces for a few moments, then turns with a shriek, barging through them and out of the hall. Mary Stokes and Robert Darley suddenly turn to Jose as if the artist is somehow vicariously responsible for the incident.

“I don’t know her,” Jose says angrily, sensing this unspoken accusation.

The group gradually disperses. It’s almost seven o’clock. Lucy Bendrill, the president of the society, flanked by Mary Stokes and Robert Darley makes a few closing remarks, following which the exhibition will close. A reporter from the local paper scribbles as she speaks, but Tanya notices him looking across to Jose. He’s witnessed both the young woman’s peculiar outburst and Jose’s skirmish with the society officers. As soon as the speech is over he’s bound to come across and want to talk to her. Making an excuse about ‘avoiding the crush at the end’ she steers Jose towards the door so they’re able to slip away quickly.

“Why are you in such a hurry?” Jose says.

“Dinner’s on me,” Tanya says, “if we’re quick we can get to Gianni’s before this lot turf out.”

With this she leads the puzzled Jose up the hill to ‘Gianni’s,’ Italian restaurant. Over a good meal and a couple of bottles of wine they forget about most of the evening’s events although ‘the strange girl’ as Jose calls her, periodically returns to the conversation.

“What was she on about?”

“Drugs,” Tanya says with an emphatic finality that she doesn’t believe.

“But why all that talk about Carina Fennell?” Jose says doubtfully.

“With her being in town it’s the topic of the moment.”

Jose is still unconvinced and Tanya changes the subject. Jose temporarily forgets her contretemps about the bounced cheque, but the following morning she's at Edward Hall by nine o'clock. It's the time for the collection of all the unsold pictures and she's determined to revisit the issue.

Robert Darley has arrived early and the front door is already open. Jose steps in. She can hear his voice. Other people arrive and they walk in together. None of the unsold pictures have been removed from the panels. This is unusual. Robert is on his mobile phone. Mary Stokes is with him. Jose goes up to her.

"Not yet made a start?" she says aggressively.

Mary doesn't answer at first. Robert comes off the phone.

"They're sending someone round," he says.

"What are you talking about?" Jose says, "Who's coming round?"

"The police."

Mary turns to Jose.

"When we arrived we found a broken window in the back room. There's been a break in during the night."

Jose glances toward the rear room, expecting to see dishevelled furniture and empty panels.

"But it looks alright," she says.

"That's what's odd," Richard says, "only one thing seems to be missing, your picture, *Restful Haven*."

2

CHRIS Stover's day starts with a grim duty. They've found a number of documents on the body, but there has to be a formal identification. Carina Fennell had no known relatives. Yesterday he contacted her agent's address in London.

"Carina Fennell's in Darrasea."

"Yes...I know. Can I speak to her agent?"

"Wendy Arbon's in Darrasea too. They're making the first of the new series of 'Your Town My Town."

Chris gets the details. They are all at the Plaza. Filming should be well under way. Except Chris knows it probably isn't and when he arrives some of the technicians are beginning to pack up. He speaks to the hall manager first.

"How long will they be here?"

"At least three days. That's what they've booked, but they've not started yet because..."

"Yes...I know."

He finds Jeremy Charlton and Wendy Arbon together in heated discussion.

"Can't waste another bloody day just hanging around," Jeremy is saying.

Wendy shakes her head dejectedly.

"I think we should wait just a little longer."

Chris introduces himself.

"God, what's this?" Jeremy says, "One bloody disaster after another, I can't take much more. Something's happened to Carina, what is it?"

"I can't say at the moment," Chris says, "Will you be remaining the rest of the day?"

"Well that depends on what you've got to say. Without Carina..."

"If you don't mind sir, I would like everybody to remain in the hall."

"Everybody? I can't speak for Dominic Mathers and Harry Willard, they're not my staff."

"If you could pass the word."

"But they'll need to know, what do I tell them?"

"It'll be clearer later."

Then Chris speaks to Wendy before taking her to the mortuary.

"We have reason to believe it's her."

He mentions how the body, especially the face has been disfigured.

"We do need to be sure, though I'll understand if you'd rather not."

She's not deterred, though chatters all the way, asking where and when the body was found. He can't tell her, but she persists. Nervousness fuels her gabbling. Will she cope with the shock? When they arrive he tries to prepare her. It really is bad. No, she's alright. How many times before has he heard that until the sheet is removed and...this time it's even worse. Utter silence, then the hands to the face, eyes closed, then opened again, have to make sure, a soft whimper and then she turns away. Yes, it's her. That is Carina Fennell.

"I'll take you back to the Plaza," he says.

"I'd rather not, perhaps...if you could drop me off outside... a short distance away."

He's reluctant. He's already despatched officers. They'll ensure everyone remains. She should be there. But, it's been quite a shock, better perhaps to talk to her alone. At least for now.

"As you wish. You've known her for long?"

"Twelve years or so, almost since she started out."

"When did you last see her?"

"A couple of weeks ago."

"Were there any problems in her life?"

"None that I knew."

"No one who would have wanted to do her harm."

She hesitates.

"That's a hard question. People in the limelight, no matter how popular they are, there's always somebody they upset. It's the nature of the work. But this...to kill her...and...in such a way..."

Her voice crackles and breaks up. She wipes a tear from her face.

"I'm sorry. She was more than a client, a friend, it's such a shock."

"It's quite understandable."

They drive back to Darrasea in silence. He enters the town at the marina and turns into the front near the slipway, deliberately avoiding the Venture rocks.

"Anywhere here," she says.

He stops the car on the promenade close to the clock tower.

"Are you sure you'll be alright on your own?"

"I'd rather be alone for a while. You'll be telling the others?"

"Of course. Are you up to a few questions?"

She has a hand on the car door, but releases it.

"Yes, I'm okay."

"Tell me about her programme?"

"Have you watched it?"

"Only occasionally."

"It was originally scheduled for a six week run and here we are, what eight years later and still going stro...it was going strong. Like all good ideas, it's very simple. Ordinary towns, ordinary people and the extraordinary stories they can often tell. Of course, it's much more than that. The strength of the programme is Carina. It's her unique blend of old fashioned star quality and such a winning way with everybody. Carina can talk to a duke or a dustman in the space of a few minutes and make both feel she speaks *their* language, as if she's one of them. It's a very rare gift. Then there's the team behind her. There's a wonderful spirit in every production. Naturally it's led to other programmes, film work, books and so on."

"Making her a very wealthy woman."

"Yes, but she's remained the same person."

"That must be a very difficult thing to do," he says sceptically.

"Not if you're a very unusual person. The programme has never lost it's solid base in ordinary people's lives."

"Some of the stories have been very remarkable."

"You said you've not watched it much?"

"It's often talked about."

"Will there be an announcement...about Carina?"

"There'll be a press conference later this afternoon."

"Is that all?"

"Yes, for now."

She gets out.

"...and finally a bizarre story from Darrasea tonight. On the last day of the annual art society exhibition, a visitor disturbed the normally sedate event when she claimed a figure in one of the paintings was moving! She kept on saying it and at one point grabbed the picture before being stopped. She fled from the exhibition, shouting she could see Carina Fennell in the picture! The famous television personality is known to be in the town though no one has seen her and certainly no one at the exhibition recognised her in the picture. And now for the weather, it will..."

Richard Tanner, reporter on the 'Darrasea Advertiser' is returning from the Edward Hall when he hears the newsflash on his car radio. Somebody in the exhibition must have tipped off 'Darra Sound' and by now virtually everybody will have heard it. Assigned to recording the predictable speech by the art society president he'd gone with no especial enthusiasm. He'd done it last year and the year before. Lucy Bendrill's words had hardly varied. He could have written up the piece in the office without bothering to turn up at all. Fortunately he'd resisted the temptation, otherwise he would have missed the really interesting events of the evening.

Hovering near Mary Stokes' table ready to catch Lucy he'd seen Jose approach and heard every word of the skirmish over the bounced cheque. Then he'd heard the young woman's outburst and carefully noted down her every word. He'd wanted to catch both her and Jose, but one had fled and the other evaded him. Neither Mary Stokes nor Richard Darley wanted to talk either. The first saying it was 'a private matter,' the second that it was 'a storm in a teacup.' He'd scoured the front, but couldn't find the others.

His editor also hears the radio report and is keen to make it the lead for the week.

"Have you written it up?" he says first thing in the morning.

"As much as I can," Richard says, handing over the copy.

The editor peruses it quickly.

"Alright as far as it goes, but we need first hand comments. Find that girl. We go to press this afternoon and need more for the story."

"What if I can't find her?"

"Then we'll have to run with what we've got."

Richard's quest to find either of the vociferous women isn't successful. Jose is not at her flat in a block on the hill, overlooking the sea. He's sure the other is local and asks in every pub and café in town, but draws a blank. Then on a hunch he speaks to the familiar bearded figure in the centre. He's always there with his dog outside the shops. Today he's selling the 'Big Issue.'

"Sounds like Kelly," he says when Richard describes her, "She'll be at the front."

Unfortunately he can't be any more specific. Starting at the Venture rocks Richard paces the front from one end to the other. It's been a warm summer and many of the regulars who frequent the shelters and seats are still around. Some won't talk, not sure he really is a reporter and even if he is, suspicious of his motives. A few, girding their plastic bags and sleeping bags closer, affect not to know whom he seeks, though Richard knows they are lying. The mysterious young woman must be known to some of the dossers and might be one herself. Then as he reaches the clock tower, a dishevelled character emerges from one of the covered benches, rolling a cigarette so thin it bursts into flames when he lights it.

"Have you seen Kelly," Richard says.

The young man turns to him with narrow, penetrating eyes.

"Who wants to know?"

"I just want to talk to her, I'm from the local paper."

"What's she done?"

"Nothing to get her into trouble."

"She's not around."

"Has she left?"

"No, just not around."

Richard starts to walk away.

"Is there money in it?"

"Depends," Richard says, scenting he's getting warm, "There could be."

"I could give her a message."

Richard hands his card.

"She don't use phones, where you gonna be?"

Richard glances over the road to the 'Warren.' It's almost lunchtime.

"I'll be in the pub."

Chris Stover watches Wendy until she turns the corner. He stares out over the estuary. The sun flickers between the clouds, sending streaks of light onto the far hills. A train hoots in the distance and then appears, seemingly sliding south like a worm beside the coast. Barred from the crime scene by the rocks the Council workmen have resumed their sand shifting at this end of the beach. It's colder than yesterday and they keep their coats buttoned up. The place is still busy, people strolling along the promenade, plenty on the beach though most keep moving. A few intrepid kite boarders skim along the water, catching the wind and the waves. A tranquil scene, an ordinary day in an ordinary resort, except Darrasea isn't so ordinary now.

He drives back to the crime scene and wanders along the sand. With this end of the beach taped off and so many people denied access, a lot of talking will be going on. Darrasea is that sort of place. Everybody knows everybody else or wants to. It'll give the local paper a lot more to fill its pages than society meetings and school prizegivings! A lively, talkative place, but not used to murders on the beach. Not good for tourism. Then again, it might well be. They say the population goes up ten thousand with the summer influx. Ghouls are always attracted and with such a famous woman by how many more will it be swelled now?

But why here? Tom Allenby wasn't sure whether she'd been killed here or not. A fairly good place to put the body. Without the storm the sand would have been undisturbed for a few weeks, but it's open. The murderer might have been seen, unless she was moved at night. Only need to move her at all if she was murdered somewhere even more conspicuous. In which case how well was it planned? An argument that went wrong? Tom said the murder weapon could have been a large stone or a rock. Tempers are frayed. Someone picks up a large stone. So what would they be arguing about? Time to investigate the background of the delectable Carina Fennell. She doesn't look very attractive now, poor woman. Everybody knows her. The beaming face, for years the universal warm hearted woman at the forefront of family friendly television. Her programme 'Your Town, My Town' is immensely popular.

He returns to the production company in the Plaza. It's quieter than before. Most sit around, a few dulled conversations, even the technicians have ceased clearing up. Everyone turns as he enters. It's as if they know. Jeremy comes across. Get it over with quickly. He tells Jeremy. His colour drains.

"My God, what do we do?"

Is he concerned for the welfare of his staff or the sudden end of the programme?

"No one is to leave," Stover says, "We'll have to question everyone."

"You're absolutely sure it's her?"

"Wendy Arbon has identified the body."

"She's not here?"

"No, understandably she was very upset. It's not a pretty sight. I've already spoken to her."

There's a rumble of apprehensive chatter in the hall.

"Time to tell them?" Jeremy says.

Before Stover can respond, Jeremy claps his hands and steps forward. The hall is immediately silent.

"Can I have your attention everyone? As you can see, the police are here and they've brought bad, indeed tragic news."

Stopping abruptly he turns to an irritated Stover, who feels suddenly upstaged as if another actor has stolen his opening lines.

"Ladies and gentlemen, yesterday a body of a young woman was discovered on the beach. We are now sure it is Carina Fennell and we are treating her death as murder."

A deep, drawn out groan sears through the hall as stunned groups huddle with shaking heads and hands over mouths. It's as Wendy said. The collective shock is deep and palpable. Stover's sergeant has already arranged one corner of the hall with a number of tables and chairs for interviews. Pausing only slightly as the assembled company struggles to take in the disastrous news Stover makes his next announcement.

"I know this is a difficult time for you all, but as part of our initial enquiries I must ask you to remain in this room for the time being. We'll need to take statements from everyone. Hopefully this will not take too long, but I would appreciate your cooperation and patience."

He turns to sergeant Barrow.

"Got a full list, Amanda?"

"Everybody's here," she says, passing him a sheet of names, "I've arranged them into groups. I thought you might like to question this lot yourself."

He nods as she points to four names.

"I've already seen Wendy Arbon. I'll start with the director. Let's get going."

Apart from bewailing his own difficulties now that 'Carina's no longer with us' Jeremy contributes no more than the others. He's not seen her for weeks, was totally bemused by her disappearance and has no idea who would want to kill her. Stover moves on to Dominic. He's shaking and at first finds it very difficult to answer any questions.

"It's been a very great shock," he dribbles out.

Stover waits patiently.

"I'll be alright in a bit."

"'Course you will," Stover says.

Dominic occasionally looks across at Stover, gauging the reaction perhaps or even hoping the interview might be postponed. It takes a few moments, but eventually he stops his snivelling. Stover immediately challenges Dominic's very presence.

"You're not directly involved in the programme, are you?"

"What you might call essential moral support, looking after her subsidiary needs so to speak."

"Was she in need of support, she seems to have been a very strong person?"

"Indeed so, but however strong you are you can always be made stronger. I like to think I've made a small, but valuable contribution to her success. Anyway what you see is not always the real person."

"And what sort of person was she?"

"Dynamic, absolutely dynamic. I've never met anyone with so much sparkle and verve. She electrified everyone around her. It was like being in the presence of a fantastic source of energy. She was so...alive..."

He stops abruptly.

"You've known her long?"

"About a year."

"A serious relationship?"

Dominic hesitates.

"That would have been up to Carina."

"You have no feelings?"

"It's not that I don't have feelings. You didn't know Carina, I was never entirely sure of her. A very attractive woman, she could easily choose."

"Then you were a lucky man?"

Dominic grimaces, then curls his lips in what might almost be a smile only to harden them again.

"There have been many relationships and even..."

"Other relationships at the same time?"

"I'm not saying...I had no reason...no, I didn't know."

"But you suspected?"

"It crossed my mind occasionally."

"Recently?"

"The last couple of weeks when I couldn't raise her...I wondered."

"Any idea who else she might have been seeing?"

"No one I could be sure of."

"Anyone you couldn't be sure of?"

Another hesitation.

"No," he says at last.

"What about you. How did you feel about potential rivals, you were angry?"

Dominic turns furiously.

"No! Not that angry. I didn't kill her."

Stover asks about Dominic's movements two weeks ago. He becomes detached, almost cold. His replies are vague and imprecise. He was mainly in London and didn't go out much except to try and track down Carina. He has alibis for some days, but not all.

"What do you do yourself, Mr. Mathers?"

"Do, what do you mean?"

"Apart from hanging around the making of television programmes you're not actually involved in."

Dominic's calmness goes.

"I don't hang around as you put it."

"What do you do when you're not here?"

"This and that."

"Would it be true to say that you're very dependent on Carina Fennell and I don't mean emotionally."

"It's difficult being dependent on someone when you don't see them for two weeks and don't know where they are."

"Any disagreements between you?"

"Nothing serious."

"Do you know any reason why she would come to Darrasea two weeks before the programme was due to start production? Something or somebody she was trying to escape from perhaps?"

"No idea."

There's much about Dominic Stover finds distasteful without being able to pinpoint it exactly. It could be his peculiarly mixed reaction of apparent devastation and almost clinical calm. It could be his gold digging tendency. It could be the hidden smirk that never quite appears. It could be he's not telling everything he knows. Amanda comes up after he's finished with him.

"Made a few enquiries in London. Carina withdrew a considerable quantity of money out of her account a few weeks ago. It hasn't reappeared anywhere else."

"How much?"

"Over five thousand and then another two thousand two days later. The next day was the last time she was seen alive."

"Even wealthy people don't usually carry around that kind of cash. Why would she want so much?"

"Blackmail?"

"Possibly. I'll see what her accountant has to say."

Harry Willard displays much more than his forty years. His eyes heavy, the lids weighed down so much he finds it difficult to keep them open. His cheeks are pale, untidy wisps of hair hang over his forehead, which he keeps brushing aside and his lips quiver slightly at the edges. His tenseness has notched up considerably since learning of Carina's murder. Unlike Dominic, he shows this by his silence and has to be prodded into answering.

"Did you know her well?" Stover says.

Harry doesn't respond immediately, his sad eyes opening a little more as he looks across blankly.

"Yes," he says at last, "I suppose I did. Ten years or more."

"You were her accountant."

"Oh much more, I was her financial advisor, but I like to think I was a friend. Someone always willing to give advice."

"You advised on accountancy matters?"

“Of course, but much more. She had extensive financial interests.”

“She was a wealthy woman.”

“Indeed.”

“Was she in the habit of carrying large sums of money around with her?”

Harry looks bewildered. Stover explains the large withdrawals. Harry seems shocked.

“I’d no idea, but though I gave my advice freely, she didn’t always take it.”

Asked about Carina’s ‘extensive financial interests,’ Harry trots out a catalogue of wide and varied investments.

“You managed these for her?”

“In the main.”

“Not them all?”

Harry grimaces.

“There were a few she preferred to manage herself and there were some...”

He stops. Stover prompts him.

“It’s just...I was beginning...just lately, some of the investments ...I wondered if I really knew about them all.”

“What makes you think she had other investments?”

Harry hesitates, half smiles nervously and wrings his hands slightly.

“Just...just a feeling.”

“These large withdrawals. Why would she want the money? Did she have financial problems?“

Another hesitation, then he says, “No, I’ve no reason to believe she had.”

“So far as you know.”

“I would have known.”

“Even though you’ve just said she may have had investments of which you were not aware?”

Jolted from his somnolence Harry explodes.

“It’s not the same!”

He regrets it immediately, apologises for his ‘unnecessary forthrightness,’ then speaks very softly.

“You see, she was in so many ways a truly golden girl.”

Wendy wanders along the front. She's not yet full realised the dreadful event even though Carina's battered and deformed face keeps staring back at her. She looks to the sand and the sea and the sky, desperately trying to ward off the recent memory, but the mangled features shimmer in the waves, leer through the clouds and are drawn in the lines on the beach. She'd expected to be shocked, almost geared herself up, but was utterly unprepared for what she found. It wasn't the face she'd admired for so long. That's what she must tell herself. She wanted to go back to the Plaza and face the others, but what would she have said when they asked about Carina? She hears the chatter from the 'The Warren.' Strangers in there, they won't know. It'll be better. It'll stop her thinking.

She gets a drink and looks for a seat. There's a table near the window. Two women are at the next table.

"It was on the radio last night, " Tanya says.

"Didn't listen to the radio," Jose grunts, "too tired, went to bed."

"All about that strange girl who was shouting at your picture, saying she saw Carina Fennell and how she moved and..."

"Very convenient for Mary Stokes and Richard Darley. While everybody was busy listening to that stupid idiot they sloped off out of my way."

"You could have gone back and argued with them."

"How could I do that after you'd whisked me out the door?"

"Yes, well," Tanya says, lowering her voice and leaning forward over the table, "I was getting you away from the reporter."

"What reporter?"

Tanya grabs Jose's arm and pulls her closer to the table.

"Shush! We don't want everybody to know. He was there. I'm sure he heard every word between you and them. He was writing it down and then again when the girl started crying out."

"Oh my God! That caps it all. Not just losing money for a picture I'm going to be plastered all over the local rag."

"Could be worse."

"What do you mean?"

"They say there's no such thing as bad publicity, you might sell more paintings."

Jose laughs.

"Oh yes, the Van Gogh of the Devon coast, discovered at last!"

"Don't mock, these things have a way of turning back around."

"Never mind about drumming up future business. At the moment I'm more concerned to get paid for the pictures I've already sold before thinking about those not yet painted. That damned woman yapping on about 'the normal procedure.' I'll give her normal procedure. And as for that good for nothing treasurer, running away when the flak starts. If he doesn't give me my money there'll be hell to pay at the next meeting."

"You don't go to the meetings."

"I'll go to the next one. I'll be the star turn!"

"It'll be too late by then."

"Not if I get my money back."

"But what if you don't?"

"They wouldn't dare."

"I'm not so sure. You know how pedantic they can be. You've said yourself they make up rules when they're not needed to make life more complicated than it needs to be."

"Even so..."

"You knew the risks, we haven't got facilities for guarantees, Mrs. Pearsall," Tanya says, mimicking Mary Stokes.

"Oh yes and they'll say the same about the picture that's stolen. It'll be my fault. You knew the risks, we don't take any responsibility. What about the building...?"

"But is that down to the society?"

"It is if they've not checked it before they leave. I wouldn't be surprised with all the fuss last night the windows were never closed properly."

"I suppose they could have been distracted."

"No excuse."

"No, but they'll wriggle out of it."

"So what do I do?"

"Strike while the iron's hot. Go after the bounced cheque, surely they have an address?"

"Should be in the sales book."

"Have you seen it?"

"Checked it this morning."

Richard Tanner is at the bar, imbibing his pint, awaiting his pasty and chips. He's known in the 'Warren.' One of the regulars sits opposite at his usual place, leaning against the wall.

"Got it on the radio. You lot gonna cover it?"

"We always cover it," Richard says, guessing he's probably referring to the incident at the Edward Hall.

"So we'll read all about it in the Advertiser?"

Richard glances at the clock. The deadline's past. The paper will have gone to press with his story without any interviews.

"Yes, you'll read all about it."

"What did Jose Pearsall say?"

"Who?"

"The artist, surely you've spoken to her?"

"She left so quickly, didn't catch her last night."

A glass is lifted and a little finger flicked in the direction of one of the tables by the window.

"She's over there."

Richard's pasty and chips arrives. Balancing these with his glass he negotiates his way across the crowded room. The pub has filled up and there are not many places to sit. A woman is at the next table to Jose and Tanya. She glances nervously as he eases into the vacant chair beside her.

"Then you can follow it up," Tanya says, "Is it far?"

Jose scrutinises a crumpled paper in her bag.

"Not that far, Yaverton."

Richard leans over, "Jose Pearsall?"

Jose looks at him quizzically.

"I'd like to talk to you about last night."

Turning away from him, Tanya mouths 'reporter.'

"The young woman who took such an interest in your painting, do you know her?"

"Where are you from?" Jose says.

Richard introduces himself.

"I was there, I heard what she said."

"Then you don't need me to tell you."

"Why do you think she was so sure she saw Carina Fennell in your painting? You know she's come to Darrasea?"

"I heard."

"Did you see her when you painted the church?"

"If I had I'd've put her there, wouldn't I? Did you see her in the picture?"

"No."

"Sure? You looked at it carefully?"

"I did."

"She's just a nutter then, isn't she, this girl?"

"Even so, she said..."

"In any case I was painting the church, not Carina Fennell."

"I was just wondering if there was anything special about the picture, something you included perhaps..."

"We're never going to know now, are we?"

"I don't follow?"

"Well it's gone, hasn't it? *Restful Haven* was nicked last night from the exhibition."

Richard gets out his notebook. Tanya shakes her head.

"How did this happen?"

"You may well ask. I arrived this morning to pick up my unsold picture to be told it had gone in the night."

"How was it taken, was it a burglary?"

"That's something you'll have to put to the officers of the society, I'm just an artist."

"It's very unfortunate."

"It certainly is. I say my unsold picture, but then of course there's the one that sold, but for which I haven't got the money, due to their negligence."

There's a briefly shocked silence across the table. The woman next to Richard is also listening now. Then Richard recovers.

"Whose negligence?"

Gesticulating on the table with her fingers and raising her eyebrows frantically, Tanya tries to forestall Jose, but to no effect.

"I've already told you, the secretary and treasurer and the committee of the art society."

"So, you're saying they are responsible for the loss of your picture?"

"Both pictures, *Restful Haven* stolen because of their laxity, *Waiting for the Tide* effectively stolen by fraud because of their administrative failures."

"That's a very serious allegation."

Tanya intervenes, leaning in front of Jose and smiling broadly, but nervously towards Richard.

"What Jose means is that..."

"What I mean," Jose says, elbowing Tanya aside, "is that their crass stupidity has deprived me of two paintings."

"Of course you can't quote this," Tanya says, "Jose is speaking off the record."

Richard smiles mischievously.

"I shall deny she said it," Tanya says.

"You forget I was there last night," he says, "I heard the argument you had with Mary Stokes."

"Not an argument," Tanya says, "just a firm difference of opinion."

"Very firm," Jose interjects.

Richard switches tack.

"The painting that girl shouted at, *Restful Haven*, there must have been something she saw, something perhaps you included without realising its significance, though now we won't know..."

"I know what I painted," Jose snaps.

"And we all heard what she described," Richard ripostes, "Do you know Carina Fennell?"

"No I don't know her, I've hardly even heard of the woman."

"Then why did she see her in the picture?"

"You'll have to ask her that."

"Can you explain why she said Carina was moving, was it because of the way you painted her?"

"I've told you I didn't paint her."

"Perhaps there's a connection between the church and Carina Fennell?" Richard persists.

"I neither know nor care. My only interest at the moment is the recovery of my pictures."

"Do you have any idea who might have stolen *Restful Haven?*"

"Of course I don't. If I did I would be after them now. But it's different with *Waiting for the Tide*. I can go after that one."

"This is the picture with the bounced cheque?"

"Precisely. They're not getting away with that. The money or the picture, but not both."

"What are you going to do?"

"I know where they are. I'm going to get my picture back!"

"Very interesting, thank you very much," Richard says before quickly finishing off the last of his lunch.

"Do you think that was wise?" Tanya says after he's left.

"Don't care," Jose says.

"That's his headline, 'I'm going to get my picture back.' It's an even bigger story now."

"It was your idea."

"It wasn't my idea to tell everybody. Quite apart from drawing attention to yourself, you've alerted the people in Yaverton who have your picture."

"I'll be there before it comes out. In any case the paper will be too busy following up Carina Fennell."

While Tanya has tried to keep her voice down Jose has been gradually raising hers and Wendy, sitting at the next table has overheard almost everything. It seems she can't escape Carina even temporarily, however hard she tries. Talk of the pictures intrigues her.

"You put too much reliance on Carina Fennell," Tanya says, "The story of her in town is just a passing thing. This is much more juicy and..."

"Well I've said it now!"

Jose glares at Tanya. The talk of Carina is too much for Wendy. She thought she could escape, get away from the world she orbits, but she can't for it's in her head and she's carried it into the pub. That's why they talk about her. They can't escape either! She may not be able to face them in the Plaza, but she has to tell someone about Carina.

"You're wrong I'm afraid," she says, "Carina Fennell won't be a passing thing."

Tanya and Jose turn to her.

"I'm sorry, I couldn't help overhearing. I do hope you've not compromised yourself with that reporter – I know from experience it's an easy thing to do – but you're probably right, the paper will be more interested in Carina. The news will be out this afternoon so there's no reason why you shouldn't know now. My name is Wendy Arbon, I'm Carina Fennell's agent, the nearest she has to a family, I suppose. I've just identified her body."

Wendy feels better as she explains. She's tearful again, but it's a release. Her instinct was right. She can talk to these two and they understand. She leaves out the gory detail and they don't ask.

"Fame lasts such a short a time and quickly passes," Tanya says, "but not usually so suddenly, so violently taken away."

"Yes," Wendy says sadly, "A showy suit of clothes we put on and take off, but in this case... someone else took off."

They are silent. She wipes her eye and apologises. They ask if there's anything they can do.

"Tell me about the picture," she says, "someone saw Carina?"

Hardly pausing for breath afraid Jose might suddenly interpose, Tanya quickly relates last night's events. But Jose listens calmly even when Wendy asks lots of questions, saying how amazing it is, where is the strange girl and 'there must be some kind of connection.'

"That's what the reporter kept saying," Jose says.

"It's just in that silly girl's head," Tanya says, not wanting Jose provoked into a further explosion.

Wendy takes the hint and talks about the bounced cheque.

"Are you really going after it?"

"I have to recover my painting," Jose says.

"You have the address in Yaverton?"

"Oh yes, I checked it out this morning."

"Yaverton's what, forty miles away?"

"I'll go tomorrow."

Tanya offers to come too even though it means taking time off work, but Jose refuses.

"It could be a little hazardous. If there's going to be trouble it'll be of my making. Only I should take the risks."

Tanya reluctantly accepts, but reminds Jose of their recent conversation.

"But don't do anything stupid, it's not always wise to say exactly what you think."

"Action not words," Jose replies, adding in response to Tanya's reproving look "Wise action, of course."

After Wendy leaves Tanya says, "She's very interested in your bounced cheque and where the picture is."

Stover and his team have completed their initial interviews at the Plaza. Jeremy leads away any not required for further interview with a final melodramatic farewell.

"We are the remnants of a remarkable people. We will remember these times, treasuring them forever in our hearts."

Stover looks on dubiously. He's sure Jeremy's sorrow is driven by irritation if not anger rather than mourning, but this isn't so with all. There are few dry eyes as the dejected and miserable band shuffles out to load the vans. Others are told not to leave either Darrasea or London without advising the police. This includes Jeremy, Harry, Dominic and Wendy. Now Stover has to prepare for the press conference.

"Anymore from London?" he says to Amanda.

"Neighbours haven't seen her for a couple of weeks."

"In big cities people often never see each other at all," he says gloomily, "It might be difficult to get a precise last sighting."

"Two weeks and two days ago," she says, "They saw her regularly or at least heard her up to that time. Carina was quite the party girl. Often came in very late and not very quiet. Usually accompanied by noisy friends. Then there were frequent parties at her own place."

"Not popular with the neighbours?"

"Mixed views. Some didn't mind her lifestyle, live and let live, said it didn't interfere with them. Others didn't like the noise."

"Anyone she'd recently quarrelled with or had a grudge against her?"

"They didn't really know them. No one in particular stood out."

"What about friend Mathers?"

"Sometimes he was there, sometimes he wasn't."

"Not exactly the love of her life then?"

"Doesn't really seem anybody was."

"A good time girl, eh?"

"Well, yes and no. One neighbour across the road, the only one who seems to have exchanged more than a few words with Carina was less critical. She says she sometimes thought Carina was quite a sad person."

"In what way?"

"Despite all the visitors, Carina seemed alone, surrounded by lots of acquaintances, but no real friends."

"Was this based on anything Carina said herself?"

"Partly. She always had to be asked about her so called friends, never volunteered information and when asked always spoke about 'the group' or 'them' as if they had no individual personalities."

"But still no one who might do her harm."

"It was more they were irrelevant."

"That fits with what Harry Willard said. He mostly talked about money, but his view of Carina seemed softer, more thoughtful. He called her the 'golden girl."

"Did he know her when she was very young?"

"I don't think so. Why?"

"Because Carina used to live in Darrasea. I was talking to one of the waitresses in the bar. She recognised her from school. Said she was very surprised to see her."

"Did she know her well?"

"No, she was a few years younger and only remembers her by sight. The waitress was about eleven at the time and she believes Carina was sixteen."

"But surely she'd've known she was coming?"

"Apparently not. She didn't connect Carina with the girl at school. I've checked the school records. There was a Carina *Armstrong*. It seems Fennell is her mother's maiden name."

"Interesting."

"Isn't it? The waitress doesn't remember seeing Carina Armstrong after her first year in the secondary school and believes she left the area."

"Do we know anymore, relatives in the area?"

"It seems not."

"Follow it up. There might be something in this local connection. Strange she changed her name."

"As if she wanted to put the place behind her."

"We also need to follow up all we can about Willard and pretty boy Dominic Mathers."

Amanda laughs.

"Something funny?" Stover says.

"Dominic as a pretty boy."

"Oh excuse me, he just strikes me as a man likely to be attractive to women, but of course..."

"Oh yes, I suppose in a *pretty* way, but not my type."

"Obviously he was Carina's."

"Maybe."

"But surely...?"

"Oh I'm sure she thought him attractive, but how much is a different matter."

"I'm not with you."

"Carina Fennell was successful in so many ways, wealth, fame, reputation, possessions...perhaps that's how he was important to her. A pretty thing like a work of art, an expensive painting perhaps. It's just a feeling. I may be wrong, but I wonder whether she was parading him almost as a trophy."

That evening, after leaving Tanya, Jose walks up to the lifeboat station and looks west across the estuary and the long sweep towards the slipway. The five colour spectrum of the promenade lights in their gold and red, yellow, blue and green twinkle against the white faced hotels and the clock tower. Further along the shrouded lights of the 'Warren' glint through the trees. Even at ten o'clock people stroll along the front. A few on the beach walk their dogs. She hears the faint hum from the pub. The white waves slurp onto the beach. It's a peaceful night, warm but cloudy, hardly a star, presaging the morning rain.

She sits on a bench and watches the sliver of moon winking between the clouds, casting intermittent yellow splintered shafts, rippling across the leather like dark greyness of the water. In the stillness she listens to the water on the sand. From the faint lights of Sumston she can make out the outline of the hills and shore and the bobbing boats in the river. It's a scene to be savoured, but the clouds thicken and soon the struggling moon will be masked and the spectacle lost. Not seen again until another night like it returns. If ever the same night is exactly repeated for every moment is unique. For isn't that what painting is truly about? Capturing the unrepeatable composition of light and shape and feeling? She waits until the cloud finally encloses the moon and the blackness of the night descends over the river.

To capture that fleeting, magical, charged evening before the dancing light, the bobbing water, the soft breezy air in the elemental confluence of land and water are gone. That would be a truly great picture, but how to do it? Memory will trick her. A high quality camera with very fast film might record such a magnificent night. Could an authentic atmospheric picture be reconstructed from such a lasting, accurate reminder? Surely snapping with a camera only produces a painted photograph, the artist fabricating a fakery? But how 'authentic' is any painting? It's not photos that undermine the picture, but the artist's 'licence,' her individual 'interpretation' so beloved of pompous critics. So how 'real' is any painting?

The welcoming, warming exuberance of the 'Warren' entices her again, but she walks on to the slipway, then right around the marina, looking down at the boats and in at the trendy town houses.

"Never painted here," she thinks, "perhaps I should. Plenty of money to buy views."

By the time she gets back to the promenade she thinks better of it. That would make her even more of a hack, churning out pretty things for pretty people. Further away from reality, whatever that is. The best artists seize the essence of a scene, parcel up the senses, transferring them to the viewers so they feel them too. Is that what the strange girl 'saw' in her painting, grasping the feeling of the moment, seeing what was *really* there? Was Carina Fennell at the church that day, two weeks ago, just before she was murdered?

Next morning the soft drizzle, drifting over the hills follows Jose east, petering out just before she reaches Yaverton. It suits her mood, subdued but determined. She smiles to herself as she remembers Tanya's final words.

"Wise, quick, silent and unheard."

She's not told Tanya, but she wants to do this alone.

She listens to a recording of the previous afternoon's news conference on the radio. Stover is measured and precise, with far less detail than Wendy, sparing the public the worst of Carina's horrific injuries.

"Carina Fennell was attacked with sustained ferocity."

Responding to questions he said they 'retained an open mind' and called for potential witnesses who may have seen Carina around the town a couple of weeks ago to come forward. It reminds Jose of the stolen painting and the strange young girl who 'saw' Carina. Had Jose also seen her, subconsciously inserting her in the picture, a hidden image, capable of being uncovered by someone with special gifts? Ridiculous.

She reaches the edge of town and checks the name and address. Mrs. M. Hyde, 85 Lawson Road. It's not difficult to find and within ten minutes she's at the end of a row of neat semi-detached houses. She stops, with a twinge of nervousness she's not felt before. All the predictable doubts come to mind. Better to have put it in the hands of a professional debt collector, but that would be expensive and effectively negate the project. Perhaps she should have written first, giving the recalcitrant a chance to redeem herself. After all, it could be a genuine mistake. Giving them plenty of warning. No, the element of surprise is essential.

She parks near number 85. Tidy front garden, a well maintained house, nothing unusual, very ordinary and respectable looking She goes to the door, rehearsing for the umpteenth time the alternative versions of what she'll say. The quiet approach, are you Mrs. Hyde, you know when you visited Darrasea, I'm sure this is a mistake, however... or a more aggressive attack, what have you done with my painting, screw up the worthless cheque and demand proper payment...

After several rings of the bell she gets no answer and returns to the car. She waits and watches for a couple of hours. Someone must come to the house, but if Mrs. Hyde is working? She gets hungry. Lack of planning. She should have brought sandwiches and a flask. Tanya would have organised it. She's too impetuous, too quick to sally forth. Maybe this isn't such a good idea. If Mrs. Hyde is out at work there's little point waiting and starving. Launching an attack on an empty stomach isn't sensible.

She's goes into town, finds a café to sustain both mind and body, but can't settle and finishes the meal quickly, intent on returning to the house. She parks a little way off, able to see the front door, but not close enough to invite attention. There's little coming and going until the local primary school turns out and for twenty minutes the road is filled with children's skipping and chattering. Then it empties. A relatively quiet time, a half hour window until people start returning from work. There's been no activity in the houses on either side of 85. Jose is restless. She tries the doorbell again, more for appearances than any realistic chance of finding someone in and then, glancing furtively to either side, walks to the back, peering in windows. It all looks very ordinary, not the obvious hideout of a fraudster, but then what do they look like anyway? She tries the back door. It's locked. Then she hears a sound from next door and flits quickly back to the front and the security of the car.

She sits, shivering slightly and turns on the heater. That was foolish. She could have found out from the neighbour when Mrs. Hyde is likely to return. But that would give the game away, more advance warning with the neighbour seeing her before Jose can get to the door.

"Oh, Mrs. Hyde, there was a funny woman here earlier, looking for you, she wouldn't say what she wanted."

The minutes become an hour. Five, six o'clock. Jose gets stiff. She'll walk to the end of the road, keeping a wary eye on number 85. If any one returns she'll double back. But the same neighbour might see her walking up and down. Would she be challenged? Better stay put. Seven o'clock. Where is this woman, does she never return from work? Perhaps she's on holiday. Eight o'clock. It's getting dark. Enough to give her confidence in taking that stroll, but walks only a short way, afraid she might not see her quarry return. The darkness comes down suddenly and the streetlamps cast a dim light. She scuttles back to the car.

There she broods for another hour. Is it time to give up, return to Darrasea, lick her wounds, ingratiate herself with Mary Stokes, appeal to her and Robert Darley's better side? Surely the funds of the society can stretch to reimbursing her pending legal action against Mrs. Hyde? Don't be stupid Jose, they haven't got a better side and could she really humiliate herself in such a grovelling way? Would she ever be able to look Tanya in the face again?

If the cheque has bounced the picture has not been paid for. It remains your property and Mrs. Hyde has no right to it. Yet she holds it, somewhere in this house. In effect she's stolen *Waiting for the Tide*. Whenever possible, stolen property ought to be recovered. Her picture, her creation, held against its will, her will, in that house. That isn't right. She has the right, not this Mrs. Hyde, this thief and she should exercise it. She reiterates the thought for a further half hour. If she took it she would not be the criminal for the crime has already taken place, Mrs. Hyde has stolen it.

After nine. No one stirs in the closed curtained deserted road. Time to act. She didn't come to sit in the car and waste her time. The wretched woman isn't here. She doesn't deserve the courtesy of an explanation. She didn't give Jose one. She gets out and steps quickly to the front garden, up the path to the door. Should she ring the bell one last time just in case someone is in? But how would they get it in, over the garden hedge and in through the back door? There are no lights. She looks around. No one about. She stabs the bell and waits a minute before making her way along the side of the house. The light is on in next door's kitchen. She sees no one, but hurries past nervously. She tries the back door again. Still locked. She turns the corner and reaches the back of the house. At least here it's dark. The houses at the rear are some way back. No chance of being overlooked. The garden is quiet and almost black. She can only just make out the short path and patio.

What now? She paces along the rear of the house, peering in the windows, but can only make out vague shapes of furniture. This is a wild and ultimately unproductive exercise. The patio doors are fastened hard. She tries the windows of another room, but they too are locked. Ready to give up she shuffles back along the house wall towards the corner. Then she sees a small window slightly ajar. It's probably on a catch, but she'll try. It's too high for a small woman and she looks around for something to stand on.

There's a shed near the patio. She walks over and stumbles noisily against something hard at its side. She freezes and looks around. She hears nothing, but waits anxiously for a few minutes. It's a large plant pot. It should take her weight. She lifts it over beside the house and stands up, pushing her hand through the gap. She can get her hand right through and leans down the inside of the glass until she feels the catch of the larger window. She twines her fingers and pulls. It gives slightly. Her arm is fully stretched. She pulls again. Her arm aches. As she pulls her shoulder is yanked against the window and her foot slips on the plant pot. It sways under her weight and, unbalanced she starts to slide sideways. She grabs the window with her other hand and manages to steady herself. Then she feels the catch move and with a distinct 'click' the large window is freed. She pushes it from the inside, then pulls it outwards until it's large enough to climb through.

She lands on the top of a toilet cistern, then slides to the floor, staggering forward and clattering against the door. She stands still and waits. Silence for a moment, then she hears a faint, distant creak. It could be someone on the stairs. In a second she'll hear footsteps, getting closer to the toilet door before being thrust open to reveal her. She feels for the bolt on the door, though that will only confirm her presence to someone on the other side. She waits and listens. Nothing. The creaking timbers in an autumn night. No more.

She carefully unbolts the door and steps into a wide hall. The street lamp's dim light comes from the front door. There are two large rooms and a kitchen. She hesitates at the bottom of the stairs, unsure which way to go. Her eyes gradually adjust to the gloom and she looks into the room facing the back with the large patio doors. It's very dark, but with the hall door open she can see clearly enough to get round and examine the walls. There are a few photographs, but no pictures. Her painting may not have been hung. It could be stored in a cupboard or might not even be in the house at all.

She retreats back to the hall where there's more light and walks into the front room. This is a little brighter with more light at the window, flickering through the trees from the street. It's larger than the other room, less cluttered with little furniture though dominated by a large dining table in the centre. She lingers by the door and scans the walls. She can see two pictures on the wall facing the window and a third on the wall next to her. Even in the gloom she can tell these are the wrong size, one too large and the others too small, but she scrutinises them to make sure. None are familiar. She's about to turn back to the hall when she sees a dull shape against the lightness of the wall next to the window. It's rectangular. It could be a picture, but in the dimness too far away to be made out. To see it better she moves around the table into the middle of the room.

Now she can see it more clearly. The right size. She gets closer. The frame is the type she uses. It's still too dim. She can only make out vague shapes. She leans forward over the table. Then one of the trees bends in the breeze and for a moment the light from the street lamp strikes the wall and she can see the picture clearly. Yes, there's no doubt...there it is...*Waiting for the Tide!* All she has to do is get round the table, take the edge and lift it off. She moves to her right, but then she's hit. A heavy blow from behind and she goes down.

3

CHRIS Stover is returning to the incident room mobile. He likes to take an early morning walk along the front at Darrasea. It's his first case in the town. He lives and is based in Darraton, ten miles upriver. He's been down here a few times before, but doesn't know it well. It's always struck him as a vibrant place, a resort that's also a real town with a distinctive character from the rest of the area, quite different from Darraton, a city four times its size. Vigorous, even rowdy sometimes, but not fundamentally violent, though this murder changes his whole perception of the place. Yet the victim wasn't local and as yet there's no evidence the murderer was either.

He leaves the road and trudges along the sea washed light brown ribbon where the sand is firmer. Having tramped the two mile expanse for several mornings he recognises the same dog walkers or early strollers. Walking east he has the light, but slightly cool wind behind him. On his left is Cliff Road, a blue plaqued enclave of Georgian houses, former homes of the widows of famous poets and admirals. Apart from a few thatched cottages it's the oldest part of town, distinguished survivor of the original eighteenth century resort. Many of the houses have been converted to flats. Stover envies the residents. High on the cliff they enjoy magnificent views across the sea and the estuary.

When Cliff Road was built there was no sea wall and the lower ground close to the 'Warren' and the slipway frequently flooded right back into the town centre. The nearby Edward Hall, named after a local benefactor is a 1950s structure, a welcome post war amenity, relic of a less affluent, more innocent, perhaps wiser age.

He passes a man with a metal detector and wonders how often anything more interesting than cans, pen tops and old spoons are found. Yet now it'll be known for a more gruesome find than buckets and spades, ice cream cartons and discarded towels. The place is first mentioned a thousand years ago when the local landowner led a successful force repulsing a Viking attack from the Channel. Resolute from the beginning, maybe it's not such a peaceful place after all? Peaceful or not, his overriding impression of Darrasea is its amazing parochialism. To many of the inhabitants Darraton is more like a thousand rather than ten miles away.

No different perhaps from similar towns of the same size, but Darrasea also has a tremendous need to know. Everybody likes to know everybody else even if some are people they'd rather not know. New businesses have to rapidly 'fit in' or are quickly ostracised. A seasoned observer like his sergeant, a native, is a highly skilled assessor of success or failure. She'll remark on some newly opened shop with a curt 'it won't last' and is invariably right. A town where everybody knows everybody else and it's difficult to keep secrets whether you're 'in' or 'out.'

He watches the man with his metal detector for a few moments as he snakes along the beach, waiting, wondering if he'll stop and scratch away with his shovel. He slows down a couple of times, kicks the sand, but then moves on. No rich pickings today, no Viking helmets or Saxon jewellery. Hopefully for both him and Stover no unwelcome organic discoveries either.

Why was Carina Fennell in Darrasea two weeks before production of her programme was due to start? Why did she run away from London and all the people she knew? Jeremy was ambivalent about her death, irritated, shocked, concerned for the effect it had on his team, saddened perhaps, but hardly devastated. Does his superficial grief conceal a more sinister satisfaction? How comfortable was Carina with her new director? They had worked together before and Wendy Arbon's bitchy remarks implied some unpleasant previous history while other members of the team noticed 'needle' between them. Did he bring unwelcome baggage, old cold disputes resurrected and warmed up, uncomfortable reminders, even threats during one of their rows?

No love lost then between Jeremy and the agent, but what of Wendy herself? Supportive, attentive, even finding the time to follow her a hundred and sixty miles to shoot a television programme. She's either short of other work or Carina Fennell represents such a valuable commodity she can't bear to be too long away from her. Perhaps both, but whose interests does she really support? She must know much more about Carina, but how much of that is for public consumption?

Harry Willard, more than a dutiful accountant and trusted financial adviser. How far could Carina really trust him and how much of his involvement was purely financial? Her death seems to have affected him more than most. More than a client he counted her a friend, but what sort of 'friend' and what pressing financial issue made it necessary for him to come down here? Perhaps money is at the heart of the mystery.

Then there's Dominic, suave, slippery, superficial, but is he sinister? Stover doesn't like him, but tries to keep his personal prejudice under control – it could undermine his ability to think clearly. Is Amanda right? A glorified male doll Carina liked to parade around when it suited her? Was Dominic happy with that or did he resent the part? An unprincipled gold digger may be happy as long as he's comfortable, but comfort may not have been enough. Amanda may not be the only one to see through the relationship. The razor sharp tongues of influential people can inflict real wounds. Stover has no experience of showbiz, but he assumes Carina's world was filled with tigers and crocodiles, saying things they didn't believe, commending those they hated, sophisticated endearments that seared with tooth and hacked with claw.

Only those with the thickest brain or skin would fail to get the real message. Dominic is neither. Hurt pride may have made him yearn to turn the tables. If the world unjustly labelled him why not tell the world the real story about Carina? Must have been worth a few bob. Or perhaps nothing less than the ultimate retribution would suffice. A man scorned may be as dangerous as a woman.

London gossip is that Dominic's lifestyle outstrips his resources, confirmed by enquiries on his finances. Evidently his occupational 'this and that' was insufficient to keep pace. So long as he remained a pleasing animated decoration Carina probably propped him up, but even her money may have reached the limits of endurance. Stover sees him as a bloodsucker. Perhaps she ran away to Darrasea and he followed. She won't give him any more money and he loses his temper.

Carina was certainly running, but the cause is not yet clear. Did she arrive on the day of the murder or had she been in Darrasea some time? Couldn't have been more than a day or two because she was seen in London not long before. Where did she stay? How did she spend her day? Despite their enquiries around the town no one has reported seeing her. The real Carina is elusive. The media image – direct, honest, wholesome, unaffected sits uneasily with the alternative emerging from her set and her neighbours – frantic, hedonistic, superficial. Only one element is consistent. She was popular with both the public and friends and acquaintances. But popularity is a fickle master. Are you popular for yourself or for what you can give people? Her public yearned for the tasteful, warm, accessible softness that she crystallised. A Sunday afternoon cake the family looked forward to all week. What did her London group desire? Attachment to success, security in belonging to a 'personality' greater than themselves, but willing to generously share her glitz. But what did she get from her two 'publics?' That may be the clue they've yet to find out.

He reaches the mobile at the far end of the front. A few officers are around. Amanda hasn't arrived yet. He slumps into his chair. The local newspaper, the 'Darrsasea Advertiser' is on the desk. The front page headline is predictable – *Carina Fennell found murdered on beach.* The main story is a good account based on the press conference with useful background information on Carina, her career, her programme, her fans, nothing about her life in London. Not really of local interest, though it might become so later. Let the local journalists make the most of it. It's not every day a national television personality is murdered on their patch. Next week it'll be back to WI jampots and the local football. No, not that quickly, this should run into next month or perhaps a little longer if something turns up to extend it. There's a reference to page four and a 'linked story' entitled *'A Tale of Three Women.'* Intrigued, he opens up the paper.

"It could be a tale of three women. What began as an unfortunate blip disturbing the smooth running of a long standing local event became a bizarre, but still local incident. Now it's a national tragedy, but played out in our own community.

Local artist Jose Pearsall's pleasure at selling her painting 'Waiting for the Tide' at the annual Art Society exhibition quickly turned to bitter disappointment when the purchaser's cheque 'bounced.' Understandably she was furious and her anger spilled over into the exhibition itself, a bitter row erupting on the last evening between herself and society officers when she demanded recompense for her loss.

To add insult to injury, another of her paintings, 'Restful Haven' was stolen from Edward Hall on the same night. Mrs. Pearsall, a forceful lady, blames the society officers for both her losses.

"Restful Haven' was stolen as a result of their laxity and 'Waiting for the Tide' was lost through fraud because of their administrative failure."

Society treasurer Robert Darley said both incidents are currently being investigated. Society secretary Mary Stokes said "these are internal matters," but confirmed that she told Mrs. Pearsall the society "does not have facilities for guarantees."

There was a further twist when a visitor to the exhibition made a startling assertion that in the same painting 'Restful Haven,' she had seen famous television personality Carina Fennell. The painting depicted the main west entrance of the parish church of St. Nicholas in Seymour Street. The young woman was loud and vociferous, continually pointing to the painting saying 'She's there' and at one stage that she even saw Carina moving. Many people witnessed the incident including the artist herself, who did not know the woman and denied any connection to Carina Fennell. No one could recognise any of the people shown in the picture at the church, so it remains a mystery why only this particular visitor 'saw' Carina Fennell. The young woman is also a mystery as she rushed out of the exhibition and has not been seen since.

These events, unusual and disturbing in themselves, were thrown into sharper focus when the badly mutilated body of Carina Fennell was subsequently discovered on Darrasea beach. Police have confirmed she was murdered and are keeping an open mind as to the likely motive or who might be responsible. Carina Fennell was due to film a sequence for her programme 'Your Town, My Town' and the production crew had already arrived in town.

Carina Fennell was murdered around two weeks earlier and it is unclear why she would be in Darrasea at that time. Her arrival also coincides with when Mrs. Pearsall was painting 'Restful Haven.' Meanwhile, Mrs. Pearsall has not given up on 'Waiting for the Tide,' vowing to "get her picture back."

Stover puts the paper down. It may be useful to talk to Jose Pearsall even though she says she's unconnected to Carina. She may have seen more than she realised. It's even possible her picture of the church was painted on the same day Carina was killed. He glances at the town map. The church is about half a mile from the murder site. Then there's the elusive young woman at the exhibition. What's her connection to Carina? The newspaper says she hasn't been seen since and doesn't give a name. There were plenty of witnesses of the incident so it should be possible to get a reasonably good description.

Amanda arrives. He points to the newspaper.

"Yes," she says, glancing at the front page.

"No, page four," he says.

She turns it over and reads the 'three women' article.

"This would have been the front page in an ordinary week," she says.

"What do you make of it?"

"We can talk to the artist when we go to see the art society."

"Why are we going there?"

"They've asked us to investigate the burglary at Edward Hall where the picture was stolen."

Stover grunts. A mere burglary is beneath consideration.

"What about Carina Fennell, do we have anything on her background here in Darrasea?"

"We now know why she left Darrasea, at least what appears to be the reason. When she was a young girl, about sixteen there was a terrible accident, one of her friends was killed. It seems she never got over it, eventually eating her up so much she had to get away. "

"Why didn't we know this before?"

"Because Carina changed her name, remember? Originally she was Carina Armstrong. She adopted Fennell, her mother's maiden name when she left Darrasea and she's been known as that ever since. Nobody in Darrasea ever seems to have connected the young Armstrong girl as one and the same as the national personality."

"Very odd. You'd think somebody would've made the link."

"It seems not, that's why there appeared to be no connection."

"What happened?"

"The local paper carried the story. Carina was devastated. They were very close, inseparable apparently. So Darrasea was a place with bad memories."

"Or one bad memory that wiped out all the good ones."

"Not a place she'd want to come back to if it upset her that much."

"Maybe that's why she came down early, to try and exorcise the ghosts so to speak."

"I've arranged to see the secretary and treasurer of the art society at Edward Hall, do you want to come?"

"Yes," he says, sighing resignedly, "Let's get it over with. I don't suppose we'll get any peace until this burglary is sorted out," he glances at the newspaper, "we'll probably have this stroppy artist on our backs too."

Stover wants to go on afterwards so Amanda drives them the short run along the promenade to the Edward Hall. The clouds have cleared the estuary and the sun is higher than earlier. It's going to be a bright, warm autumn day. His spirits lift. Maybe the separate strands of Darrasea and Carina are really coming together though as yet he can't see how closely they're connected.

Robert Darley and Mary Stokes are 'supervising' the final clearing up of the exhibition. Others are packing away the stands and boards. A few unsold pictures remain to be collected by the artists.

"We usually have everything sorted out by now," Mary Stokes says, standing in the large empty space in the centre of the main room, shaking her head.

"We weren't sure when you'd get here," Robert Darley says as if the police are responsible for their tardiness, "people are understandably upset, everything's been delayed by recent traumatic events."

"Yes, I quite understand," Stover says, "such a terrible discovery on the beach, it's affected us all."

"Oh I didn't mean that business with Carina Fennell," he says and then as if to correct any misapprehension about Stover's greater concerns, "though I appreciate the murder must be your main priority. I was referring to the burglary and the unseemly incident the previous evening."

"Yes it was an odd outburst, wasn't it?" Stover says, meaning the young woman and her 'vision' of Carina.

"Indeed," Robert continues, "It's not the sort of behaviour we expect from one of our members."

Stover looks at him, puzzled.

"I was referring to the totally unwarranted remarks by Jose Pearsall."

Stover still looks puzzled.

"The bounced cheque," Amanda whispers.

"Oh, I see," Stover says, "However, it was her picture that was stolen."

"It was," Mary says, "but it wasn't our fault."

"Was the hall secure that night?"

Robert hesitates with a 'careful what you say' lift to his eyebrows, a signal Mary either misses or chooses to ignore.

"We have a procedure," she says forcefully.

"Indeed and how did that operate?"

Robert coughs loudly.

"Whoever is on duty makes a final round before they leave, ensuring all doors and windows are locked."

"And that was done that night?"

Now she hesitates. Robert intervenes.

"Everybody was a little shaken up with the scene over the... er...unfortunate cheque and then there was the business with the young girl...er...seeing things in Mrs. Pearsall's picture. It caused quite a stir at the time, it's not really surprising not everything was checked...we were all so keen to get away."

"I see."

"The main doors were locked properly," Mary says.

"And the windows?"

"In the morning we discovered the catch on one of the kitchen windows had not been completely tightened..."

"It was closed," Mary says.

"...so I'm afraid it seems it was forced open."

Robert and Mary stay at the door, as if afraid to venture over the threshold, looking on nervously as Stover and Amanda examine the kitchen. From marks on the draining board and the floor it's clear the window was the means of entry and exit for the burglar.

"Odd the intruder only took the one painting," Stover says, "You are sure of that?"

"We've checked our inventory. No other paintings were taken," Robert says.

"How much was the painting worth?"

"190 pounds."

"And equipment, materials, things belonging to the hall?"

"Nothing else was taken," Mary says.

"Very odd."

They return to the main hall. Stover asks about the young girl. No one knew her.

"Did you see the picture that was stolen? Was Carina Fennell in it?"

They are both a little vague about the painting.

"We had over 200 paintings on show," Mary says tartly, "We can't be expected to know them all."

"But weren't they all subject to individual viewings to ascertain their suitability for selection?"

She starts in surprise. He's well informed about their internal procedures.

"You were both involved in that process?"

"Yes of course we were, as society officers, but even so, we had to get through so many very quickly, there really wasn't time..."

"Your scrutiny was only superficial?"

"No, of course not, we..."

Robert intervenes.

"Chief inspector, whether or not we saw Mrs. Pearsall's painting prior to the incident with the strange young woman, we certainly had a good look at it afterwards and I can assure you no one saw Carina Fennell or indeed anyone else recognisable in the picture."

"The figures were most indistinct," Mary says stiffly.

"You don't like her work?"

"No...it's not that I...I didn't mean...these things are a matter of taste."

"Her remarks that night," Robert says, "most unfortunate and really quite uncalled for."

"The bounced cheque, how much was it for?"

"270 pounds."

"I can understand her being upset."

"Not a large amount," Mary says, "she's not one of our more successful artists."

"Judging success by the amount they fetch?" Stover says.

"That's not quite..."she begins.

Robert comes in quickly.

"Of course she was upset, but that was no reason to berate us in the way she did. We needed time to look into the matter."

"And have you?"

"Well, we know the identity of the purchaser."

"And have you followed it up?"

Robert grimaces, unsure what to say.

"Any action we might have taken has been pre-empted by Jose Pearsall herself," Mary says acerbically.

"I was hoping to speak to her."

"You're welcome to try."

The meeting is quickly terminated. They respond to Stover's promise the police will 'do all they can' with glum and unbelieving glares.

"You were a little hard on them," Amanda says as they go round to Jose's flat on Cliff Road.

"Why so? I'd be annoyed if somebody leaving a window resulted in me losing something worth 190 pounds, especially if they're not prepared to reimburse me."

Amanda reconsiders.

"I suppose so, then there's the bounced cheque for 270, all told 460."

"Exactly. We'll see what Jose Pearsall has to tell us."

He stares out across the estuary as they wait at the door. He envies the gorgeous view, which must be even better from her second floor flat. They get no answer, but he won't give up.

"I'm going to see that reporter. Get SOCO to the burglary and then follow up anything more on Carina's movements."

Taken aback by Stover's sudden appearance at the 'Advertiser,' Richard Tanner tells of his conversation with Jose in the pub, including details not included in his article. He's not surprised Stover has been unable to locate her.

"She said she was going to track down the painting."

"Which one?"

Richard checks his notes.

"*Waiting for the Tide*, that's the bounced cheque one."

"270 pounds," Stover mutters.

"She had the address, seemed pretty determined."

“What about the girl, the one who said she saw Carina in the other picture, what do you know about her?”

“Her name’s Kelly, she’s usually at the front, but that’s all I know. I’ve not been able to find her.”

Richard can provide some information on the people who ‘hang out’ at the front. Stover knows others. They are many and varied. He parks near the ‘Warren’ and retraces the steps of his earlier stroll, though keeps to the promenade. Every time he comes here, whatever time, whatever the weather, there’s always someone around. The estuary, the beach, the Channel, the elegant sweep of white faced hotels and apartments, all magnetising and attracting people, though those he wants to see rarely stray onto the beach, preferring the benches and shelters. They like the refreshing air and get close, but not too close to sea and sand. They have that magical quality of being at the end of the land where it meets the sea, essential for people who themselves are at the end.

Which is more than can be said for Stover. He’s very much at the beginning and preoccupied by three things, a picture and two women and how they might be connected to the murder. The theft of *Restful Haven* is an oddity. Why break into the hall and steal only one picture? Even an opportunistic thief would take a handful. But if it was pre-planned, why that particular picture? Does the answer lie with one or both of the women? Who is this Kelly and why did she ‘see’ Carina when no one else did? Is it because of some previous connection? She may have actually seen Carina at the church on that fateful day and the picture reminded her. But why should it be so traumatic, news of the murder was not then public knowledge although it was known Carina was in town. Then we have the fiery Jose Pearsall, so effectively turning over the art society apple cart. Had she seen Carina when she painted the picture? Both Kelly and Jose are local and he now knows Carina also had a local connection. Were they connected to her?

He reaches the first shelter. Two men are curled up on one of the seats, at right angles to the beach, facing along the promenade towards the clock tower. The younger one, in his early twenties has a small radio on his lap and is listening to the cricket. The other, older man gets up as soon as Stover arrives and ambles away along the promenade.

Opening up the conversation, Stover asks the score. The young man waits for a lull in the commentary before speaking and then comes out in a pronounced Brummie accent with a stream of information on fallen wickets, batsmen, bowlers and comments on individual performances. Stover nods sympathetically, wholly uninterested in the cricket, but intrigued by the young man's encyclopaedic knowledge.

"You're quite an expert."

"Keep up to date," the man says dismissively, then turns up the volume and cups his ear as the commentary restarts.

Stover introduces himself as Chris and sits beside him. The other says he's always known as 'Sparrow' without indicating why. He sits on a sleeping bag and pulls a couple of blankets around his legs. Stover makes a few other remarks, trying not to appear too ignorant of the finer points of the game before moving on to the real subject of interest.

"Know most of the people who get down here?"

Sparrow nods absently.

"You might know somebody I want to talk to."

Sparrow takes no notice.

"They call her Kelly."

Sparrow glances up, then nervously along the promenade. Stover follows his eyes. He can see the other, older man in the distance. It's as if Sparrow wants to check with him before replying.

"Do you know her?"

Sparrow is still intent on the cricket.

"It's very important."

Sparrow half turns to the side of the shelter. Stover shows his warrant card.

"Is she in trouble?" Sparrow says.

"Not that I know of, but she might be able to help me find somebody who could be."

"Don't know where she is."

"But you know her?"

"Heard of her, don't see her much, not seen her for ages."

"It could be connected to the murder of Carina Fennell, you must have heard of her?"

"No, who's she?"
"She's very famous on the telly."
"Don't watch television."
"Not even for the cricket?"
Stover struggles on, but whether he's reluctant to say anything without his 'minder,' the older man, or because he really hasn't anything worth saying Sparrow isn't forthcoming. Stover eventually gives up and leaves him to the cricket. He wanders further along the promenade. He comes across more 'regulars' and marvels at the sub world of people existing on so many levels at the front. The dog walkers and other routine ordered exercisers patrol the beach and the road with almost military precision. The pubs and cafes also have their rhythmic clientele, people who drift in and out conditioned by the clockwork dictates of their stomachs. At strategic points, motor caravans are parked kerbside. Most of their doors are open, many have deckchairs positioned outside and almost all ring with the sound of whistling kettles. Stover wonders how many take advantage of overnight parking.

There's a small queue for ice cream. He's last in the line and when it comes to his turn Stover asks about Kelly.

"Couldn't say," the woman at the kiosk says, "there are so many of them. I don't know their names."

"She might have been hanging around for some time. Could be dossing down at night."

The woman shrugs.

"Many do in the summer, I wouldn't know one from the other."

A man in his sixties comes up. He's shabbily dressed in aged corduroys, a grubby cardigan and a battered woollen hat. He clutches a large plastic bag, bulging at the sides.

"Hallo Tony, my lover," the woman says, "what do'you reckon, rain later?"

He blinks several times, then looks blankly at the sky over the distant hills, glances at Stover, then turn backs to her.

"By eight tonight I'd say, yes definitely, he'll be coming over by then, from the moors, could be damp down here tonight."

He dribbles on about the weather for several minutes, getting gradually less coherent. Obviously used to these meteorological diatribes, the woman acknowledges his remarks with sympathetic nods, 'I know's' and 'isn't it's.' He's overheard Stover's conversation about Kelly and suddenly mentions her. Stover tries to get him to say more, but Tony soon deviates again. The weather, the tides and the need to discourage visitors not to feed the gulls are of greater interest. Then, he loses interest altogether and drifts into the adjacent gardens to his usual place in one of the shelters.

"Knows everybody down here," the woman says in reply to Stover's unspoken question.

"Does he stay overnight?"

"No, he's got a place in town, but he knows all those that do," she says, "but you won't get what you want out of him today."

Ignoring the warning, Stover follows him to the shelter, but his attempts to get him to talk about Kelly are unsuccessful. Tony reverts to a pot pourri of incoherent assertions interspersed with long bouts of complete silence. Even when he's speaking he stares at the estuary, never once looking at Stover directly. Only when Stover sits beside him, does Tony turn to face him and then eyes Stover with surprised, questioning irritation as if he's said something scandalous. The reason for this becomes obvious when another man about the same age, slightly better dressed and sporting a wide brimmed hat lopes up. Tony's darting eyes between him and the policeman indicates Stover ought to vacate the new arrival's regular seat. Stover gets up, not wanting to transgress what is clearly an understood regime of complicated seat possession.

The newcomer is more articulate than Tony except when the two of them engage in what almost amounts to a private language, part dialect and part eccentric jargon, but he expresses total ignorance of Kelly. Stover moves on. It's the middle of the day and with the front's daytime population reaching its zenith he encounters more habitues in their various 'pitches.' They're an interesting mixture of age, accent and appearance, reflecting the cosmopolitan town, but united in a yearning to be away from everything except the sea air.

Stover reaches the last of the shelters near the sand dunes where two men are sitting. Even though it's a mild day, one has the hood of his coat over his head, his collar turned up and a thick scarf round his neck. He's in his early twenties, gaunt and pale. Like Sparrow he has a sleeping bag and blankets on the seat. The other man is older, about fifty. His clothes are casual and well worn, but clean and serviceable. Unlike his companion his trousers and jacket are light and airy. His long, mainly grey hair with streaks of brown lops over his slightly tanned face and he has a strong, healthy frame. He wears a substantial pair of boots in good condition. This is a man used to the outdoors. The young man takes no notice of Stover, but the older man watches him with wide, penetrating eyes and a look of controlled wariness, almost aggressive. Stover recognises him as the man who'd been with Sparow.

Somewhat wearied by the lack of meaningful responses and less patient than earlier Stover makes a direct approach, introduces himself and immediately asks about Kelly. Neither reply. Sensing more non cooperation Stover demands to know their identities. The young man is still silent. The older man says 'he's a bit delicate' and is called Phillip.

"He's not done anything wrong, doesn't know anything and you shouldn't be harassing him."

"I'm not harassing him. I'm only asking questions."

"Leave him alone. He can do without the fuzz nosing around."

Stover bristles.

"Can't he speak for himself?"

Phillip appears not to notice Stover except to turn away and pull his coat and blankets closer.

"He doesn't express himself well," the older man says, "can be easily misunderstood. It's better if someone speaks for him."

"That's your role is it?"

"I look out for him. He needs looking after."

"And you are?"

"Vince."

"Vince who?"

"Vince Randall."

"Vincent Randall."

"No just *Vince*. I was named after a motor bike. Bit before your time. Vincent bikes were well known. It wasn't my choice."

Stover's eyes look him over suspiciously. Vince returns with a cold stare.

"You seem to know everybody around here," Stover says.

"I keep my eyes open. It's necessary, you never know who might drop in."

"But you don't know Kelly?"

"That's not what I said."

"I asked if you knew of her and you said you didn't."

"That's right, didn't know *of* her, not the same as knowing who she is. I don't know of her because I don't know *where* she is."

"So you *know* her."

"I might."

Stover is annoyed.

"Yes or no!"

"Yes...but I don't know her whereabouts."

"I saw you at the other end of the front with Sparrow."

Vince glares in surprise.

"Spying on me, eh? I didn't know it was a crime to walk along the front."

"You obviously get about, probably know everything that goes on."

Vince doesn't reply. Stover mentions the Edward Hall and the night of the theft.

"Were you around that night?"

Vince grimaces and screws his eyes.

"I'd have to double check the social diary with my secretary," he says, curling his lip and raising his eyebrows as he turns to Stover, "but subject to that I suppose I might have been, but I didn't see anything."

"Nothing?"

"Nothing to do with thefts at Edward Hall."

"You're not an art lover?"

"Art is all around us," he says, opening his arms and gesturing towards the sea, the sky and the road, "I don't need no pictures to tell what I can see and hear and smell myself."

"Where do you live?" Stover says suspiciously.

"Are you charging me with something?"

"No."

"Then I don't have to answer any more of your questions."

"I am investigating a murder, Mr. Randall."

There's a glimmer of concern in Vince's eyes, but is it because he's genuinely startled by the reminder of Carina's death or the implication of further police pressure?

"Let's just say I'm passing through," he says at last.

"No fixed abode," Stover mutters.

"I didn't say that."

Their eyes meet in steely antagonism. Stover hesitates. He could make something of it, but doesn't think it's worth the effort. He'll get nothing more today and despite what he says, Vince will be around for some time. So with a parting admonition for him 'not to go too far away' he leaves. Vince and Phillip watch him in silence for some minutes, then Vince gets restless.

"You alright?" he says.

Phillip grunts, nods slightly and pulls the blankets closer.

"Need a change of scene," Vince says, "Shan't be long, see you later."

He waits until Stover is out of sight, then walks briskly in the opposite direction along the promenade, past the Plaza, the ice cream kiosk, Edward Hall and the clock tower, only slowing his pace when he gets close to the 'Warren.' He walks away down a side street, intending to walk into town, but the cooking aroma from the pub's kitchen makes him reconsider. He's not hungry, but feels like a drink. Despite his bravado, the encounter has upset him. He's usually quite neutral in his attitude to policemen, but however unintentionally, Stover's intemperate speech has provoked him. He always regrets using 'resolute' language. In the next hour he'll go over everything, cursing himself for drawing attention and opening up unguarded. But then, what did he say? More to the point, what he *didn't* say. The policeman won't believe he doesn't know where Kelly is. Too bad. He retraces his steps to the pub. It'll be good to wash away the taste of authority.

It's quite crowded. Not seeing any vacant seats he perches on a stool at the bar. He loves this place, the long wooden bar with its ornately carved front and the splendid pen and ink drawings of contemporary Edwardian characters. Much more interesting than pretty views or abstract nonsense in the exhibition up the road. He downs his beer quite quickly (he always drinks faster when he's alone) and eavesdrops on the conversations around him. It's one way to keep in touch, for as Stover rightly said Vince knows virtually everything that goes on at the front. He hears nothing of interest, but it could be he's not concentrating well, his mind still regurgitating Stover's questions and his unhelpful replies.

"I am investigating a murder."

He gets another drink. His back's getting stiff and he has to keep straightening up on the stool. He looks around. It's thinned a little. There are a couple of vacant chairs at one of the tables. Just as he sits down a woman arrives behind him.

"This one free?" she says, "you're not holding it for someone else?"

"No, you're alright."

"It's getting chilly, out there," she says, putting her drink down and stuffing a packet of cigarettes into her bag.

Vince sniffs unsympathetically. He gave up smoking twenty years ago and is now a zealous oppositionist.

"They could at least provide a proper facility for smokers," she says, "perhaps like one of the shelters on the front."

"Technically the shelters in the front are inside," he says crisply, then adding after a short pause, "you're not supposed to smoke in them, but people do."

"You know what I mean."

"Unfortunately I do."

"You don't approve?"

"It's your life."

"Yes it is and we have to make the best of it while we can. We can never be sure what disaster might lie ahead at any moment."

He looks at her quizzically.

"I'm sorry," she says, "I've just lost someone quite close."

"Sorry to hear it. A relative?"

"Not in the normal sense of the word, but as good as."

She picks up her drink and gulps quickly, then fiddles with her fingers as if about to take out a cigarette, then realises that's impossible and puts her hand on the table before smiling nervously. Vince watches her. She seems familiar...if only...he wracks his brain...then it comes to him.

"You knew Carina Fennell well?" he says.

She turns to him sharply and is about to speak.

"I saw you coming out the Plaza," he says, opening his hands in a gesture of innocence, "so I assumed you must be involved with the television crew."

"You watch the programme?"

"No, I don't see much television."

"You must be one of the few people who's not seen it."

"I've heard of it."

"You're remarkably observant," she says, with a little disquiet, "to remember me."

"It's not difficult noticing such a well publicised event. Do you appear in the programme?"

"No, nothing like that. Wendy Arbon, I am...was Carina's agent."

She waits for him to reply, eventually saying, "...and you are?"

"Vince.""

"Vince?"

"Vince Randall."

"And what do you do?"

"Things."

"But always around the seafront?"

"Usually."

"So you see *things*?"

He stares piercingly, his eyes betraying a slight twinkle, his lips parting but not quite reaching a smile.

"Oh yes, usually. I don't miss much."

She returns his stare for a few seconds, but then looks away anxiously before taking another nervous swig from her glass.

"Did you hear about the burglary?" he says.

"You mean the painting stolen from the exhibition, yes I was speaking to the artist in here."

"You get about too."

"It was purely coincidental. We just happened to be in the same place at the same time."

She feels oddly embarrassed with her conversation with Jose being 'found out.' There's no reason why she should. Perhaps it's his continuing penetrating stare as if he's saying 'I know about you, much more than you're saying and you might get even more uncomfortable because I know a lot more.'

"Funny business," he says, "just taking the one picture."

"So I believe. You read about it in the local paper?"

"I don't often read newspapers."

"Then how do you..."

"On the night of the theft I was outside Edward Hall."

"Have you told the police?"

"No."

"But I suppose just being around, there's nothing important to tell them?"

He shrugs.

"Depends what you think is important. When I say I was there I mean much later when the exhibition had closed. That's when I saw somebody coming away from the back of the hall. It could have been the thief."

Stover meanders between the cafes, becoming adept at distinguishing between regulars and occasional visitors. Only the regulars are likely to know where Kelly is, but no one helps. A couple of the proprietors recognise the description and have seen her, but not today and don't know where she can be found. He even speaks to a few young women who could be Kelly themselves, but isn't thanked for his presumption.

He wanders back towards the Plaza. Temporarily it seems to capture the world of Carina Fennell and her 'realistic' programme, providing a locus for his investigations, but in that role it's unreal and not part of Darrasea at all. He walks away, the seafront and its motley people beckoning him back. The two mile stretch is more than sand and dunes, a place to beach divergent humanity. But it's real and may yet hold more clues to Carina Fennell's mysterious death than anything in the facile masks of the Plaza.

He's almost reached the end of the promenade. A man in his late sixties sits on one of the last benches. He has a magnificent grey beard and long hair to his shoulders, an old denim jacket, heavy trousers with a thick brown belt and well worn but substantial boots. Stover sits beside him. Unlike his other encounters with the 'regulars' he's surprisingly affable.

"Fine day," he says, continuing to stare at the sea.

"You look like you're out here come rain or shine," Stover says, staring into the weathered and time worn face.

The old man turns, smoothing the long moustache hairs around his mouth, his eyes bearing into the policeman.

"Most days I'm here. Now who is it you'd be wanting to see?"

"Why should I be looking for someone?"

"Because people don't have time to sit and talk about the weather unless they're after something or somebody they think I might know."

"I'm looking for a young woman called Kelly."

"Then your search is over, she's right over there by the van."

He points to the mobile snack bar, parked near the end of the promenade and about as close to the murder scene as its possible to get without scrambling over the rocks. A few people are waiting to be served including a slim woman around twenty.

"She'll be treating herself to a hamburger or something equally unhealthy," the old man says, "she does that if she gets some money."

"Is that often?"

"No, she's usually broke," the old man chuckles.

Stover thanks him and crosses to the snack bar. Kelly is munching into a hamburger as the old man surmised. Stover stands away from her, pretending to look out to sea. She's dressed in the same long purple jumper and tattered jeans. Her face is pale, consistent with someone who until recently has spent most of her time inside rather than in the sea air.

He glances at the old man as if to challenge whether this really is Kelly. She's the right height, build, dark unkempt hair, the studs in the nose – it has to be her. She finishes the hamburger. He can see her more clearly now, The large, almost empty eyes, moving slowly around. Do they take things in or just bounce images onto an unreceptive mind or does she absorb what other don't see?

She sits on the wall next to the beach. Stover looks around. There are still a few people at the snack bar, but not many on the promenade itself. The old man is walking slowly away. Stover moves over and stands next to her. She doesn't take any notice, continuing to stare like the old man towards the beach. How constantly the sandy ribbon fascinates. The tide has turned and washed by the sea it's very clear, resembling a micro desert with all the empty mystery of the Sahara. Perhaps that's it's magnetism.

"Are you Kelly?" he says quietly.

At first she doesn't stir from the sea, then turns slightly, her wide eyes staring with mixed apprehension and irritation.

"Your friend over the road told me," he says, needful to explain how he knows her and pointing to the old man's contracting back, "I thought you might be able to help me."

Still she doesn't answer, her eyes darting across his face from one feature to another, anxious to detect some explanation.

"It's about somebody you may know," he continues cautiously.

She turns back towards the beach ostrich like. If she ignores him he might go away. Time for Stover to up the pressure a notch.

"You've probably seen Carina Fennell's television programme."

She keeps staring ahead, apparently impervious, but he sees the slight shudder. The name is familiar, though not necessarily welcome. Still she's silent.

"I know you must know her because..."

"Everybody knows her," she snaps, still intent on the sea.

"Yes, but I understand you've seen her quite recently."

No response. She still doesn't look at him, but purses her lips. He still might go away.

"You know she was in Darrasea?"

She bites her lip and turns.

"Yer, but that was before..."

"...she was killed."

She says nothing and turns back, staring at an empty part of the beach.

"Did you see her before she was killed?"

"Yer... o' course...on the telly," she mumbles.

"I mean in Darrasea, in the street perhaps?"

She turns aggressively.

"Look mister, what's this about, why are you harassing me?"

Stover steps back, emphasising a non threatening approach.

"I just want to ask you about..."

She stands up and steps out towards the road.

"Stop asking me questions, who do you think you are?"

"But you saw her, didn't you, in the painting?"

She steps further away and flings her arms out towards him.

"Shut up! I didn't see nothing."

He moves towards her.

"Keep calm, I'm a police officer. There's no reason to be alarmed. I only want to talk to you about the painting."

She raises her voice and screams out. The people around the snack bar look on in some alarm.

"Police? I've not done nothing!"

"Of course not," he says soothingly, moving slightly closer, "Please, if you can just tell me..."

"Why are you asking me?" she shrieks.

He moves gradually closer and smiles, trying to reassure her. He turns his back on the onlookers and lowers his voice.

"I am investigating the murder of Carina Fennell, if you could..."

It's no good. Mentioning 'murder' incites Kelly and she shouts at him hysterically.

"Murder! I've had nothing to do with no murder!"

Everybody within a hundred metres hears her and everything stops. Dogs are no longer walked, joggers take a breather, ice cream licking dries up, sandcastle building is suspended, hamburger serving is held off. Everybody listens. Everybody waits. Stover glances at them all nervously. Then he turns back to Kelly.

"If we could..."

"Get away from me, leave me alone!"

He moves towards her, but she flings her arms out again, screaming once more.

"Get back!"

He stops and hangs his arms down, palms outstretched, trying to calm the situation, but it's too late, he's lost it. She turns away, then runs past the shocked and gobsmacked crowd, along the promenade away from the snack bar, the rocks, the scene of the murder towards the halls, the cafes, the town, anywhere. He considers giving chase, but it's useless. She runs faster and is soon too far away to be caught.

4

THE cell reminds her of a bathroom. It must be the tiles. Clean, functional, soulless. The cells are in the basement, out of sight and most of the time out of mind except for those officers with specific custodial duties. There's a very small window high in the outside wall, well out of reach, allowing a little light, but its inaccessibility emphasises her isolation. In times like these she appreciates the important things too easily taken for granted. Like fresh sea air and the sun glinting on the estuary. Things she sees nearly every day and to which she never gives a second thought. Not so today, not just a second or a third or a fourth but many thoughts.

Last night she'd not been totally aware of what was going on and even now her memory is hazy. She remembers coming round at the house in Lawson Road and two women yapping hysterically. Then she must have lost consciousness again. The next she remembers is the police in the house. They asked her who she was and what she was doing, but she doesn't remember clearly how she replied. The two women were still there, but only one was talking. Then it goes blank. How did she get here? Oh yes...she was in the police car. Then blank... no, it's clearing again...she arrived at the police station and complained of the bump on her head. She was questioned, but was very vague and just like now everything kept going blank. They called in the doctor, a small, gruff man with little eyes, hardly the bedside manner. She didn't like him and had been quite short with him. Every time he asked a question she said 'isn't that obvious' or 'of course, I am.' Thinking about it now, he'd actually been very patient, but at the time he was just an irritation. He said something about there was no evidence of her having been drinking. Damned cheek! She hadn't touched a drop for a couple of days.

No one was interested in her account,. Something about a 'complaint' and her story 'wasn't credible.' It must have been one of those two women, whoever they were. One was probably the toe rag that took her picture without paying. It's her that should be in here. Then she passed out again and woke this morning in the cells. There'd been more questions, but still no one believed her.

They could at least get somebody to paint some nice murals on these bare tiles. Why should a cell not be aesthetic? It's not as if it's rarely used and artistic surroundings might have a beneficial effect on the drunks and other prisoners. It would certainly make her feel better. Assuming it was a tasteful picture of course. Knowing the police they'd probably get somebody like that dreadful Mary Stokes to paint it, though she's probably forgotten how to hold a brush let alone get oil or gauche on a surface. But it would be better to wake up to some colour rather than this interminable whiteness. It's probably meant to intimidate, deliberate, psychological as well as physical imprisonment. After all, police stations aren't supposed to be holiday camps. But it doesn't intimidate Jose, only annoys and provokes her. Reds and yellows for the dawn, as it is over the sea and blue, plenty of blue like the sea and the sky.

In the first disoriented minutes she imagined she was at home in her flat on Cliff Road. She would turn over and slip across the room, open the curtains and look out on the hills and the estuary. But the moment passed as it was bound to do and she knew she really was in a police cell forty miles from home. She longed for the comparative routine. Getting up, shower, breakfast, brushing teeth, sort out the washing, all the glorious boring mundane existence of a normal morning! Yet not all the monotonous comfort of a predictable existence. There's enough spontaneity scattered throughout an ordinary day to make life interesting. How do you make a morning in a white tiled police cell interesting? Pepper it with images of her usual regime. Sea and sand and sky taken for granted every day as if she never notices them at all. How many accumulated hours has she stood at her window, staring out at her circumscribed world, individual to her yet universal for anyone who cares to do the same?

She holds the shimmering morning for another instant, then it's gone. She's not standing at her window, but sits here, disconsolate, enclosed, unable to see beyond the porcelain encrusted slammer. It goes dark and she's back at 85 Lawson Road, but one more detail is added to the hazy remembrance. There's no picture on the wall, no *Waiting for the Tide*, briefly glimpsed before she...before what? She did see it, but then...it went dark...and when she came round...it was gone. She remembers now. She told them. She told the police at the house, trying to be heard above the screeching rattle of that woman. Then at the police station she told them again. She told them about the picture, how it was there and then gone. Someone stole it! Someone had beaten her to it. Taken what was hers, taken what she'd come to recover, stealing what's already been stolen? They wouldn't listen.

Two stolen pictures, one looted from the exhibition, the other taken without paying and now taken again. Some people have gone to a lot of trouble to get their hands on those pictures. People...or person...for has the same person taken both? What's the connection between them? The church and the front, both of Darrasea, but otherwise unconnected. Except they were painted on the same day. She finished the church in *Restful Haven* around eleven in the morning, then walked down the hill to polish off *Waiting for the Tide* outside the 'Warren.' Someone must have earmarked them from the catalogue, but how could such vague titles trigger an interest? She'd been in such a hurry not to miss the exhibition deadline the titles had actually been submitted *before* the pictures were painted. So the titles alone couldn't have been significant. Whatever the interest it had to come during the exhibition itself. There were plenty of views of Darrassea including her own other two pictures. All four were of the town or the front and all painted on the same day. Is it the town or the day or both?

Then came the inane outburst from that ridiculous young girl. Seeing things in the picture, including somebody actually moving...but not anybody...she saw Carina Fennell...who was murdered. Though she couldn't have known that at the time, but she did know she'd been in the town...yes that's it, it was in her mind...she'd probably been drinking or worse...so when she saw the picture she remembered Carina and 'put' her in the picture even making her walk! Ridiculous.

It's not so easy now to dismiss Kelly as 'mad' as she sits in this dismal excuse for a bathroom warehouse contemplating a future as empty as her confinement. What was she really at? Her bizarre behaviour could have been drug induced or the culmination of some twisted 'happening,' making a point about fame and fortune. Carina symbolises the superficial success so lacking in the young drop out's miserable existence, a mixture of outraged iconoclasm and old fashioned envy. It's an explanation. Trouble is, it isn't really convincing.

No one believed her. The local detective, what's his name, Templeman, was almost laughing when she told him about the bounced cheque.

"I've heard a few excuses for breaking into houses in my time, but this..."

She exploded, calling him all sort of names. She realises now that was a mistake, making him even less inclined to believe anything she said. She had no explanation for her mysterious assailant.

"Somebody hit me on the head, when I came round my picture was gone."

The doctor said it wasn't serious and she could have hit her head when she fell down. She hadn't fallen down. She'd been struck from behind. That was her story, but there was no one to back her up. Someone in the house did it. No, they found her on the floor. There were witnesses and they denied striking her. Their stories tallied. She's surely not suggesting they conspired against her? What possible motive would the neighbour have for fabricating a defence even if (which

Templeman doesn't believe anyway) the woman was out to get her? But she took my picture. What picture? The one she took away after leaving a bouncing cheque. The one she's now hidden away. We've only your word for that, but there's no disputing you broke into the house. Jose went quiet then. There's been a formal complaint. They have to act on it.

Stover gets no answer from Jose's flat on Cliff Road. To add to his frustration he draws another blank trying to find Kelly at the front. He sees none of the people he saw before except the cricket absorbed Sparrow, who's totally unresponsive on every other subject. He still knows nothing of Kelly's whereabouts and hasn't seen Vince either. Stover suspects he's mouthing what Vince told him before going to earth. He tries one final tack.

"I suppose he'll be at his tent."

Sparrow rounds quickly.

"He's not in a tent, he's got his camper."

"Camper?"

"His VW, it's old, but in good nick. He looks after it."

"And where would that be?"

But having opened his mouth too quickly and perhaps suddenly conscious he may have to explain himself to the redoubtable Vince, Sparrow eases back and turns up the radio. Stover repeats his question.

"Dunno, not seen him lately," is the terse reply.

Stover returns to the incident room a little dejected, but his mood picks up as he thinks it over. Kelly and Jose Pearsall are distracting sideshows. The first is a ludicrous eccentricity, the second only relevant to the burglary, itself a relatively trivial irritation. But then why was only one painting stolen and what did Kelly actually see? There has to be a connection, but he can't see it and must press on with the main investigation. He goes over what they've got, including his interview with Harry. Then Amanda comes in and reopens his earlier thoughts.

"That artist you wanted to see, Jose Pearsall. She's turned up in Yaverton."

"What's she doing there?"

"Getting her painting back – at least that's what she' been saying."

He remembers the reporter saying she'd gone in pursuit of the purchaser with the bounced cheque. He'd put it to the back of his mind. Now Amanda explains Jose's arrest.

"You'll have to go there to interview her," she says facetiously.

"Precisely," he says, to her surprise, "that's exactly what I will do."

A call to inspector Templeman and he's there an hour and a half later.

"You've done me a favour," he says, "I've been looking for this woman in relation to the Carina Fennell murder."

"Is she a suspect?" Templeman says darkly.

"Not as such, but she may shed some light on the background. It's all to do with her paintings."

"Tell me about it," Templeman says and explains Jose's 'cock and bull story' about the picture.

"It could be true, "Stover says.

"I thought you wanted to question her about the murder?"

"Well, not directly."

Templeman is puzzled.

"I'm about to charge her with breaking and entering. The householder is due any moment to finalise her statement. Once we've got that..."

"Can I sit in?"

"Well, after we've charged her, if it's to do with the murder..."

"No, I mean the woman at the house."

"I don't see."

"I might be able to help."

"Okay."

Marilyn Hyde arrives a little later. She's in her early thirties, medium height and build. Her dark flashing eyes and slightly squeaky voice are familiar to Stover, but he can't have met her before. After a few preliminaries from Templeman, his 'sitting in' is soon activating and he asks most of the questions. Marilyn resents having to make a formal statement. She's already explained everything to the detective who came to the house. Stover apologises for any inconvenience. He's only just been assigned to the case and has to follow appropriate 'procedures.' She calms down and even seems flattered when he emphasises the importance of her statement to the enquiries. After a few minutes they get to the essential details.

"I owed it to my neighbour, Mrs. Sanders."

"Owed her?" Stover says.

"I couldn't just leave it, could I? Complete stranger breaking into your house, particularly after what she'd done."

"You mean what *she'd* done, Mrs. Sanders?"

"Of course. She saw this woman, the woman you've got, at the side of the house. Wondered about it, but didn't do anything at first. Thought she might have been a friend of mine. I'm usually back earlier, so naturally she thought she was just waiting for me. But it preyed on her mind, so she came out to make sure and the woman wasn't there. She looked at the front of the house and up the street. Her car was there, she knew it was her car 'cause she'd seen her in it earlier. Should have called you lot in then shouldn't she, when she saw somebody suspicious hanging about?"

She pauses to catch her breath. The outburst comes across to Stover as a smokescreen to her own action. He reminds her to get back to the break in.

"That's it, you see. Mrs. Sanders was sure she was still around, so she came round the back of the house. She'd already noticed the open window at the back. It was then I came home. She heard me at the front door and came up to warn me. We went in together. I suppose we should have rung you and waited, but you don't think like that do you at the time? You know somebody's in your house, going through your things, the bare faced cheek of it, you feel you've been violated. You can't let people get away with it."

"You were very brave," Stover says encouragingly.

"We were pretty scared, I can tell you. I opened the door carefully, didn't want to warn them. Didn't dare put a light on either. It was really quite dark. Funny isn't it, how you find it difficult finding your way round your own house at night when all the lights are off? Anyway, we got around, creeping about like mice. Then I found her, bold as brass, sitting beside my settee, staring at the wall. Hardly flinched when we came in. 'Who are you?' she says as if it's her house rather than mine. 'Who the bloody hell are you?' I said, 'and what d'you think you're up to?' Then she sort of fell back on the settee. Mrs. Sanders went over. She was alright, but out for a few minutes. That's when I called you."

"And nothing was taken?"

She pauses slightly before pouring forth again.

"Only because we managed to stop her. If it wasn't for Mrs. Sanders being so vigilant and so conscientious and us both coming in as we did..."

"Was the house disturbed, anything damaged."

"No."

"Then you've really been very lucky."

"Yes, but even so, my house was broken into."

Stover confers with Templeman and checks on what Jose has told him. Then they go back and talk to Marilyn.

"What do you know about Mrs. Pearsall's picture?" Stover says.

Marilyn shakes her head.

"Don't know what she's talking about."

"She says you bought it from the exhibition in Darrasea."

"That doesn't give her the right to come and take it."

"Where is it?"

Marilyn is silent, her eyes darting nervously.

"She says she saw it."

"Then she must have taken it."

"You said nothing was taken."

"I meant nothing *else* was taken."

"But she didn't have it with her when you found her. Is it in the house?"

She hesitates.

"Well...no...it's not."

"Where is it?"

"I...I've...er...to tell you the truth I did think it was in the house, but now I'm not sure...Unless she took it...yes, she must have had an accomplice, that's it there were two of them."

"And did the vigilant Mrs. Sanders see a second person?"

"Well...no...but that doesn't mean there wasn't one."

Stover looks doubtful.

"Another one of her paintings has disappeared following a burglary at the exhibition hall in Darrasea. Do you know anything about that?"

"No I don't. She's the one that breaks in, you should ask her."

"She's hardly going to steal her own painting."

"Whether she does or not, I'm not in the business of collecting all her paintings."

"She says you paid for the painting with a cheque that subsequently bounced and therefore she..."

"That's ridiculous, she can't prove that," Marilyn explodes and then turns to Templeman, "I told you before that's got nothing to do with this and you agreed."

In the adjournment Stover queries this with Templeman.

"I may have mentioned that it was a civil matter," Templeman says.

"What about the neighbour, Mrs. Sanders, was she with Marilyn Hyde at all times in the house?"

Templeman shrugs.

"They went in together."

"Marilyn said *she* found Jose Pearsall. Was Mrs. Sanders with her then?"

"Mrs. Sander examined her, said she was only knocked out."

"But that may have been after Marilyn struck Jose."

Templeman grimaces with a look that says 'you're not being serious?'

"Whatever happened she'll back up Marilyn Hyde. We only have Jose Pearsall's word for an alternative version of events," he says, adding adamantly, "Mrs Sanders has eyes like a hawk."

"So where is the painting?" Stover says.

Templeman laughs and shrugs.

"Probably somewhere else in the house."

"You don't buy this accomplice idea?"

"It's a row about a lost painting. The only important issue is Jose Pearsall broke into the house."

"Maybe so, but there are wider issues to consider," Stover says, "The bounced cheque story is genuine. She had a legitimate reason to be at the house."

"But she didn't have to break in."

"No, but it might be connected to the murder."

"You'd better see her."

Jose is glad to be out of the cell, but uncomfortable when she sees Stover. At first he doesn't mention the murder investigation. He didn't speak to her at the beach, but she recognises him. It makes her uncomfortable especially as it seems from his questioning that he's brighter than Templeman. She feels better when he doesn't mention Darrasea. Though why should she be nervous? She only discovered the body. She feels better, but then gets irritated when she has to go over the incident in Yaverton all over again. The night in the cell has done nothing to deflate her anger.

"Have you ever met Marilyn Hyde before?" Stover says.

"Fortunately not," she says, then stupidly adds, "If I had I would have throttled her!"

She immediately regrets it. If she's to get out of here she must curb her bombastic tongue!

"Why would you be so antagonistic towards her?" he says.

It's no good. She can't contain herself.

"You wouldn't believe me if I told you. I've already explained why I came to Yaverton, but no one believes me. Alright, I'll say it again. When..."

"You mean the bounced cheque?"

"Of course. That woman stole my picture. I was only retrieving my own property."

"By breaking into her house?"

"I didn't break in, she left the window open."

"It's still an offence if she chooses..."

"She deserved it!"

"But the picture isn't there."

"Because she took it down after she bumped me on the head."

"There's no proof of that. Now, when you came round...?"

"I'm not answering any more questions about this so called break in!"

"In which case you can answer questions related to my investigation into the murder of Carina Fennell."

It pulls her up. Suddenly she feels back in the police cell, alone and vulnerable.

"I had nothing to do with that," she says gravely.

He asks her about the pictures, whether she had any connection with Carina and finally about Kelly.

"I don't know her. I didn't even know her name until you told me."

"That's surprising from somebody in Darrasea."

"What's that mean?"

"People in Darrasea seem to know everybody else."

"A very sweeping generalisation of 30,000 people."

"Just an observation."

"You don't like the place."

"I didn't say that, a lot of people seem to know everybody else's business."

"Should be useful for a policeman."

"It would be if they were more forthcoming."

"Maybe it's a place where people care."

"Care enough to murder Carina Fennell?"

"She could have been killed by somebody outside."

"You're not local, are you?" he says, curling the word 'local' with particular emphasis.

"I've lived in Darrasea for six years."

"In all that time you must have come across many people, like Kelly, but you can't help me find her?"

"Assuming I want to find her, I wouldn't know where to start."

But she's no longer uninterested in Kelly and between his questions slips in queries of her own about the elusive and mysterious woman. Grudgingly he tells of his fruitless enquiries amongst the regulars at the front, lingering over his suspicions about Vince, hoping she might know him.

"I'm sure he knows about Kelly and where she is."

Jose doesn't pursue it and appears unconcerned, but she's made a mental note of Vince and what he may tell about Kelly. Her only immediate concern is to get out the police station. Her remaining there is not in Stover's interest either. He has a gut feeling she may be useful to his investigation, and so needs her back in Darrasea. For that she may have to jettison any hope of recovering her picture even though its whereabouts seem inconsistent with Marilyn Hyde's story. He suggests Templeman looks into Marilyn's background. Perhaps the break in complaint can be dropped.

He returns with Templeman to see Marilyn. At first she's reluctant, but Stover indicates he has suspicions on both sides. He asks where Mrs. Sanders was when she found Jose Pearsall. Marilyn hesitates, but before she can answer the opportunity is lost as Templeman changes the subject, suddenly implying the bounced cheque issue could be taken further. Even then Marilyn starts to come round.

"It wasn't deliberate, just a temporary financial hiatus."

"In which case it may be possible to resolve this matter quite amicably," Templeman says with relief.

Stover wants to pursue a possible assault by Marilyn, but that would require further questioning of the neighbour and Templeman is reluctant.

"We can clear it up easily," he says, "In any case it would be one word against the other and Mrs. Hyde has agreed."

Stover sees Jose again.

"Forget about the cheque!" she thunders.

"In exchange Mrs. Hyde won't press charges on breaking and entering."

"I didn't break anything."

"I assume you want to get out of here without being charged with a criminal offence."

"What about my painting?"

"She doesn't have the painting."

"'Course she does. Have you searched the house?"

"No."

"And she attacked me..."

"It's not clear who..."

"Alright, alright," Jose says, "But you'll have to search the house, otherwise there's no deal."

Stover isn't sure which is the more difficult, convincing Marilyn her house should be searched or Templeman of its necessity. Neither are models of cooperation. Only after considerable badgering of the one and grovelling to the other do they agree. Even then Templeman insists Stover supervises the search himself. It isn't a pleasant experience.

"You won't find anything," Marilyn says, "The picture's been mislaid."

"Then if you reimburse Mrs. Pearsall, everybody will be satisfied," he says.

"Okay," she says doubtfully, "But only after you're sure it isn't here."

During the 'search' she hovers constantly and is always in the way of the officers, hampering them as much as possible. Several times he has to remind her to 'give them space to work.' The ubiquitous Mrs. Sanders also appears. Ostensibly to provide 'moral support to her neighbour,' more likely to see if the intriguing painting really has been salted away. They find nothing and Marilyn gloats, saying they 'shouldn't suck up to that bloody criminal.' Mrs. Sanders looks a little disappointed. So too is Jose. She reluctantly accepts the situation, but makes it clear she's less than satisfied with his handling of the situation even after he says Marilyn has promised to 'send a new cheque shortly.'

"Oh yes and will that one bounce too?" she says, as she collects her belongings from the duty sergeant, "This is how so many crooks get away."

Templeman shakes his head as she's released and hopes with grumbling irony that Stover 'will have more success with his other investigation.' With these endorsements ringing in his ears Stover returns to Darrasea.

Interesting as the Jose Pearsall diversion may be he can't give it too much time. He must attend to other pressing matters. First, he makes for the Excelsior for another discussion with Carina's financial adviser. At the centre of the elegant sweep of white faced Victorian hotels and flats with fine views across the estuary, it's the best place to stay on the promenade. Harry Willard is in the lounge when Stover arrives. He puts his newspaper down when he sees the detective approaching and drums his fingers nervously on a coffee table. Whatever causes his edginess it's not diminished in the last twenty four hours. He stands up, putting on a jittery, plastic smile. Stover sits opposite. Harry looks at him, then from side to side as if awaiting permission to resume his seat.

"A wonderful prospect," Stover says, waving to the window, "good for the soul."

Harry stares back bewildered. Stover wonders if accountants have souls. Harry is probably calculating how much the sea is worth as an asset to the hotel.

"Very pleasant," Harry mumbles, glancing briefly at the window, then turns away as if the sea is some disagreeable reptile, "I wasn't expecting this...visit... how can I help you?"

"You've been staying here all your time at Darrasea," Stover says, still staring out the window, then turning directly to Harry, "Even before the programme was due to start?"

"I find it very convenient."

"When exactly did you come to Darrasea, Mr. Wllard?"

The fingers of Harry's right hand have not stopped drumming the table, now they accelerate until under Stover's pained stare, he slows them, finally putting his other hand over as if they have to be forcefully stopped.

"I came down for the programme, that would be..."

"Yes, but why was it necessary to arrive two weeks before the rest of the production?"

"I...er...I'm not sure if I did..."

"I've checked with the hotel."

"Well...right...yes...okay, yes I did."

"That would be around the time Carina Fennell arrived in Darrasea and when she..."

"Don't say it! I know when it was. I can read the papers and watch the television, but just don't say it!"

He starts shaking, only gradually controlling himself until apart from occasional twitches he sits quite still.

"I'm sorry. It's just...it's still a terrible shock."

Stover waits patiently and then puts his question again, but gets no satisfactory answer other than vague references to 'coming down to get prepared' (it's unclear for what) or 'taking advantage of the sea air.' (even less plausible judging by his obvious disdain for anything remotely maritime)

"We know within a day or two when Carina Fennell came to Darrasea and you were here too. Did you see her?"

"No."

"You weren't looking for her?"

Harry shrugs without answering.

"Can you account for your movements at the time?"

"I was in the hotel most of the time."

"You didn't go out?"

"I went into the town and along the promenade...it's very...pleasant."

He can't be more specific.

"So at the time of Carina Fennell's mu...(Harry flinches violently)...when she...you were in Darrasea, but you have only a hazy recollection of what you were doing and no one can vouch for you."

Harry nods gloomily and then brightens up slightly.

"I went to see the paintings."

"What paintings?"

"There was an exhibition along the road here at one of the halls..."

"Edward Hall?"

"Yes, that was it. The local art society had a display. There was some quite interesting stuff."

"Art is an interest of yours?"

"Not really. I don't know anything about it, but I like to look around. It's very...pleasant."

"I don't understand why you had to come down at all."

Harry doesn't reply. He's already said what he can, which isn't much. If he says anything more it'll only increase Stover's suspicions.

"Did you know Carina was coming to Darrasea?" Stover says.

"I was unaware of her movements, though I suppose it wouldn't have surprised me."

"So you were hoping to find her here?"

"I knew she'd left London. I won't deny I was hopeful she might be here, had the same idea as myself so to speak, though I would never presume...if I'd seen her it would have been...pleasant."

"You must have had some idea why she might come to Darrasea."

"She didn't usually confide in anyone, let alone me, when she decided to take off."

"She took off frequently?"

"Not regularly, but from time to time."

"So why should she..."

Up to now Harry's been addressing most of his remarks to the coffee table with only upward occasional glances. Now he looks directly at Stover with a pained, slightly annoyed expression.

"That's an impossible question to answer, Mr. Stover. You have to understand Carina Fennell was not like other people. You might even say she could only be judged by her own rules."

"If you mean the law," Stover says sternly, "We are all subject to the same rules."

Harry sighs, nods and smiles indulgently.

"Of course, you say that as a policeman, but that's not what I mean. There are three types of famous people ; those whose fame is already made, those who get it by rejecting what they have and those that *make* it themselves. Carina *made* everything about her. Some people said she was very lucky to do what she did, that she was really quite ordinary and just happened to be in the right place at the right time. Nothing could be further from the truth. There was nothing ordinary about Carina. Everything about her was *extra*ordinary. Some said her programme made her. It wasn't true. She *made* the programme. She had this incredible rapport with people and that was the essence of her success. On the programme she was a constant mimic. Those that said she must have worked so hard at it didn't know her. Those few who knew her really well never said any such thing for they knew she was like that all the time. It reflected her incredible ability to connect with everyone. She was always ringing up pretending to *be* somebody else. She could be anybody."

Harry pauses, recovering his breath and some emotional balance.

"I would have thought she also started out with certain advantages," Stover says mischievously, "A woman with her looks was bound to be noticed anywhere."

Harry is irate.

"A typically sexist remark, utterly unjustified. I've told you she made everything herself."

He starts shaking, his body flexing as if he's about to lunge at Stover, who tries to speak, but Harry cuts him off.

"Carina was truly creative. I've told you how her mimicking on the programme was famous, but there were also her amusing stories. There was usually one in each programme. She pretended they were true. Some were, but many were not and no one knew until the end of each programme. No one could ever guess. Everything was down to her. There were no scriptwriters. She was very talented."

"For her accountant you're remarkably knowledgeable about these things."

"Why shouldn't I know, even financial advisers can think."

Harry stops shaking, but his lips twitch slightly. He's high, but nervous.

"What about you, Mr. Willard? As her financial adviser, what did you *make*?"

"What are you implying?"

"I wonder whether Carina running away to Darrasea had some financial motive."

"She had no financial motive, as you put it, to run away from."

"These various investments you looked after, how much of those were to your own personal advantage? She might have been running away from you, from something financial you *made*."

Harry starts shaking again, but his anger spills over.

"This is preposterous! Unless you have specific allegations I advise you to..."

"I'm not making allegations, I'm asking questions and so far I've not been getting very substantial answers."

"I've answered as fully as I can. Now please, if you've finished..."

"Why so nervous, Mr. Willard, what are you nervous about?"

"I'm *not* nervous! I just object to being hounded!"

He's becoming almost hysterical. Stover has achieved as much as he can for today and abandons the interview. He walks along the promenade. It's a fair walk to the incident room, but he needs time to think. Perhaps he's said too much to Harry. It's all speculation at this stage, but he's definitely rattled. Is it just nervousness or is there more? Nervous about questions he'd rather not answer? Is the nervousness just an act, a ruse to cover up what he really knows? Is it like a lot of other things...made up?

He muses on Harry's description of Carina. He was certainly struck by her. How does Harry fit in with Amanda's theory about Carina? He's hardly a catch of any kind, let alone something to be paraded as a trophy. Did he realise she could never see him as more than an accountant or was he so enamoured he was blind to everything? But then maybe he was her real man and the likes of Dominic were distractions, intended to fool everybody, even his usually shrewd sergeant. That would make Harry's grief much more genuine than Stover has given him credit. No, he doesn't believe that. There's something not quite right about all this heart on the sleeve stuff. Or is that policeman's cynicism getting in the way? Some of it must be authentic. Was he so smitten he could see no wrong in anything she did?

What if Harry is much cleverer than even Stover allows? Conveniently wrapped around with his heart wrenching eulogy he gives no credible answers to his whereabouts at the crucial time of Carina's death. Does he deliberately exaggerate her for his own ends? Did he manipulate her 'openness,' using her benevolent, attractive reputation to further dubious financial deals, freely dipping into her investments, ‘making’ money for himself in the process? Did she find out and needing time to think ran away? Or was she involved in dodgy deals herself? Maybe Harry is the cold calculating financial wizard after all and wanted a bigger slice to keep his mouth shut?

Harry is obviously not going to give other than very cursory replies to any financial questioning. Amanda was working on Carina’s financial affairs. He won’t be surprised if some of the paper trails have already petered out in the sands of ‘creative’ accountancy. For the moment Stover will concentrate on that other acolyte of Carina, the ‘gorgeous’ Dominic. He gets back to the incident room. Unfortunately little progress has been made on Carina’s accounts and investments.

“Speed it up,” he says, “I’m going to see Dominic.”

Amanda grimaces.

“You may have a problem,” she says.

“He was at the Beach Hotel, but checked out this morning. He’s disappeared.”

Jose also returns to Darrasea without delay. Anxious to put Yaverton, Marilyn Hyde and the police station well behind her she drives fast along the narrow road through the hills.

She sits on the balcony of her second floor flat staring out to sea for over an hour, allowing its therapeutic calm to heal her troubled spirits. At first sea and sun and sky swallow her. She thinks of nothing. It’s enough, almost like Zen. She thinks amusingly of Vince. There’s a vibrant tranquillity watching gentle waves. It’s had this effect for thousands of years and will go on doing so for many thousands more. It’s reassuring knowing there’s more to the world than the nastiness and misery of human beings. But we are our thoughts and inevitably they intervene.

The loss of *Waiting for the Tide* is galling. If she’d been more patient, waited till Marilyn returned, then confronted her about the cheque she might have recovered the painting and not got herself arrested! There’s more coverage in the local paper, written by that reporter that pestered her in the ‘Warren.’ He’s squeezing a lot out of very little, milking the story so ruthlessly its like the dried variety oozing out of the cow.

'The peculiar events surrounding Art Society paintings gather apace. The last night of the annual Exhibition was dominated by the strange disturbance when a mystery woman recognised the murdered personality Carina Fennell in one of the paintings called 'Restful Haven.' This otherwise unobtrusive view of the parish church contained an image of the famous presenter, but no one else could see...'

It goes on in this vein for several paragraphs, repeating what's already been reported. Jose skips through it. Then, to her horror, the 'story' resumes with updated information.

'The unfortunate artist of the mysteriously stolen picture was the subject of a second misfortune when her other painting was purchased with an allegedly bounced cheque...'

Allegedly! Of course it bounced, doesn't anyone believe her?

'...is determined to recover her property.

'I know who they are,' she said, 'I'm going to get my picture back.'

It will be interesting to see whether she is successful in either recovering the painting or receiving the proper payment. She was unavailable for further comment and it seems may have left town...'

The cheek of the man...unavailable for further comment... seems may have left town! When you don't know what's going on, assume, surmise, even fabricate with innuendo. If he knows she's come back he'll be round to find out 'whether she is successful.' He'll get short shrift when he does. That's if she's in. No, don't run away, face the little squirt! She could confront the newspaper editor and complain. Great, give them even more copy. You don't put a fire out by loading on more logs! Anyway, surely he wasn't going to quote anything about her take on the bounced cheque? Tanya was right. As usual Jose had opened her mouth and said too much.

The stupid reporter, with his improvised guesswork only mentioned one other picture. A glance at the exhibition catalogue would have told him she had four on display. What about the other two, were they sold? Even if they were, they might still be at the Edward Hall. So obsessed with *Restful*

Haven and *Waiting for the Tide* she's completely forgotten them. Now she's anxious to look again at *Sea and Sand* and *The Rocks*. It'll be like going back to a youthful holiday destination. The same childhood place, but utterly different seen through adult eyes. What was then so large and long and distant, now seem smaller, shorter, nearer. Yet the wisdom of the years should make up for the lost spark of youth and much more can be seen. So it must be with the pictures. Splurging onto paper at breakneck speed, so much hidden detail must have been unwittingly captured. Keen to get the pictures finished and submitted she probably gave them only superficial scrutiny, making sure they were not too technically flawed without proper examination. With today's discerning eyes she only has to uncover the hidden gems, artlessly included in the haste and verve of the day.

She has to find them. Then she remembers. Before she left for Yaverton she'd asked Tanya to collect any unsold pictures from the hall. She rings Tanya, but it takes several minutes to put her question. Her friend is too anxious to know what's been happening.

"There's this rumour you've been arrested."

"Where did you hear that?"

"In the salon of course, you know that's where I hear everything."

"You can't believe..."

"I know, of course you can't, that's what I said to the customer, there's no way Jose would..."

"Who knows I've been to Yaverton?"

"Just about everybody."

"But how's that?"

"Well, you did say to that reporter..."

"Oh God!"

"...well I did say..."

Jose groans.

"...but as I said to the stupid woman, there's no way Jose would get herself arrested...it's just beyond belief, she only went to get her painting back...that's right...isn't it... (silence)...Jose...it is right isn't it... (more silence) ... Jose, tell me it isn't is it...(longer silence)...oh God!"

Then Jose has to tell the whole sorry story. She starts out quietly in almost a whimper, but with the detail of Marilyn and Mrs. Sanders and Templeman and the police station and Stover, she speaks quicker and louder and it all seems quite funny until at the end she's almost laughing. Then Tanya starts laughing until neither of them can talk at all. Only when they've both stopped quaking, croaking, spluttering and screeching does Jose mention the pictures in the hall.

"Haven't got them," Tanya says.

"Didn't you go?"

"Of course I went, but they wouldn't let me in."

"Who?"

"Mary Stokes. The door was locked, but I could see there was somebody inside. So I gave it a good thump and she came out, but she wouldn't let me in."

"Why not?"

"She said it was because of the break in."

"Did you tell her you'd come to collect pictures?"

"Of course, but she said they couldn't be collected until the police had finished."

"Fat lot of good they'll be doing."

"I don't think they were there. I couldn't see any police cars."

"She'll damn well let me in, police or not."

Tanya manages to get her to delay the confrontation for an hour so she can join her at lunchtime.

"She might have reinforcements," Tanya chuckles, "two of us are more likely to barge in."

Tanya hopes the delay will calm Jose down, but it also gives her further time to think. She can't get Kelly and Carina out of her mind. If she'd seen them what would Kelly have made of the other three paintings? Would she see Carina in them too? Maybe she did, but kept her observations to herself. Far from an aberration, what if *Restful Haven* was the last straw, the *fourth* frightening image of the dead woman? News of the murder wasn't announced until after the last day of the exhibition. She wouldn't have known she was dead. Or did she? Was it a premonition? Had she seen in the pictures what was going to happen? There could be only one other explanation. Kelly knew because she was involved. So why hasn't Stover picked her up?

Involved or not, all the pictures could be linked to Carina Fennell. She tries to remember the detail, but her recollection is as hazy as the estuary with the sun sparkling intermittently through the clouds on an atmospheric sea or a misty evening on the beach. Why didn't she photograph them? For the same reason she mishandled everything else, she was in such an infernal hurry! She must see for herself. If the pictures aren't sold she can find Kelly and confront her. If they are sold, she can track down the purchasers and get them photographed.

She's early outside Edward Hall and prowls impatiently around the car park. She promised Tanya not to go in alone, but she's tempted to hammer on the door and demand entry. Remonstrating with Mary Stokes is almost a deliciously appetising meal in itself! If Tanya wasn't allowed in there's a good chance the society hasn't allowed the collection of any unsold pictures. Mary Stokes didn't say whether they were sold. The normal arrangement is for sold pictures to be collected at the end of the exhibition. If they'd kept to their own rules *Waiting for the Tide* would still be there and the bounced cheque exposed without loss! What if the others have been sold and they've also been released? Surely not another set of bounced cheques! Sold pictures are only usually released to purchasers out of the area. She has to hope that any sales have been to local people.

Tanya arrives. The front door is locked. They station themselves on either side with Jose on the 'blind' side, relatively unseen when the door is opened from the inside.

"We're going in," Jose says, "whatever she says."

Tanya raps the glass loudly. No one appears. She raps again. Then Mary Stokes emerges from the inner door. She waves her hand and shakes her head.

"We're shut!" she shouts.

"I have pictures to collect," Tanya shouts back.

"You can't get them."

"I have to collect them."

This continues for some minutes with Mary saying she can't come in, Tanya saying she must and demanding she open up. Eventually Mary comes to the door. Tanya steps back. As soon as Mary opens the door, Jose flies in and pushes her aside. Tanya follows quickly.

"I've already said you can't come in," Mary says.

"Well, we're in," Jose says, "so I'll take my pictures."

"We're not sorted, what with the police and..."

"Don't be ridiculous, the police have nothing to do with it."

Jose walks into the main room. The display stands have been taken down and are leaning against the wall. The room is otherwise bare and empty.

"Where are they?" Jose bellows.

Mary doesn't reply at first, standing with her arms crossed, tight lipped and intransigent. With Jose at its far end and Tanya near the door she looks isolated, vulnerable in the middle of the room.

"Where are the pictures!" Jose screeches.

Mary jumps slightly, her arms falling to her side. Then she recovers, re-crosses her arms and with a defiant glare says, "I thought you'd gone to Yaverton."

"Well I'm back!"

Tanya moves innocently towards her, but Mary takes this as a threat and steps away, only to face Jose.

"In the store room," she says, pointing to the door behind her and stepping aside again.

Jose and Tanya brush past and go in. Hundreds of pictures are on the tables and stacked against the walls. Jose starts to examine one side and motions Tanya to the other.

"Why haven't these been sorted," she shouts to Mary, "everybody must be crying out for their paintings to be returned."

"We've told people how difficult it's been with the burglary and having to explain to the Council and with the police... everybody's been very patient."

"Ridiculous! None of that is any excuse, it didn't stop you returning pictures...what about the ones sold...have you seen them yet Tanya."

"No."

"People have been very patient," Mary mumbles.

"Well, I'm not!" Jose says, noisily dragging out paintings.

"Be careful!" Mary says, walking over.

Jose turns on her.

"You should have been careful when that criminal gave you that damned cheque!"

"They're not here," Tanya says as she gets to the end of the stacked paintings and goes over to the table.

Jose reaches the end of the other wall.

"Where are my paintings? Have some been taken away?"

"It's very confusing," Mary says.

"You can say that again though confusion must be normal these days."

"I mean we were all so confused the last night of the exhibition after that...unpleasantness and that girl making that unfortunate scene and then the next day with the burglary..."

"When my picture was stolen...oh God, that's it, isn't it... the others have been stolen...why wasn't I told...?"

"It's not that, it's..."

"I'm holding you responsible for all my losses!"

"There haven't been any more losses, at least none that I know of, but there is..."

"Exactly, none that you know of, that's precisely the problem, if you had..."

"Shut up Jose and let her speak!" Tanya shouts.

Jose turns to her and then back to Mary.

"Well?"

"As I said, it was all very confusing that night and the following morning. I wanted to get the pictures sorted out, but there was no one to help me and Robert was anxious to check on the insurance situation. He's not been back since, but he did take some of the pictures with him. He said it was for safe keeping."

"Were my other two pictures sold?"

"I'm afraid I don't know. Robert also took the sales book with him."

"So I have two pictures gone, both stolen and now two more which may have been stolen or may have been sold or may be with the treasurer!"

"You'll have to hope they're with him," Tanya says.

The front door opens and there are footsteps in the main room.

"Mary, are you there?"

It's Robert Darley. He comes into the store room, stopping abruptly when he sees Jose.

"Oh, it's you Jose," he says, then turns in an aside to Mary, "I thought no one was coming yet to collect..."

"Have you got her pictures?" she says.

"No, no I haven't."

"Do you know where they are?"

"Well, there was the burglary and..."

"No, she had two other pictures, what happened to them?"

Jose and Tanya come over.

"Stop whispering like a couple of kids at the back of the class," Jose says, "Do you know what's happened to my pictures, you'll find them in the catalogue, *Sea and Sand* and *The Rocks?*"

Robert takes books and papers from his bag and spreads them out on the table. He checks the catalogue and then the sales book. He takes a long time. Jose sighs impatiently.

"Yes," he says at last, "here they are. Let me see. Yes, they've both been collected."

"So you've broken your own rules again," Jose explodes, "I suppose this is going to be another bounced cheque!"

Robert checks his ledger nervously, then looks up with relief.

"No, there's no problem. I can give you a cheque for both pictures, fully paid up, the purchaser paid in cash."

"One purchase, they were both sold to the same person?" Jose says.

"Yes, both pictures. I wouldn't normally have allowed them to go, but he was most insistent."

"Well of course," Jose sneers, "If you're going to have rules, the first thing is to break them!"

"Not quite. It was most unusual. He wanted to take them immediately and when I said he couldn't he offered to make an extremely generous donation to the society charity raffle, really most generous, I really don't see how I could refuse especially as he was paying in cash so there was no risk."

"Do you have his name?"

"Yes, Mr. Harry Willard."

5

IN a quiet section, about three quarters along the promenade the occupant of a turquoise and white VW camper in excellent condition for its thirty odd years is stirring. At this time of the year parking is free and those who choose to stay over the winter can usually get away with it so long as they move the vehicle fairly regularly. This one has been static for three days now.

It's a late start for Vince. He likes to be up and about by seven thirty except on overcast December days. The dark mornings hang like a black shroud over the beach, the charcoal clouds blotting out so much sun. He usually regrets such decisions, for it only makes the day more difficult to bear. Even the little glimmer of midday light is worth the effort in staving off the winter blues. But bright, frequently warm days are usually the norm in late September and this morning he should have been out and along the front before breakfast. Something preyed on his mind during the night and sleep hadn't come easy until about four. After that he inevitably slept in. It's after nine. It can't be helped. He dresses quickly, opens the curtains and starts breakfast.

The camper is cramped by modern standards, but for a man on his own, relatively detached from material needs and creature comforts other than keeping warm and dry it's more than adequate. The secret is being organised, everything in its proper place, making the most efficient use of space. Tidiness has never come easily to Vince, but over the years necessity has overruled predilection and he's instilled an effectively ordered regime.

He sits near the windscreen, facing the sea, sipping coffee and munching toast. The sun creeps round the headland, the long fingering shadows receding across the sand, gradually turning the dull brown to an orangey yellow and glistening the sea. It's still relatively quiet. A few dog walkers are on the beach, but few on the promenade. He doesn't like being disturbed, preferring to be away on his travels or outside with his chair, but today he's sluggish. He puts on more toast and picks up the local paper he bought yesterday. He's not a regular reader, but has recently been following the long controversy over the proposed redevelopment of land on the estuary beyond the marina. The council's proposals have successfully done what no other issue had managed in the previous two hundred years, uniting every element of the community in violent opposition! There's only a brief reference to the latest machinations on page five and Vince desultorily skims over other pages in search of something interesting. It's full of football matches, society meetings, weddings, school achievements, planning applications, promotional offers by shops, the usual bread and butter of the local press. Vince hardly concentrates as names and dates flicker through his mind like individual playing cards when shuffled on a table. He turns to the letters page in the hope of finding something outrageous or at least amusing before venturing out, but they're all disappointingly mundane, trivial or petty. Then a short headline catches his eye, *Artist Arrested in Yaverton.*

"Troubled artist Jose Pearsall was this week arrested in Yaverton. She was at the centre of the bizarre event on the last day of the annual art exhibition when a mysterious woman said she saw murdered television personality Carina Fennell in her picture 'Restful Haven.' This picture was stolen from Edward Hall the same night while her other painting 'Waiting for the Tide' was the subject of a fierce argument between her and society officers over an alleged fraudulent

payment. As reported in our last edition Mrs Pearsall vowed to recover the painting and travelled to Yaverton where she understood the purchaser lived.'

'To add to all her growing anxieties she has now run into trouble with the police. She is alleged to have forced entry into a house in Yaverton where she believed her painting 'Waiting for the Tide' was situated. At the moment she is being held at a police station in Yaverton and it is not known whether she will be charged. However, we understand the elusive painting has not been recovered and Mrs Pearsall is making accusations that a second of her paintings has been stolen! For obvious reasons the indefatigable Mrs Pearsall is not available for comment, but we look forward to reporting her version of events when or if she returns to Darrasea.'

Vince is fascinated, but detached. It's nothing to do with him, though it has a certain amusement value. Then he remembers that night, *Restful Haven* and Kelly and above all the theft. Despite getting up late he can't avoid his normal routine and continues to sit impassively, communing with the sea and the sky and the universe before full meditation. He tries to do this at least once a day and early morning is usually the best time. He concentrates on the distant headland as he's done so many times before, but his mind wanders and flitters irresponsibly. This is not efficient and it's not usual. He blames the activity on the front. He's left it too late and there are too many people about. But that's not the real reason. He shifts his point of contact, staring out to sea, but it's increasingly difficult to remain detached. The picture, the cheque and above all Kelly dribble and disturb his mind. Finally he gives up, clears away breakfast, locking the van and striding away down the front. He has to find Kelly.

Darrasea is a town with many cafes. Some close after the end of the season in October, but the majority stay open all year round. Vince knows them all. He has his favourites, more usually determined by price than any other factor, though location and ambience (though he would never use such a word) also figure. The 'Copper Kettle' is an exception. The name alone might normally put him off and it's not the cheapest, but it has its uses. Most important it's favoured by others from whom he might find Kelly. Tucked at the end of a side street behind the Methodist Church it gets little trade from visitors, so must attract a loyal local clientele to survive. That can be problematic in Darrasea. The natives, flexible, open and friendly, can be fickle in their loyalties. Once accepted, shops, tradesmen, professionals, businesses can rely on a faithful following, but that acceptance is sometimes hard won. In the past many a newly opened café or store has been greeted with rumbling remarks that 'it won't fit in.' Darraseans are not taken in by trendy movements or the positive opinions of other, more prosperous places. They require value for money, but once their loyalty is acquired it's not easily lost.

Vince and the 'Copper Kettle' have one thing in common. They've both been 'accepted,' at least in their respective spheres. He's known in the café and exchanges banter with the owner and the waitress. He with an impeccable local accent is half Italian and half Irish. She speaks with her unmistakable Lancastrian origins and like Vince arrived years ago seeking pastures new, never bothering to move on. He can't see Kelly, but decides to stay. Having started late most of his routines are already disrupted. He sits by the window and finishes off the local paper over a large mug of coffee and an early brunch.

As the old saying goes, sometimes he sits and reads, sometimes he sits and thinks and sometimes he just sits. Deprived of his usual early morning reflection, this latter activity slightly rejuvenates his spirits. Concentrating on the funeral director's garage doors or the jeweller's window, he doesn't notice Jose enter the café and hover at the door. She looks around, pays no more attention to him than he does to her, then talks to the waitress at the counter. Even when she comes to his table, he hardly notices.

"Do you mind if I sit here, only it's a little crowded?"

He looks around. There are spare chairs at other tables.

"Certainly," he says, opening his hands before returning to the paper.

She looks across, sensing he's not concentrating on the paper.

"Are you Vince Randall?"

He lowers the paper and peers at her again as if struggling to place her.

"Who wants to know?"

"Jose Pearsall."

He still looks. The large blue eyes fix him. He knows the name, but can't place her. Then he looks down at the paper, open at the letters page and the story about the artist. He looks up. She too has noticed the page and is smiling.

"The painter?" he says, "There's a lot about you in here."

"More than there should be."

"Why, isn't it true?"

"So far as it goes, it's a little sensational."

"*...the indefatigable Mrs Pearsall ...we look forward to reporting her version of events...*Have they caught up with you yet?"

"I don't think they know I'm back."

He looks down at the report again.

"How did you get away from the police?"

"They wanted me back in Darrasea, so they let me out. It was all a misunderstanding anyway."

"What about your painting, did you get that back?"

"No."

"So that's two you've...mislaid as it were and..."

"They've not been mislaid, they've been stolen!"

"Okay, okay, " he says, holding up his hands defensively, "they were stolen. So, what do you want with me?"

"I'm looking for Kelly. I was told you might know where she is."

"Everybody wants to find Kelly, first that hack from the Advertiser then the fuzz, now you."

"The police, who was that?"

"Name of Stover."

She nods.

"You know him?"

"He's the one got me out of Yaverton. What's he want with Kelly?"

He shrugs, then says, "Maybe the same as you."

"Do you know where she is?"

"How did you find me here?"

"I asked around. Most people know you at the front. They said you might be here."

"They don't usually talk to complete strangers."

"Everybody talks to me."

He looks into her bright eyes with their inviting combination of innocence and fascination. He can easily see why people will find it so difficult *not* to talk to her.

"It's a rare gift," he says grudgingly, "Not one I've ever been blessed with."

"Perhaps you don't need to talk to people, they just follow you anyway."

"Why do you say that?"

"The impression I get from talking to people."

"Even though you only wanted to talk to me about Kelly. That figures, few want me for myself," he says, then adds with a gruff smirk, "It must be my sartorial elegance."

"Looks aren't everything."

"I've never been accused of being one of the beautiful people."

She doesn't reply. Clearly not something she wants to contradict, he thinks while she wonders why he wants to talk about anything except Kelly.

"Middle of the week, plenty of time to wander along the front noseying about, time on your hands," he says.

"I get by."

"On your own, divorced I'd say."

"You're very observant...or a good guesser...what about you?"

"Let's just say I'm best when I'm alone."

"The beach combing individualist."

"We're all stereotypes, the whole idea of individuals is a foolish illusion."

"What are you then, the middle aged drop out, a latter day hippy trying to live the life that passed you by in your twenties when you were probably ultra conventional?"

It may be less obvious, but he too has an ability to get people to talk, she thinks. Interesting how she's freely told him her personal situation, but he's said nothing about his. She lets it go. He laughs.

"I was unconventional by being conventional during those flower power days."

"You don't fit easily."

"I try not to."

"Not even into a stereotype."

"Then that's my tragedy."

"Do you always contradict yourself?"

"As much as possible, but I'm frequently unsuccessful. It's a lifelong pursuit, refusing to be labelled. One way to make contact with ultimate reality."

"Sounds like Zen."

"It is," he says authoritatively.

Her wide eyes penetrate.

"There's only one ultimate reality currently exercising my mind. I need to talk to Kelly and you know her."

"According to you I know everybody."

"It's not everybody I want to talk to."

"I don't know where she is."

"Did you come here to find her?"

"I told you I don't know where she is."

"All the more reason to come here."

The sparring continues for several minutes. Vince could leave, but he stays, even extending the discussion before finally getting to the heart of the matter.

"It's all to do with that picture, isn't it, the one you rightly say was stolen?"

"It could be."

"I know it was stolen because I saw the burglar."

"What that night?"

"Just before midnight."

"What were you doing at Edward Hall at that time of night?"

"I get about. It was you said I know everybody and everything at the front."

"Have you told the police?"

"No."

"Why not?"

"Maybe I think it's their business to find out. Anyway, they're a bit like tax collectors, sometimes the less they know the better the rest of us are."

"It's not the same. I'm no better off because you've not told anyone."

"I didn't say I didn't tell anyone, only that I didn't tell the police."

Jose looks at him incredulously, waiting for him to go on. Surely he's not going to leave it up in the air now! But he says no more and she has to break the silence.

"Who was it?"

He shrugs.

"It was too dark, I couldn't even say whether it was a man or a woman, but definitely carrying something, the right size for a painting."

"Not much use then," she says with some disappointment.

"Maybe not, but worth reporting."

"But you said you hadn't..."

"Exactly, but neither did anyone else."

He says this with a twinkling 'know what I mean?' She finds this jumping between inconclusive titbits irritating. His pinteresque obscurantism is annoying, but then he's said enough already. He must want her to know.

"I've not been approached by Stover. A bit odd, you might think?"

"Meaning whoever you told didn't tell him?"

"Exactly."

"Who was it?"

"Wendy Arbon, Carina Fennell's agent."

"She might have thought *you* were going to tell him."

He lifts his eyebrows.

"Of course, now you've told me, I might tell him."

"Feel free," he says.

He's so relaxed. Is he testing her as he tested Wendy?

"Do you intend confronting Wendy about it?"

"What, have a go at her for not telling the fuzz?"

"Well, black kettles and pots come to mind, but if you suspect..."

"I didn't say that."

"You implied she had a reason for not going to the police."

"As I might have one."

"You could, but then why tell her and me?"

"I could be the burglar myself."

"In which case you should immediately hand over the painting to it's rightful owner."

He smiles whimsically, then abruptly changes direction.

"That Dominic isn't around either."

"Who's he?"

"Dominic Mathers, Carina Fennell's latest man friend."

"And he's been in Darrasea?"

"Was. Gone now."

"How do you know?"

He taps his nose.

"I know where he was staying."

"Is it important?"

He shrugs.

"Do the police know?"

He shrugs again, then says, "And was your trip to Yaverton a complete failure?"

She eyes him carefully, trying to read his intentions. Is this a question or a statement, as if he either already knows the answer? He delights in dropping bits and pieces like he might feed a dog. She resents being treated like a pet. If he knows he should tell her, but before she can react he dribbles some more.

"What about the person who bounced the cheque, whose house you...entered?"

"She's called Marilyn Hyde. The picture was there, but she denied it. I had to drop the bounced cheque business in order to get off the burglary charge."

"It still rankles?"

"She's still not sent the new cheque I was promised. I don't trust her and I don't just mean the money. I'm sure she's got some connection to the picture."

"Ah yes, the pictures," he says, opening his arms wide and smiling broadly.

"It's not funny!"

He puts his hands down and frowns.

"Why did you say *pictures*?" she says, "the plural."

"Because they're both your concern...or perhaps there were even more than two?"

"I put four in the exhibition. The other two were sold."

"But now you're thinking all four have a special relationship."

"You make it sound like diplomacy!" she laughs.

He remains grim faced, his lips closed and tight. Then he says, "Diplomacy often hides sinister things."

"Anyway, you're right. It's the pictures that matter, which is why I want to talk to Kelly."

He sighs resignedly, changes the subject, wandering down conversational dead alleys, but is finally worn down by Jose's persistence and mounting anger.

"You know where she is!"

"Okay, okay, I did come here looking for her, but as you can see..."

"Have you no idea where she is!"

He pauses to let her vehemence subside slightly.

"I've one idea..."

"And you'll take me there..."

"Yes...she might be at the front. One of the beach huts – it's let to a couple of retired women, they love to sunbathe in the summer – Kelly often goes and talks to them. We could try it."

They leave the café, walk up the hill, then down the bank towards the front. Jose asks lots of questions, but Vince becomes unresponsive as if regretting his sudden cooperation.

"Do you do nothing now?" she says.

He stops and turns to her.

"Why must people always *do* something? That's the tragedy of their lives, forever being labelled with jobs or even worse, careers."

"I take that to mean you don't do anything."

"What about you?"

"I have my painting."

"You can't make a living out of that."

"I don't need to, I..."

She stops short, unwilling to say she'd made enough from her business to effectively 'retire,' but he's got the unspoken message.

"Aha!" he cries gleefully, "The unmistakable smell of an entrepreneur."

"But one who gave up and is no longer labelled as you put it."

He seems satisfied and walks slightly ahead, but she catches him up.

"And how do *you* afford to live without something to *do*?" she says, determined not to be outdone.

"I used to be a management consultant," he says quietly and then as if it expiates, "it's a fair time ago."

She laughs, loud and long. He stops and waits for her to stop, then says, "Tell me about your pictures."

They reach the promenade. The grim lipped expression returns. He seems serious. Briefly she describes the four pictures. He listens carefully, then nods to himself.

"And you believe these are all connected in some way to Carina Fennell?"

How has he figured that out, can he get into her head? She answers guardedly.

"I'm beginning to wonder."

"You painted them all on the same day and went from one location to the other, three out of the four on the front. That was at the time the police now believe Carina Fennell was murdered."

"It could be the exact day."

"The places are as interesting as the date."

"Because they are connected to Carina?"

"Maybe."

After the lifeboat station Vince quickens his step and crosses the road to where the first line of beach huts begins. He's seen something, Jose thinks. The sun is high now. A number of the hut doors are open and a few people are sitting outside, one couple sunbathing. Vince ignores them all, marching further along the line. Near its end Jose sees someone younger than the others, sitting alone, half in, half out of the hut.

“Don’t frighten her,” Vince says, “she’ll be nervous of you.”

Kelly is nodding and shaking slightly. At first Jose thinks there’s something wrong until she notices Kelly has earphones connected to a small radio. She doesn’t see them approaching. Jose heeds Vince’s warning and hangs back while he steps slowly round into Kelly’s sight line. Even then she pays little attention other than a vague circling wave to acknowledge his presence. He draws two of the chairs from inside the hut. He sets one beside her and sits down, motioning Jose to the other on his other side. He gestures to Kelly to take off her earphones, which she does reluctantly. She’s dressed in the same shapeless jumper and sits like an Egyptian statue, arms at her side, hands on her hips. Her large, vacuous eyes stare suspiciously at Jose, who smiles, trying not to appear intimidating.

“This is Jose,” Vince says without further explanation.

Kelly continues to stare as if she expects Jose to say something.

“On your own?” Vince says.

“Elsie and Margaret have gone into town,” Kelly says, “I’m minding the hut.”

“Will they be long?”

She stares at Vince with a vacancy that questions the necessity of the question. Then she shrugs. He tries an alternative approach.

“When did they leave?”

She shrugs and grimaces.

“Dunno...couple o’ minutes, five, ten.”

“Not long.”

She nods absently, then looks again at Jose.

“Who’s she?”

“I told you, Jose Pearsall.”

“Do I know her?”

Jose loses her brief, artificial smile. She dislikes being spoken of in the third person as if she’s not there.

“In a way,” Vince says, “You remember that picture you saw in the exhibition...the one of the church...”

Kelly's eyes open wider and for the first time seem to focus properly. She shudders slightly. Vince breaks off and Jose tries to look less forbidding, both afraid Kelly might suddenly erupt uncontrollably. It passes.

"Yer?" she says to Vince, keeping her eyes on Jose.

"Well, Jose is the painter."

"Oh yer, yer, I remember now," Kelly says, "I saw her name in the bottom corner."

"You remember my signature?" Jose says.

Kelly stares silently for a moment, again as if the question is irrelevant.

"I remember everything about that picture."

"Yes, it was called..."

"...*Restful Haven*...see I know, it was of the church."

She stops suddenly and looks back along the front as if she's looking for or has seen someone. Vince and Jose follow her gaze. Jose glances at Vince for explanation. He lifts his eyebrows in ignorance.

"I wanted to ask you about the painting," Jose says.

Kelly turns back, her eyes wide, wild and looking out to sea, beyond Jose.

"No, no, I don't want to talk about it."

"It's only..." Jose begins, but Vince puts a hand on her arm and she stops.

Kelly pulls the jumper up around her neck.

"Have you been into town lately?" Vince says, changing the subject.

"No, just been around here."

"You should because..."

"Don't want people seeing me," she says sternly.

"People see you all the time."

"Nar, not here, not like in town."

"How's it different?" Jose says.

"'Cause people look at you there and I don't want them looking."

"Why, what is there to look at?"

Kelly's sudden aggressive expression tells Jose she's said the wrong thing. She's about to say she didn't mean anything derogatory, but it's too late and Kelly cuts in.

"See, you're the same, 'what is there to see?' That's it in'it? I'm not worth seeing, so I'd rather not be seen. Who'd want to look at me?"

"But there's nothing..." Jose begins. Vince tries to stop her, but she waves him aside and continues, "There's nothing wrong with you, nothing that a bit of tidying up wouldn't put right! That's the trouble with you young girls, you're too obsessed with your looks and imagining you've got problems when you haven't. You've got a pretty face and a good figure, at least you would have if you stopped covering it up with that ridiculous jumper, it does nothing for you!"

Kelly sits back, rebuffed, eyes wide, mouth open and for a moment it seems she might retaliate. Then she starts to whimper and Jose and Vince are afraid she'll retreat into herself, but it turns into a halting titter and then a proper laugh. Jose laughs too.

"Don't know what you're laughing at," Kelly says, "not just young girls that are obsessed with their looks. Older women do too. How long did you spend looking into the mirror this morning?"

"A lot longer than you did," Jose says, "If you'd spent as long as me you'd know what I mean and go out and make something of yourself."

Kelly laughs again, but it's a little forced.

"That's if you own a mirror," Jose says.

"I don't think..." Vince says with gritted teeth at Jose.

"Shut up you," Jose says, brushing him aside.

"'Course I've got a bloody mirror," Kelly says, "but...it's not like you say..."

"It's nothing to do with mirrors or looks," Jose says, "it's about confidence. You've got to stop worrying what other people think."

"I don't care what other people think."

Jose shakes her head and stares knowingly at Kelly.

"Is that why you're here? Too many people doing you down, making you feel guilty for just being yourself, even for just being born?"

A long oppressive silence follows. Vince shuffles uneasily. Jose's said too much. He's not going to be able to get Kelly out of this very easily. Damn the woman! Who does she thinks she is? If she can't get her brain engaged she should keep her big mouth shut! Yet Kelly is not really put down and keeps her eyes on Jose.

"I've been there," Jose says, "Don't listen to them, listen to yourself."

"Them?" Kelly says.

"Your family...isn't it?"

Kelly turns away.

"You've said too much, leave her alone," Vince says and then quietly to Jose, "What do you hope to achieve by this?"

Before she can reply Kelly turns round.

"You don't look like a painter."

"What do painters look like?" Jose says.

"You know, long hair and big hats and big loose coats and..."

"A little untidy?"

"Well, yer."

"You don't have to *look* like anything to be able to paint any more than to do anything else."

"Well you don't look like a painter, you're too small and you have curly hair and you don't look washed out."

"Thanks for that. If I don't fit the image I only hope the pictures are okay."

"Oh yer, they are, I like them, well the one I saw, the one of the church with the big tree and big cross on the headstone and the two cars, one blue the other yellow and there were six people in front of the door and..."

"Good God, you remember all that!"

"I remember everything about it."

"You must have been in the exhibition many times."

"No, only that once."

"Had you been in very long?"

"About ten minutes. I'd been past a few times before and thought about going in, but put it off, I didn't want..."

"...to be seen?"

"Yer, something like that, but I like pictures, though I've not seen many."

“You seem to have an amazing memory for what you have seen.”

“I suppose I could have looked at more that night, but then I saw...you know...I saw her...”

“Carina Fennell.”

“Yer, her.”

“At the time I was standing a little way away, so I didn’t really know what was going on. Can you tell me more about what you saw?”

Kelly turns away again.

“No, no, I don’t what to talk about it. I’ve said enough.”

“Why don’t you want to talk about the picture?”

“Because of him,” she glances at Vince.

“Vince?” Jose says.

“No, no, not him, that guy that came looking for me...that policeman.”

“She means chief inspector Stover,” Vince says.

“Oh him!” Jose says, “Yes, I suppose he is a bit of a pain in the arse.”

“Sounds like he got you out of the nick.”

“Well, yes, that apart.”

Jose has continued to look at Kelly, who’s pulled up her legs around her knees and her hands around her mouth almost in a foetal position.

“It’s not him that’s asking now,” Jose says gently, “Whatever you say I won’t laugh, nor will I tell anyone else.”

“What do you want to know?” Kelly says quietly, almost inaudibly, speaking through her fingers across her mouth.

“Where was Carina in the picture.”

“Near the door of the church.”

“With the other people?”

“No, they were away from her. She was coming out of the church.”

“You’re sure she was coming out?”

“Yer, ’cause she was walking away.”

Vince and Jose glance at each other. Vince shakes his head slightly, but tentatively Jose goes on.

“She was definitely walking out of the church, she was... moving...?”

"Yer, but not at first, only after I'd been looking for a bit."

"How long, a minute or two?"

"No, not that long, a few seconds maybe."

"And was...anyone else...moving...?"

"No, they were just standing around."

Kelly describes the other people, their build, what they were wearing.

"What about Carina?" Jose says.

"She was all in red, you know top and trousers."

"A suit?"

"Yer, it was you know, good, pretty posh."

"So Carina was wearing a good quality red suit?"

"Yer."

"Anything else?"

"She had very nice shoes, they were real good like..."

"Stylish?"

"Yer, that's right...stylish."

"That's incredible, to notice her shoes in the picture."

"You must know, you painted her."

"How did you know it was her?"

"I saw her picture once in one of the papers."

"You saw this recently."

"No, don't see papers much, it was one o' them, you know, picture papers, Hello, Goodbye or summat."

Jose glances at Vince. He nods.

"But it was quite a small painting, Carina must have appeared very small, how could you be sure it was her if you'd only seen her in a paper some time ago?"

"Never forget pictures, never forget what I see in papers."

Kelly stares hard at Jose as if to say 'I won't be forgetting you either.'

"Have you...seen things like this before?"

"What do you mean?"

"Well, unusual things...like..."

"Like people moving?"

"Well...yes..."

"Yer, a few times."

"Have you told anybody?"

"No, don't like to...in case..."

Jose touches her arm.

"It's alright, I said I won't tell anyone."

"I like pictures, I'd like to see some more."

"What about the other paintings you sold," Vince says, "they might also be interesting to Kelly, she might be able to see things in them too."

"That's if I can get to see them again myself," Jose says.

"You've been seeing into quite a few things lately!"

Engrossed in their own discussion none of them has noticed someone standing beside the door of the beach hut. All three turn to see Chief Inspector Stover.

"How long have you been there?" Jose says.

"Long enough to be sure who you're talking too, Ms Pearsall," he says, staring across to Kelly who turns away nervously.

"Leave her alone," Vince says.

"Who?"

"Kelly, she's not up to your questions."

"Which is why you obstructed my enquiries by not telling me where I could find her?"

"She wasn't here then."

"But she is now."

Jose gets up and approaches Stover.

"Vince is right, she really is very delicate. This isn't the time nor really the place."

"But it is for you, I suppose?"

"You led him here," Vince shouts, pointing at Stover with one arm and shielding Kelly with the other, "sitting here all innocent and protective, all along giving him time to get here!"

"Of course I didn't," Jose says, "I no more want him here than you do."

"So you're also intent on obstructing my enquiries."

"Don't be ridiculous!"

"Either way, both of you can now leave," Vince says, getting up, "I'm not leaving Kelly alone with you."

"You've no choice," Stover says grimly, facing up to Vince, "besides she won't be alone."

Sergeant Barrow steps from behind the door.

"I see you come well prepared," Jose says, "Who's she?"

"My sergeant."

"Well, I'll stay if you don't mind, to give Kelly moral support," Jose says.

"As it happens I do mind. Kelly isn't being questioned under caution, it's merely a preliminary discussion, it'll take a few minutes."

"Then it won't matter if I stay," Jose says adamantly.

"It matters very much," Stover says, getting angrier, "You're making a habit of interfering with my enquiries. You've only just been released from custody in Yaverton."

"I was innocent."

"That may or may not be the case, but you had no business going to see Dominic Mathers' sister."

"Who did you say?"

"Let's be polite and say you *entered* the home of Marilyn Hyde."

"Yes, yes, but what did you call her?"

"Marilyn Hyde, the woman who's house you..."

"You said Dominc Mathers' sister."

"Yes, Marilyn Hyde is Dominic Mathers sister."

"You didn't say she was his sister in Yaverton."

"That's because in Yaverton I didn't know, but I'm wondering now what was your connection with her and him."

"Until you told me I had no idea she was his sister. You should talk to him about any connection."

"I'd very much like to, but unfortunately he's not available. Despite assuring me he would remain in Darrasea, Dominic Mathers has left town."

"I'm staying," Vince says, moving slightly away from the beach hut, "the pavement is the public highway, I've every right to be here."

Stover sighs and grits his teeth.

"I'm having no geriatric hippy wasting my time. Now, just move along."

"You can only communicate in outdated stereotypes," Vince says, folding his arms resolutely.

"Nick him for obstruction, sergeant," Stover says.

"Come on, Vince," Jose says, taking his arm, "This isn't doing Kelly any good."

He pushes away her arm, though not aggressively and edges away. Jose also steps from the beach hut. Kelly shrivels up even more, her eyes darting nervously between Vince and Jose, then to Stover, finally to Amanda, then back to Vince again.

"Don't leave here," Vince says to her emphatically, "I'll be back for you," and then to Stover, "I'll be around."

"Before we go, chief inspector," Jose says to Stover quietly, turning away from Kelly, "I assume there's no longer any problem divulging information on what Carina Fennell was wearing when she was murdered?"

"Why would you want to know?"

"Indulge me, please."

He grimaces.

"Would you at least confirm she was wearing a good quality red suit?"

"Yes," he says grudgingly.

"And shoes, which could be called fashionable, stylish even?"

"Yes, is that all?"

"Just one last thing. Though it's not confidential, this information has not yet been released publicly?"

"No."

"Thank you, you've been most helpful," she says, smiling graciously, then turning back, "Come along, Vince."

They retire a short distance to the Estuary café. Vince is so worried about Kelly he insists on sitting at a window seat where he can see up the promenade towards the beach huts, though he can't see either her or Stover.

"He won't be long with her," Jose says reassuringly, "Leave it a quarter hour and you can go back when he's finished."

He remains uneasy and then apologises for erupting when Stover arrived.

"It was understandable," she says, "but you can see he and I aren't exactly the best of friends. In any case there's no need for you to act the minder."

"As long as she doesn't wander off in a state."

"She won't wander off, she's in charge of the hut remember."

"Even so, you shouldn't have spoken to her like that."

"Like what?"

"About her family, it was..."

"Presumptuous? Maybe it was, but it needed saying and it worked."

He keeps looking up the promenade nervously. She'll have to get his mind on other things.

"When we were talking about the pictures, what did you mean about the places being as interesting as the date?"

"Did I?" he says, at last moving his attention away from the front.

"When you said I might think they were all connected to Carina."

"The bounced cheque picture, what was it called..."

"*Waiting for the Tide.*"

"You painted that outside the Warren?"

"What about it?"

"If it's the day I think it is, Dominic Mathers was there, maybe inside, but definitely outside the pub."

"How do you know?"

"Because I saw him."

"But how do you know it was him?"

"Kelly isn't the only one with a good memory. I may not remember pictures, but I know who's at the front."

"Did you know him then?"

"No, but I've seen him since and I'm sure it's the same man. He had a very distinctive green jacket."

"Why didn't you say before?"

"I never thought of it till Stover mentioned him. Interesting coincidence and him also being the brother of that woman who bounced your cheque and took your picture."

"It certainly is. Stover should be doing something about that. What was Dominic doing at the Warren?"

"Just hanging around."

"Did he look suspicious?"

"I didn't think so at the time. A lot of people hang around at the front every day, but now it does seem..."

He stops, reluctant to talk through the full implications of what he's begun.

"You're wondering if he was looking for Carina?" she says.

"It's possible, but that pub, it's..."

He stops again. She waits.

"Those other pictures," he continues, "remind me again, what they were."

"*Sea and Sand* near the clock tower and *The Rocks* at Venture Rocks."

"The clock tower, Venture rocks and also the church and the pub," he muses.

"A connection with Carina?"

"Not exactly...or maybe...it may not be anything. When she was young Carina lived in Darrasea."

"Did you know her?"

"No, no, I didn't live here then, but I've heard..."

"What *don't* you hear?" she laughs.

"Whether the police have picked it up...there's someone in town who knew her in those days. I hear they were great friends. Carina used her mother's maiden name when she left town, she was originally Carina Armstrong."

"So this friend won't necessarily connect her with Fennell?"

"Possibly not. Her name's Lisa Weldon. I've not seen her lately, but she was a regular in the Warren."

"Perhaps she's keeping her head down."

"She also lives near the clock tower and works on Seymour Street, near the church. Which means three of your pictures are connected to her."

"They're probably also connected to a lot of other people."

"Maybe," he says doubtfully, "but how many of them are connected to Carina Fennell?"

"What do you know about her early life in Darrasea?"

"Enough to know it wasn't much like her life afterwards."

He mentions the accident and tragic death of Carina's friend.

"It must have devastated her," Jose says, "but how does Lisa Weldon fit in?"

"Because she was involved in the accident that killed Andrea Curran, Carina's friend."

"What happened?"

"I don't know except it was somewhere near Venture Rocks."

Jose whistles.

"You don't like all these coincidences?" he says.

"No, but there's one in particular I intend to follow up. I'm going back to see Marilyn Hyde."

"Because she's Dominic's sister?"

"Because she knows where my picture is."

"You've been warned off by Stover."

"Things need explaining and if he's not prepared to find out I'll have to do it. I'm not letting that copper push me around."

"It could still be dodgy. I don't think you should go alone."

"You'll be telling me you're coming along," she laughs.

"That's exactly what I am saying."

"Whatever for?"

"As you say, too many unexplained connections."

She laughs again.

"Isn't this too 'grasping' for a Zen practitioner? Chasing, or helping me to chase after a picture, even worse its temporary owner, that's grasping at something, what is it...the continual destructive striving...always wanting...the perpetual unquenchable craving? No, it really doesn't equate with your Zen principles."

"Zen is in everything," he says quietly, "even in the recovery of lost paintings and after all your pictures may contain some profound reality. Missing that might be something I'd regret for the rest of my life. Besides, as I said, it might be dangerous."

"How do I know you're not just tagging along to keep an eye on me? You could be another Dominic or this, what's her name...Lisa ...afraid of what I might find out. Rather than a friend, you could be the enemy."

"I could, but I'm not. When are you leaving?"
"Straight away, is that too soon for you?"
"No, but first I must check on Kelly."
Twenty minutes passes. Vince is concerned Kelly may have 'wandered off,' but Jose is right. When they return to the beach hut Stover has gone and Kelly is still there. She's huddled on the chair and pleased to see them.
"Are you alright?" Vince says, "Did he bully you."
She shakes her head and relaxes.
"Nar, just asked me same things she did (Kelly nods to Jose), di'n't tell him much."
"So he asked about Carina?" Jose says.
"Yer...just said I saw her, that's all."
"Did you say you'd seen her...moving?"
"Nar...he'd'a laughed..."
Kelly seems unaffected by her grilling from Stover. The anticipation far worse than the actual event, though Vince remains nervous until the two elderly ladies who rent the beach hut return. Even then he wants to stay, but Jose is anxious to get off to Yaverton. He's finally knocked out of his unnecessary protectiveness when Jose says, "You can stay if you want" and starts to walk away. After assuring himself Kelly is safe he joins her.
"Stay put, whatever happens," he says to Kelly, "and keep calm, we'll soon be back."

Stover's interview with Kelly was a long shot, which had to be tried, but was predictably inconclusive. She couldn't tell him anything more than he'd read in the 'Advertiser.' She only knew Carina through picture papers and didn't even know she was in Darrasea, let alone knowing her personally. She was incredibly nervous. At one stage he'd almost abandoned the interview when she became particularly incoherent, but Amanda intervened and calmed her down. From then at least he'd got rational answers even if most of them were monosyllabic. She denied knowing Jose Pearsall, saying they'd only met just before he arrived. He didn't believe her, but couldn't make any connection between either of them and Carina. She hadn't actually seen Carina at the church or anywhere else in the town. In the end he concluded her 'vision' was just that and no more, the silly imaginings of a slightly disturbed and impressionable young woman. Amanda was less sure, reminding him Jose's knowledge of Carina's suit and shoes must have come from Kelly.

Back at the incident room he concentrates on more tangible leads, though nothing especially forthcoming grabs him. He followed up Templeman's message about Marilyn Hyde, but she'd not heard from her brother, Dominic. No obvious lead, but worth keeping in mind. The more intriguing link is with Jose Pearsall, then to Kelly and her wretched pictures! A gut feeling tells him there's something related to the murder, but with no substance, no evidence! He turns over the file again. There's at least a connection between Jose's painting and the assorted group at the Plaza. Why did Harry Willard purchase two of her other paintings? Is there some other connection to Carina? Time for another chat with nervy Harry who's maybe not so nervy at all. He'll go alone. It's a good walk to the Excelsior Hotel. The fresh air will do him good as long as he doesn't bump into Jose or Vince. He's had enough of those two for one day.

Harry's not in the lounge when he arrives.

"Mr. Willard?" the receptionist says, "Oh I'm afraid not, Mr. Willard checked out this morning."

6

MARILYN Hyde's house is large for someone who lives alone. Jose surmises there must once have been a 'Mr. Hyde' and this is what was once the marital home. Jose is keen to go in as soon as they arrive and 'confront' her, but Vince wants first to make sure neither Mr. Hyde nor anyone else is around. It's seven o'clock. They've been here an hour and there are still no signs of activity at the house.

"She could be inside," Jose says impatiently.

"There's no one there," he says.

"How do you know?"

"There are no lights on..."

"Even so, it doesn't mean..."

"...and I get a feeling about a house that's unoccupied."

She doesn't argue. It's probably prudent to delay and make sure. She went steaming in last time and got hit on the head and that was when the house was empty! They wait another hour. Jose talks a lot, not because she's nervous. She wants to find out more about Vince, but his greater skills are in listening so she ends up talking more about herself. How she finally realised she wasn't cut out to be an employee, however distinguished, and launched out on her own. She even mentions in passing how this decision coincided with the even greater one of splitting up with her husband.

"Not the best time to start out in business," she says.

"I'm sure it was very successful," he says.

So it was and she's never looked back. She tries again to get him to talk about himself. After a lot of prodding he admits to having once held an enigmatic 'senior position.' Then he gets evasive again, effectively turning the conversation back to her.

"Like you, I wasn't very good at working for other people."

"Does that matter if you're at the top?" she says probingly.

"You don't escape. The higher you go you're still accountable to people, more important people, more influential, more difficult, more dangerous."

Her sense of unreality increases. What does she really intend to achieve coming here again? And why with Vince? She can cope perfectly well on her own. Why didn't she stop him coming? What is it he's after? Then she talks about Kelly.

"I can't dismiss the 'vision' and have a nagging belief it must mean something. If only I could figure it out."

She looks to Vince, but he says nothing. She tries a different approach.

"It's ridiculous of course, just the pathetic ramblings of a dimwitted girl."

This is intended to provoke Vince, but fails.

"She's not a dimwit," he says dryly.

If not, Jose wonders about her motives. Was Kelly actually at the church that day? Perhaps Jose inadvertently painted her rather than Carina. When Kelly saw the picture she panicked. Maybe it was a reminder of her hang up about her appearance. She doesn't like being seen. Shouting about Carina in the picture distracted attention from herself. But why say it's Carina? Because she's well known and people would take notice. They'd hardly be interested if Kelly said, 'look there's old Mrs. Whatsisname?' She probably knows a lot more about Carina than she admits. That's why she's so reluctant to talk to anybody about it. So, why say it in the first place, why expose yourself so publicly if you're so frightened of being 'seen' at all? It doesn't add up.

The car is silent now. Jose is as quiet as Vince as she struggles with these contradictions. If only she had the picture to check. She tries to remember, but the detail fades like an accidental smudge of paint in an otherwise perfect sky. She hasn't Kelly's photographic memory. She won't have, she's an artist, into feeling, not capturing technical accuracy on celluloid. And those feelings tell her Kelly is on to something.

There are still no lights in the windows. Vince could be wrong. Marilyn could be in the back room. They could be wasting valuable time. On the other hand she could arrive home as late as she did the last time. Then Jose sees a woman walking up the road. She's in her mid to late thirties, a little older than Dominic. Jose watches her carefully, willing the woman to stop at number 85.

"Is it her?" Vince whispers.

"Not sure. I never saw her at the police station."

"But didn't you see her at the house?"

"No, I had my back to her remember before she thumped me over the head."

Marilyn steps up to the door of number 85 and goes in. They wait a few moments in silence.

"There's no one else," Vince says, "we can go in, but remember what I told you, we'll have to be quick."

Even then Jose glances round furtively to make sure there's no one in the street. She rings the bell and Vince stations himself on the other side of the door. As soon as Marilyn answers Vince forces the door open wider as Jose pushes her inside. Vince closes the door and follows. They're so quick Marilyn has no time to resist or cry out and Jose gets her into the rear room.

"You are alone?" she says.

Marilyn stares back, at first not recognising her.

"Well?" Jose demands, pushing her down onto a chair.

"You're the woman who..."

"Answer!" Jose says, jabbing her forcefully in the chest.

"Yes, yes, I'm alone. What do you want?"

Marilyn is still shocked and looks across nervously at Vince, who stands impassively by the door. She moves to get up, but Jose pushes her down again with a firm hand on each shoulder.

"I've still not got my money for the picture."

"If you wait to the end of the month then..."

"I can't wait for that. I've come for what I came for last time, my picture!"

"I told you before, we got the police..."

"Don't give me that. Where is it?"

"Why are you back, we've cleared all this up?"

"Nothing's cleared up. You knew I was here for the picture. It could have been cleared up then. You didn't have to call the police."

Marilyn is about to utter another denial, but Jose's determination, brooking no refusal and another glance at Vince, standing it seems with controlled menace, changes her mind.

"I had no choice. My neighbour was here with me. She was frightened and insisted."

"And who insisted on knocking me out?"

"Not me. You were down when we came in."

"You told the police I had an accomplice. That was a lie, wasn't it?"

"I had to say something."

"Something to cover up who actually did hit me from behind."

"I'm the innocent in all this, caught up in the middle of..."

"If you're so innocent, why did you pay with a bouncing cheque?"

"It wasn't intentional. The picture was more expensive than I intended to pay and I didn't have the cash."

"So you knew the cheque would bounce?"

"No, no...not exactly. I didn't think it would clear so quickly."

"But there were other pictures, cheaper ones, you could even have bought one of my others...unless of course it had to be that particular picture?

Marilyn is silent. She tries to get up again. Jose pushes her back down.

“Now, are you going to tell me the truth or do I have to start getting nasty?”

Jose pushes Marilyn down into the chair and pins her thumbs on her throat, squeezing gradually. Vince comes across and looks down much as a connoisseur might evaluate a particular antique.

“Okay, okay,” Marilyn splutters, “I took the painting down after Mrs. Sanders left.”

“Where is it now?”

“I haven’t got it.”

“Somebody took it, somebody who bumped me on the head?”

Marilyn says nothing. Jose squeezes a little harder. Marilyn nods.

“Come on, come on,” Jose says, squeezing even more and leering closely into her, “who was it?”

“Dominic.”

“He took the picture and hit me?”

“Yes. He’d been waiting for me. He was upstairs.”

“He’d come for the picture?”

“Yes, but when he heard you he came down. He guessed you’d come for the picture and...”

“...thought it better I didn’t get it or know what was going on?”

“I guessed what had happened when I came in. If she hadn’t been here, Mrs. Sanders, we could have got you outside and...”

“...like an unwanted sack of coal, dumped in the alleyway...”

“...got you into your car.”

“You had a damned cheek, calling the police and getting me arrested. I could do you for assault.”

“I had no choice. She was here, I had to do something.”

“So you denied you had the picture?”

“It was difficult enough getting Dominic away before the police arrived.”

“With the picture.”

Jose has relaxed her grip. Marilyn doesn’t answer and eases herself back up the chair. Jose grabs her again.

"Answer me! He's got picture?"

"Yes, yes, he's got the picture."

"And you bought it for him?"

"Yes, he didn't want anyone to know he'd bought it."

"Why was it so important, why did he have to have it?"

"He didn't want Carina to know."

"Know what, he had the picture or that he was in Darrasea at the same time as her?"

"Both. They had a row. He played it down, said it wasn't serious, but I think it was. She said she was going away, made some reference to Darrasea along with other places. I don't think she meant to mention it and tried to cover it up. Anyway, he was very suspicious. He thought there was someone else. There probably was, I always told him what sort of a woman she really was, but he wouldn't listen. So he went to Darrasea on the off chance he'd find her there, but he didn't want her to know. When he saw the picture he was afraid she'd see it too and start asking him why he'd been in Darrasea."

Jose stands back and looks at her contemptuously.

"Get it back, " she says softly.

Marilyn looks up and shakes her head.

"I can't do that. I've told you Dominic has it."

"You're his sister, just get him to bring it here."

Marilyn sits up and glares at Jose defiantly.

"No! I won't and get out of my house or I'll call the police!"

Jose pulls her from the chair, spins her round and pushes her to the floor. Marilyn tries to resist, pulling away slightly and rising on one knee, but Jose elbows her down and then locks her arm round Marilyn's neck in a vicious hold. Marilyn writhes, but Jose has her firmly. They wrestle on the ground for a few moments, but Jose though older is stronger and fitter and gets Marilyn on her back before straddling her legs without letting go the tight hold on her neck.

"Now," Jose says panting, "Get Dominic to the house with the painting."

"He won't come," Marilyn splutters, "He'll never come to the house just because I say so, he'll know..."

Jose tightens her grip again.

"If you want to keep you neck on your shoulders you'll get him here."

Marilyn speaks intermittently between further pressure on her windpipe. Vince leans over and Marilyn stares back at him petrified.

"He won't come...he'll know it's too dangerous...he'll be... suspicious...he'll know something's afoot..."

"There certainly will be," Jose says, "It'll be my foot on your head and if that doesn't work I'll set *him* on you!"

She nods to Vince, who leers threateningly, but does nothing.

"The police are on to him," he says, "If they find him with the picture, it'll be more than a bounced cheque he'll have to explain."

"Police?" Marilyn says, genuinely shocked.

"Surely you've heard about Carina Fennell?" Jose says.

"Dominic had nothing to do with that."

"Try telling that to the fuzz," Vince says

"They've figured out his true connection," Jose says.

Marilyn stares blankly, querulously. Jose and Vince glance at each other with the unspoken conversation 'has our bluff misfired, does she really know nothing, is Dominic innocent, what do we say when she challenges us?' Then Jose makes one of those innocent, impulsive stabs that hit their mark without being properly aimed.

"They understand what's in the picture. "

Vince looks at her with the same incredulous, perplexed expression as Marilyn, except hers has a hint of mystified understanding. Enough to tell Jose its worth pursuing.

"I see it too," she says.

"'Course you do, you painted it," Marilyn says.

Jose stays silent, hoping it might make Marilyn say more.

"If they find him with the painting," Vince says, also trying his hand at double bluff," the police will..."

"He told me it was the same day she was killed," Marilyn says with a hint of doubt, "He was sure he was in the picture and that put him in Darrasea on that day."

"Just what the fuzz will think," Vince says dolefully, almost to himself, but loud enough to be heard.

"He was so foolish to use a bounced cheque," Jose says, "that's what they're on to..."

"That was my fault! If only...but they told me at the police station..."

"Ah yes, but then they didn't know..." Vince begins.

"Know what?" Marilyn demands.

Vince hesitates, struggling. Jose comes to his rescue.

"They're on to him, if they find him with the picture..."

"He'll have to destroy it!"

"No! He mustn't do that!"

"Why not, it's the only way and as for the money..."

"My only interest is in the painting. If I get it back, I'm not interested in these other matters. Carina Fennell means nothing to me, but if that picture is lost I shall have no alternative..."

"We'll go immediately go to the police and tell them all we know," Vince says with an improbable firmness and fallacious resolution.

For a moment Marilyn says nothing and it seems their bluff is about to be called.

Then she says, "What must I do?"

Vince and Jose exchange relieved glances. Constructive deceit doesn't always reveal its fabricator.

"He has to understand the dangerous situation he's in," Jose says, "He can't be found with the picture. He must return it."

"But I've already told you he won't come here, he'll be too afraid the police will be watching the house. From what you've said that can't be long anyway."

"If he won't come here, you'll have to meet him somewhere else," Jose says, "Give me your phone!"

Marilyn hands it over.

"Okay," Jose says, "No nonsense, you make the call to him now."

Stover hasn't slept well and missed his breakfast. It's put him in an obtuse and grumpy mood.

"So why hasn't this Lisa Weldon come forward before?"

"Because, like everybody else who knew Carina in Darrasea, she knew her as *Armstrong*, not Fennell," Amanda says.

"Even so, by now she should have realised. Would Carina have come back to Darrasea specifically to see her?"

Amanda is doubtful.

"Probably not. After the accident they weren't on good terms apparently."

"The girl that was killed..."

"...Andrea Curran..."

"...was she close to Carina?"

"It seems so."

"What about Lisa?"

"The three were inseparable before the accident "

"And afterwards Carina and Lisa drifted apart. You have an address?"

"One of the streets behind the clock tower, nearer to the town centre."

The entrance to Lisa Weldon's flat is down a back alley behind a row of shops. The rear gate is stiff and at first they assume it to be bolted, but it opens after a good push. In the back yard a couple of overflowing dustbins and several cardboard boxes are stacked against the fence as well as empty cans and bottles on the floor.

"Not very salubrious," Stover says.

"They probably keep that gate deliberately tight," Amanda says, "this is close to the town centre pubs and the public loos close around eight o'clock."

The flat is on the second floor and access is along two wooden walkways and a steep flight of steps.

"I wouldn't want to be coming in here drunk on a Saturday night," Stover grunts.

There's no answer from the bell. Stover raps hard and long on the door. The curtains are drawn back and they can see through a rear window. There's no sign of activity. He raps again. Still no answer. Stover hammers again, even louder.

"She's out!"

A hard, high pitched, almost metallic voice from below, followed by a head sticking out from the one of the walkways with a great crop of blue-yellow hair.

"Lisa Weldon?" Amanda calls down, "Do you know when she'll be back?"

"Couldn't say, not seen her for some time."

"When did you last see her?"

"Couldn't say exactly, at least a week. What do you want her for?"

"Police."

"Oo er...I got a key if you like."

A woman in her late fifties trudges up the steps.

"Nothing serious, is it?" the woman says on reaching them, her eyes searching Amanda's face and darting to Stover.

"She lived here long?" Amanda says.

"Couple o' years, never been no trouble. You wanna go in?"

The woman opens the door before they reply and is about to lead them in.

"Thank you, Mrs..." Stover says.

"Laxton. I could show you round."

"That won't be necessary."

"You could try her at Parnells, the estate agents up Seymour Street, that's where she works."

Stover steps inside. Amanda follows, shutting the door on the helpful Mrs. Laxton. The flat is small and basic with only one bedroom, a diminutive living room/kitchen separated by a curtain. It's relatively tidy though a few clothes and other items are strewn around. Mrs. Laxton hovers outside the door, occasionally waving through the window.

"If she's gone it looks like she left fairly quickly," Amanda says, picking up a pair of tights, "too many things left about."

"We'll try the estate agent," Stover says.

It's a short walk to Parnells on Seymour Street.

"Took a week's holiday," the manager says, "but that was nearly three weeks ago. She's not been back. Not heard a word."

"Has she worked here long?"

"About six months."

"Any problems?"

"Not until now. She was coming along well."

"Was she new to this work?"

"No, she previously worked for a firm in Darraton, but they closed down. She worked there two or three years."

They get the names of Lisa's known friends and acquaintances from her employers. A further visit to the helpful Mrs. Laxton adds a few extra names.

"You must want to speak to her very badly?" she says.

"Did she ever mention Carina Fennell?" Stover asks.

Mrs. Laxton screws up her face in disbelief.

"What 'er that was murdered? No, never. Should she have done, did she knew Lisa?"

None of Lisa's friends have seen or heard of her. Nor do they know of any connection with Carina.

"Another dead end," Stover says despondently, "and now we've lost Dominic Mathers and Harry Willard. Nothing from our enquires, I suppose they've not turned up in London?"

"No one's seen them."

"What about the director, Jeremy Charlton?"

"I think by now he's even forgotten about Carina let alone Mathers and Willard."

"I'll see what the agent has to say."

Wendy Arbon has moved into a small, but select guest house on Cliff Road. The landlady says she's gone out and will probably be 'strolling along the front at this time of the day.' She expects her back around three of four, but Stover is restless and can't wait. On a hunch he goes to the 'Warren' and finds Wendy at a table by the window. She's surprised to see him and is very anxious to know how he knew where to find her. She's sceptical when he denies any informant. She looks anxiously around the pub as if she might discover the culprit.

"You've become a regular?" he says.

"It's congenial and like all good places anyone worth meeting thinks the same."

"Darrasea's a small place. You won't have to wait long before whoever you wish to see walks in."

She eyes him suspiciously, wondering what he's getting at or what he already knows.

"Who would I want to see?" she says with affected innocence.

"You tell me, you said it was convenient for meeting people."

She doesn't respond.

"I thought by now you might have wanted to go home," he says.

"You asked me to stay."

"Do you know where Dominic Mathers and Harry Willard have gone?"

"Have they left, I didn't know?"

"Any reason why either of them might have left so suddenly?"

"You're obviously very anxious to talk to them."

"I'm anxious to talk to anybody who may be able to help with my enquiries and like you they both knew Carina very well."

"Not like me!" she says vehemently, "they are wannabes and what they actually are falls well short."

"In relation to Carina?"

She sniffs disdainfully.

"You've met them. Harry is pathetic. Fawning on her like some lovesick schoolboy."

"Unlike Dominic."

She turns with a look both affronted and derisive.

"The pimply teenager rather than the schoolboy."

"I only meant Dominic is more in control."

She laughs.

"Control, control, that creep in control, you must be joking!"

"He likes to play the man about town," Stover says, deliberately hoisting up the image of the carefree philanderer.

"He's as besotted as Harry if not more, but don't be fooled by scullion Dominic."

Jose held Marilyn close as she spoke to Dominic while Vince performed his silent part, his inscrutable eyes boring into her with such deliciously initimidatory effect. They detected no odd, secret phrases, so there seems no way she could have alerted him, but Jose can't be sure. Staneman Cross is a lonely spot at the junction of minor roads about ten miles from Yaverton. It has the advantage of being known by Marilyn and Dominic as well as Jose. It wasn't the first choice for either of them, but they had to agree somewhere familiar to Dominic. The wrong place would arouse his suspicions. Even now Jose is uneasy. Perhaps the place itself gives him some signal to beware. Marilyn sounded convincing, repeating her lines about the closing police net and the necessity of handing over the painting to her safe keeping.

"They won't come looking for it here again, but they might come looking for you. Keep the picture safe until then," she said and then plaintively, "for me."

Could he have interpreted the true meaning of those last two words? Was that in itself a signal? Without the painting, what will Jose do...what will she do to Marilyn? He has to heed her words and bring it. He might still destroy it. It's the obvious conclusion. Why hasn't he done it already? Maybe it's the lure of immortality on paper, the reluctance to destroy something of yourself, even if it can be incriminating. Why didn't Richard Nixon get rid of the Watergate tapes earlier?

All the way Vince is anxious. Sitting beside him, Marilyn is also anxious. When he's not looking around he glowers at her with unintended menace. The lanes widen at the crossroads and the hedges are set back. They park Marilyn's car conspicuously on the wide verge so Dominc can be reassured the appointment is only with his sister. It's already twilight, the shadows from the trees merging and creeping across the grass as the faint sun rapidly disappears from the dull sky. They get out, leaving Marilyn in the car. Vince is wary. Unlike Jose he doesn't know the place and he surveys the ground dubiously.

"It's very open."

"Open and hidden," Jose says, walking towards the road, "Enough hiding for us to see him without being seen and open enough for him to see her car, otherwise he might think it's a trap. He'll have to stop here. We've said she won't get out of the car."

"He'll try to see her."

"If he does, you'll be waiting."

"I don't like it."

"That's why we came early, there's half an hour yet."

"He could also be early."

He glances at the car. The doors are locked and Jose has the keys. Marilyn watches them, but doesn't move.

"Did you believe that guff she gave us about why Dominic was in Darrasea?" she says, changing the subject, but moving closer to the car.

"Only if you believe the rest Marilyn says about him – that he's incredibly innocent. About as credible as you using me as a threat."

She laughs.

"You look the part."

"Let's hope I don't have to perform it."

"Nearly time," she says and returns to the car.

Vince takes up position in the trees. From there he can see all four roads and anything coming along them. It's assumed Dominic will come from a particular direction, but Marilyn was somewhat vague about his whereabouts. Perhaps she doesn't really know. Vince's apprehensions grow. What if they were followed? Marilyn could have an accomplice. She may have made a pre arrangement with the neighbour or someone else. The call was genuine. Jose dialled the number and only handed the phone to Marilyn after Dominic answered. If it was Dominic...but if it wasn't him, who was it? He hears a car. It could be him. Vince will have to be quick if he's to grab Dominic. Maybe it's not such a good idea...but as Jose says if the police won't follow him up...he has to be confronted.

The car slows, then stops opposite. Marilyn's headlights flash. Vince can see her, but Jose is well concealed. The car pulls over and stops just on the wide verge. The driver gets out. He has something under one arm. It's dim, but the jacket is the giveaway and Vince is sure it's Dominic.

"Marilyn," he calls.

She doesn't answer at first. He moves closer. Then the car window winds down.

"Just put it down, Dominic."

The words are slow, stilted, her voice tremulous, edgy. Dominic must have noticed. He puts the picture next to a bush. Vince's fears accelerate. They may not have long. It has to be now. He moves slowly and quietly from the trees, trying to keep in the shadows as long as possible. Then everything happens quickly and simultaneously.

"Go back!" Marilyn shouts, "it's..."

Then she's pulled back into the car by Jose, her hand tight around her mouth, but it's too late and Dominic turns. Vince breaks into a run and races round the car towards him. Then he sees the other car. He's been so closely observing Dominic he's not seen it glide and park a little way up the road. A figure emerges and suddenly races across the road. Dominic turns towards the picture, but the figure is closer. Then he sees Vince and looks between the two. Vince runs up to him, but Dominic runs towards his own car. The figure gets closer, shrouded by the trees. Jose gets out and runs over to the picture, grabbing it just in time. Vince races across to Dominic, but he's already in his own car. Jose turns to the figure and then looks anxiously back towards Marilyn, who's got out of the car. The figure stops, then turns to run back across the road. Vince is too late. Dominic's car roars into life and Vince has to jump aside to avoid being run down. Then the other car is away in the opposite direction. Marilyn runs towards Dominic's car, which slows as if to pick her up, but Vince blocks her and pulls her to the ground.

Stover is despondent. There's been no progress in finding either Harry Willard or Dominic Mathers and he's faced with more inconclusive information. Harry's evasion over Carina's financial affairs becomes more understandable as details of financial irregularities dribble out.

"He may have good reason to do a bunk," he says to Amanda as she wades through piles of computer printouts.

"It might not be him," she says, "Carina must have known about some of this lot."

"Convenient therefore to blame the dead."

"So why run away?"

It may not just be Carina's financial squeaky cleanliness that's in danger of becoming soiled. Coinciding with Dominic's disappearance, so called 'friends' have started creeping from under suitably lifted stones to reveal other affairs.

"How did she manage to keep this quiet for so long?" Stover says, "with all the media attention, surely someone sometime would have talked before?"

"Carina certainly wasn't the whiter than white girl next door she liked to portray," Amanda says.

"So where does that put Dominic? He must have known. Did the jealousy eat into him so much he was driven to a seaside crime passionel? Or was it a more mundane calculation, a juicy blackmail attempt that went wrong?"

"The girl next door who wasn't happy with him or with anyone else."

After their return to Darrasea Jose and Vince meet up in the Estuary café.

"Have you seen Kelly?" she says.

"She's alright," he grunts.

"At the risk of being castigated for stereotyping or even worse putting a label on you...but no I really will insult you and say you ought to discard being a protector. It's not necessary."

To her surprise he doesn't erupt.

"She's just so vulnerable."

"Like Sparrow and all the rest."

"I don't protect Sparrow, I only look out for him."

"It amounts to the same thing."

He looks down and stirs his coffee cup, producing a compound scraping and swishing sound.

"You surprised me," he says, "The demure artist wielding her strong arm on Marilyn."

"There's nothing demure about me."

"So it seems."

She moves on to more pressing matters.

"Who do you think it was?"

"I told Wendy Arbon about the burglary."

"So she also picked up on us going to Yaverton?"

"Somebody knew and somebody followed us."

"So is she also implicated with Dominic?"

"Not necessarily, she could have been acting in her own interest. It wasn't Dominic she was after."

"She was after the picture. At least I have that," Jose says with undisguised satisfaction.

"Is it safe? By now Marilyn will have told Dominic the full story. Both he and Wendy could come looking."

"Not just them, but it's safe enough."

"We need to show it to Kelly, can you get it?"

Jose nods. She's reluctant to tell him it's in Tanya's mother's Victorian rabbit warren house, safely buried in all her accumulated bric a brac. Who would know to look there and even if they did, would they find it?

"Harry Willard's also disappeared," he says.

"That name's familiar, isn't he...?"

"Carina Fennell's accountant."

"Really, but there's something...yes, he bought my other two pictures. I wanted to find him and at least photograph them...and he's gone?"

"He was staying at the Excelsior Hotel, but left very suddenly."

"Damn!"

"Not necessarily. All may not be lost. I have a contact at the Excelsior."

Jose laughs.

"Another one you protect?"

"I said a contact. He works in the hotel. I've arranged to see him later. You could come along, that's if you don't feel it too condescending to see one of my protectees."

Vince doesn't pick up Jose's reply and she refuses to repeat it, but accompanies him to the hotel. They enter through a rear entrance, wander along narrow corridors, slip through the kitchen and find a small staff room where a man in his thirties is sitting.

"Okay?" Vince says at the door.

"Yeh, sure, I'm on my break," the man says, a little nervously.

"Grant, this is Jose," Vince says, "You remember I told you, the painter."

Grant is tall, gaunt with deep set eyes beneath prominent bushy brows, which look back with a mousy reticence. Jose assumes he's fearful of being discovered with outsiders in the hotel precincts, but he looks at Vince with a separate edginess. Unknown to himself, Vince the protector may be also held in respectful trepidation by some of those he protects. Some of Grant's nervousness seems to have transferred to Jose, for he looks at her as if to say 'are you here to grill me as well?'

"Well?" Vince says in response to Grant's silence, "You said you might know something."

"It could be nothing," Grant begins, intent on losing whatever minor treasure he has, but then catching Vince's stern lips and lifted eyebrows, "the pictures may still be here."

"Where?"

"I've tried the door and it's definitely locked. Fortunately nobody's tried to get in since, but if they do..."

"Wait, wait! What on earth are you talking about."

Grant calms down, glances at the door, slightly ajar and then at his watch. Jose shuts the door.

"I've not got long," he says.

"Then be quick about it," Vince says impatiently.

Grant gathers himself up, hunching his shoulders, swallowing and putting his hands together on the table. He addresses the far wall over Vince's head as if eye contact may deflect him too much and make it difficult for him to get through the ordeal.

"It can be very quiet here at night. Opportunities present themselves," he glances at Jose, "It's a little delicate..."

"I don't think she's easily shocked," Vince says, "go on."

"There's this waitress...I'd been trying to see her for some time...it's not always easy, what with the hours and different shifts, but one night we were both on duty very late. It was my turn as night porter and there'd been a late function. There was a lot of clearing up for her to do."

"When was this?" Vince says.

"Three nights ago. Anyway the packing away and clearing up had finished and all the other staff had left. It was very quiet. All the guests were in and no one was expected until the morning. I thought it would be safe to leave the desk for a while. Up on the second floor there's a storeroom. It's quite large. It's used for spare beds, blankets, linen. No one goes there very often. Well, it's ideal, if you see what I mean?"

"We get the picture."

"We were in there at the back. It was about two o clock when we heard this noise like someone was in there with us. It was a bit creepy. She got scared, really put the mockers on things I can tell you, I was just..."

"Spare us the details, what happened?"

"I came out to have a look."

"Out of the storeroom?"

"Yes, but we were at the back, out of sight even though Chrissie...that's the waitress...she thought we'd been seen. I told her we hadn't and I don't think we'd been heard either, but she was adamant. I had to go and make sure. I got to the front, it's a big room and there was no one about, but the door was open and I'd definitely closed it when we went in. Well, I went back and told Chrissie. She was shivering and coiled up with a blanket round her. She was right scared. I got her calmed down, but she was frightened to come out. There was nothing else doing that night and time was going on, you know. I was worried about the desk. It would be just my luck for somebody to want a bloody drink or something, I'm not there and they come looking or worse get the duty manager up and in the morning, well I'm right in the shit so I said to her..."

"Yes, yes," Vince says, "but you're still here so presumably this great disaster didn't happen!"

Grant looks at him, slightly irritated as if to say 'it might only be a trivial thing to you, but my livelihood was on the line.'

"What happened next?" Vince says irritably.

"We went to bed of course...I mean actually to bed, you know...apart...she was so upset..."

"And you saw no one?"

"No, but somebody had definitely been there. I was agitated myself, you know, so concerned with calming her down, getting her back to her room and getting back to the desk I forgot to lock the door to the storeroom. It was only later, just before I finished my shift I went back upstairs. Then I found the door already locked and there was no sign of the key."

"But didn't you have it?"

"I'd left it in the lock when we went in. I should have locked us in from the inside or at least put the key in my pocket, but I was a bit carried away at the time and forgot all about it. I couldn't find it anywhere. The key's still missing. Fortunately no one's needed to go into the storeroom for anything. For obvious reasons I couldn't report it, there would be questions I couldn't answer, but it was definitely him."

"Who?"

"Harry Willard."

"How do you know?"

"Because of this."

Grant takes a white handkerchief from his pocket and lays it on the table. In one corner are the embroidered initials 'HW.'

"He must have dropped it when he locked the door."

"You're sure it was him?"

"Chrissie was right. He must have heard us. We disturbed him rather than the other way round. He was in that room for something, then he panicked and ran away. He came back later and locked the door, taking the key with him."

"If you were so sure, you could have approached him... discreetly."

"Impossible. He left during the same night. I didn't see him. Must have been in a hurry. Didn't even check out, left a cheque at the desk in an envelope for the manager. I didn't notice it. He was in that storeroom for a reason. He must have been putting something in there."

"Can you take us to the room?"

"What now, you're joking. I'm in enough trouble as it is. Besides, you can't get into a locked room without a key!"

“Did we find anything in Harry’s room?” Stover says to Amanda.

“No, somebody got there first and gave it a thorough going over.”

Stover sinks back in his chair, his despondency increasing.

“But there’s more creeping out of the woodwork elsewhere,” she says, “Friend Jeremy in London is suddenly out of work. The TV company ditched him now Carina’s programme is no more. Not well pleased, he’s been doing some digging of his own. He’s making embarrassing allegations, saying he has evidence some factual material in previous programmes is inaccurate or as he puts it ‘manipulated.”

“Fraudulent?”

“That would be our word. He’s pointing the finger at Wendy Arbon. Says she was behind it and Carina may not have known, at least not until very recently.”

“Now, let me guess. He thinks Carina was very upset and Wendy was out to silence her?”

Five to one o’clock in the morning, Vince and Jose have almost reached the rear entrance of the hotel. Vince checks his watch.

“Grant will be at the door at one o clock to let us in.”

“If he does as you agreed,” Jose says doubtfully.

“He’ll be there.”

“As instructed, though I don’t regard him as one of your proteges. He doesn’t need protection with his nocturnal activities...”

“Grant said Harry’s room had been ransacked,” he says, ignoring her remarks, “Do you think that’s why he left so fast?”

“With Grant away from the desk philandering, someone could have slipped into the hotel unnoticed, gone up to his room...”

“If Grant is right and Harry was looking for a place to hide the pictures, he must have had an idea someone was after him.”

“Or after the pictures.”

"He must have meant it to be temporary. He waited around until Grant and the waitress disappeared, came back and locked the door. Then he went back to his room, saw the mess, panicked and left."

"Probably before Grant got back to the desk."

"Who do you reckon it was, Dominic?"

They get to the door. Vince tries it, but it won't budge. He knocks gently. It opens slowly and Grant peers at them through the gap.

"You'll have to be very quiet," he says, allowing them to pass, "you won't do any damage, will you?"

"Just take us up," Vince says.

Grant is very nervous. He walks slowly along the corridor, glancing furtively at every corner and frequently checking on Vince and Jose behind him. He'd rather not be here at all. He's not on duty and has stayed up specially to meet them. Vince was so persuasive, making it sound the most natural thing to take them to the storeroom. Vince lives in his own world in which individuals' own doubts are the only real barriers. To the determined everything is possible, but Grant doesn't live in that world. He'd willingly agreed, but away from Vince's peculiar ability to impart blind faith in which the extraordinary becomes utterly ordinary, fear gripped him and he'd reconsidered. He thought about not letting them in, but was afraid Vince would turn nasty and land him in even greater trouble. Vince talks with the ease of someone who takes nothing seriously, which appeals to like minded people. Except they aren't really like minded. Vince means what he says and will carry it out. Now it's too late.

They creep up the stairs and along the corridors, Grant stopping frequently to check their footfalls haven't woken anyone. Then they proceed again. On the first floor they hear a noise between a clatter and a scrape seemingly coming from the bar. The wait is longer this time, their tramp not resuming until Grant is sure every mouse, spider, microbe is at rest. At last they reach the storeroom. Vince tries the door.

"I told you it was locked," Grant whispers.

"Don't suppose you've found another key?"

"No."

"Never mind, needs must," Vince says, drawing a piece of stiff wire, similar to a hat pin, but thicker, from his pocket.

Grant looks at it incredulously.

"You're not going to..." Grant says.

Vince nods and bends down to insert the wire into the lock. Grant suddenly turns and runs along the corridor.

"Probably got another appointment," Jose says sniffily.

Vince takes only a few seconds before he pushes the door open.

"Must have been an unusual kind of management consultancy where you learnt such skills," she says.

As Grant had said the storeroom is much larger inside than indicated by the modest door, a short passage widening out to a large space behind the adjoining bedrooms. They mooch around quietly, lifting piles of blankets, and peering behind the beds. Several times Jose puts her fingers to her lips as Vince scrapes the metal on the floor as he investigates every fissure and cranny.

"There's nothing here," she whispers.

But he won't give up and continues to the rear of the room.

"Grant and his ladyfriend will have been at this end," she persists, "Harry would have been nearer the door."

Acknowledging this, Vince returns to the short passage, dislodging a pile of sheets with his foot, from which a thin, small, rectangular object falls onto the floor. He picks it up, reads the label on the back and turns over, revealing *Sea and Sand*.

"Anything more about Carina Fennell's friend that was killed ...?" Stover says.

"Andrea Curran? Not as such," Amanda says cryptically, "but I've got something interesting that might be connected. This isn't the first time Lisa Weldon has left Darrasea very suddenly. She left not long after the accident. Didn't go down well at the time. Running away from her own guilt, some said."

"Guilt because she couldn't save Andrea?"

"Or worse, though nothing could be proved."

"You mean it might have been deliberate?"

"So some evil tongues said at the time."

"But she came back?"

"Yes, eventually, but it was many years later and some never forgot and never forgave. In some eyes she still lives under a cloud."

Kelly makes her way around Jose's spare room like a child discovering Aladdin's cave, picking through the scores of paintings leaning against the walls and neatly stacked on the tables. She says nothing, but her wonder filled eyes tell all. For over an hour she methodically pulls the pictures out, scrutinising with the practised eye of an apparent connoisseur. She was reluctant to come. Jose's flat is unknown territory, where unspecified danger might lurk. But it's private, she'll not be exposed, so eventually succumbed to Jose's reassurances. Jose regarded it as a major personal triumph when Kelly trudged up Cliff Road from the front. She was accepted, almost on a par with Vince, a commendation to be savoured.

They wait for her in the lounge. Vince says she needs time to acclimatise. Jose doesn't argue, but neither thinks she needs so much time. Perhaps she's deliberately prevaricating, knowing the real purpose of her visit. Tanya brought *Waiting for the Tide* earlier. With *Sea and Sand* it lays unseen, face down on the lounge table. That avoids pre-empting or jeopardising Kelly's proper viewing. Jose's patience is ebbing and she glances across at the table, keen to release any suppressed energy in the pictures. The exercise marks the denial of all her earlier conceptions. They're only paintings, knocked out quickly in the middle of a day, of no especial artistic merit, albeit sufficient to attract buyers, but surely that's all, well composed, pleasant, innocuous, not harbingers of same fateful event.

Kelly comes into the room, her face brighter than Jose has seen it before. She sits with her back to the table. For a quarter hour, hardly pausing to draw breath she talks continuously about the paintings, recalling title after title and describing in detail compositions, colours, figures, but above all atmosphere and feelings. It's a revelation to Jose, disclosing depths to her unconsidered trifles she'd never envisaged. It's as if they're someone else's work. What Kelly reveals could be from a catalogue, almost a critique, but sparkled with insight and deprived of pretension, yet this is what *she* has done, not someone else! While she speaks Kelly loses all hesitancy, incoherence and repetition. There are no 'you knows' and 'likes' and 'sort ofs,' all is fluid and mellifluous, her voice lilting and intense as if she is really in the pictures she describes, part of the scene not looking at them from without.

Then without warning she stops and the room is strangely silent except for unheard resonance in Jose and Vince's heads as if a great bell, tolling for hours suddenly stops and its echo reverberates throughout the tower. The play is over, the audience must leave their seats and move to the exits, the stairs, the main doors and the cold reality of the dark and dismal streets. Kelly loses her composure and sits on the edge of the settee, her shoulders hunched, her knees quivering as if she must soon bring them up to her chin while her fingers stroke the sides ready to drum pointlessly, obsessively. The gauche, slightly frightened girl returns.

"You must come again," Jose says, smiling reassuringly.

"If I had somewhere to hang one..." Kelly begins.

"I would give you the one of your choice," Jose says.

They look at each other silently. Kelly has closed her box of delights, unable to control her own retreat into actuality. Jose looks, oddly helpless, the non swimmer standing at the river bank beside the drowning woman. Vince watches them both with mounting irritation and concern, conscious of Kelly's reversion and its effect on Jose, making her diffident, unsure of the direction to take and reluctant to make the essential jolt. They could circle each other like this indefinitely if he doesn't intervene, however blunt that must be.

"And now the main course," he says, getting up to the table and turning the pictures over.

He holds up *Waiting for the Tide*. Jose gets up.

"Come and look," she says to Kelly, taking her hands and gently pulling her.

Kelly doesn't resist, but her eyes have dulled and dart apprehensively. Jose turns her towards the table where Vince holds the picture high in front of him. We're making too much of this, Jose thinks, she'll see what she believes we want her to see.

"Take your time," Jose says, "Just look at it like you looked at all the others. We're not asking you to..."

"She may see Dominic," Vince says, glancing down, "if he was there at the pub..."

"Shut up, Vince, don't lead her!"

Kelly stares at the picture for several minutes, her eyes fixed and intent. Jose stands behind her, watching for any sign of distress and shaking her head for Vince to be quiet. The silence stretches. Outside a car reversing to park, invades with unnatural loudness.

"Show me the other one," Kelly says.

Vince puts *Waiting for the Tide* back on the table, then picks up *Sea and Sand*, holding it in front of him. Kelly stares impassively as before, her face giving nothing away, but her eyes, wide and receptive, seem immersed in the picture.

"Now both," she says, "can you hold them both together?"

Vince takes one hand away and prises up *Waiting for the Tide*, then holds both pictures, one in each hand. Kelly watches for a few moments, then turns away.

"I see her," she says.

"Carina?" Jose says.

"She's in both pictures."

Jose kneels down in front of Vince, staring into the pictures.

"There are figures in both, here and here and here," she says, pointing at the pictures, "but I can't tell who it is."

Kelly turns back and points at one and then the other.

"There! See the woman dressed in red. And there!"

Jose looks more closely. Vince peers down. The pictures slip, he almost drops one.

"Vince! Hold them still!" Jose says, then as she looks between the two, "Yes, she's right, there is a figure in both pictures and she could be dressed the same, but I can't see the face."

"Of course you can," Kelly screeches, "Look, there...the face... it's clear...it's her... and... she's moving."

"No, no she's not," Jose says, glancing back and forth between the two images.

"Where?" Vince says to Kelly, "how does she move at the pub?"

"She's looking in at the window."

"There are several people outside the door," Jose says, "but I can't..."

"And at the clock tower," Vince says, "is she coming or going towards you?"

Kelly shakes her head.

"I'm not sure, but I see her arms moving...it could be she's walking away...or maybe the other way...I can't tell...I'm not sure..."

"But you're sure it's her, Carina?"

"Yes, yes, yes, it's her...and she's definitely walking towards me."

"What about...?"

"Vince!" Jose shouts, "That's enough!"

She leads Kelly back to the settee and sets her down. Vince puts the pictures back and joins them. Jose turns to him quietly.

"Did you see Carina?"

"No," he says, "I can't make out any of the faces."

"Neither can I."

"But it doesn't matter we don't see it. She says she does and I believe her."

"So do I."

"And she saw Carina in the picture at the exhibition. Now we have to find the final picture, because I'm sure she'll see her in that one too!"

7

VINCE and Jose sit in the Estuary cafe, nursing respective cups of coffee and tea. Vince eschews tea, saying it's bad for 'his innards.' He remains nervous about the paintings and continually asks Jose whether they are safe at Tanya's mother's place. For someone who's spent many of his prime years on the road with a conspicuous distaste for 'possessions,' he's suddenly very security conscious and old women's attics or spare rooms, however cluttered and dense, don't satisfy his requirements. She reminds him the room is locked and the front door locked and bolted. He grimaces doubtfully and mumbles incoherently.

"There's only the one entrance from the main shopping street," she says, "which is very public and then they'd have to climb the stairs next to the estate agent. It's not the easiest place to creep about unobserved."

"What about the back yard?"

"If you mean the rear entrance, that door is never used."

"Even so..."

"If anyone came in that way they'd also be seen and heard."

He backs off for a time, but brings up the subject again with a grunting 'you are sure everything is alright at that place?' She reassures yet again having checked only this morning.

“Locks can be picked,” he says.

“So I’ve noticed, how did you learn so well?”

He returns with a look that keeps the door on his past firmly closed, eventually replying with his usual explanation for many things, ‘Contact.’

“Your paintings tell a story,” he says, “a story somebody doesn’t want told. I’m worried about Kelly.”

“Where is she?”

“Around,” he says, gesturing widely with his arms, “I told her to make herself less conspicuous.”

“Gone to ground?”

“If you like. If they can’t find the pictures they’ll go for whoever they think has them.”

“Dominic? Harry?”

“Either or both. You also need to be careful.”

She laughs.

“What have I to be afraid of?”

“The same as Kelly. Dominic knows you have his picture.”

“It’s not his picture, he didn’t pay for it.”

“And Harry put the other one away for safe keeping. He’ll be back to find it. You’re the artist. Everybody knows you want them back.”

“Then there’s *Restful Haven*, stolen from the exhibition, who has that?”

“Somebody who’d like to get their hands on the others.”

“But why?”

“I told you, they tell a....”

“Yes, yes, they tell a story, but which one?”

“The one about the famous television personality who got herself killed at the seaside.”

“Do you really believe that?”

“Don’t you?”

She shivers, but not with cold.

“It’s the only explanation,” he says, “People are going to a lot of trouble to get hold of all the pictures you painted on the day of Carina’s murder. Everybody also knows Kelly’s seen her in one of the pictures. We know she’s seen her in two others. It won't be difficult for them to figure out the same and then there's the fourth picture. Harry has that."

"He was quick to snap up his two, one went to Dominic..."

"...who thought he was in *Waiting for the Tide*."

"Kelly didn't see him."

"But he was there, at the 'Warren.' I saw him."

"Afraid Carina would see him in the picture and know he was in Darrasea – or so Marilyn Hyde said."

"More likely it would be evidence he was around on the day she was killed."

"Is it the same with Harry, is he afraid he's in the pictures? He might be in the one he's still got, *The Rocks*. If we find that we find him."

"What about *Restful Haven*?" she says nervously, "Did he steal it? (he doesn't answer) If he didn't, have we got two killers?"

"I don't know, but I've found more about Carina's past life in Darrasea. The three girls were inseparable, even called the triplets – Carina, Lisa Weldon and Andrea Curran. The accident changed everything."

"How did it happen?"

"Lisa and Andrea were out walking on the beach near Venture rocks. Exactly what happened was never clearly established, but it seems they were larking about and Andrea slipped, fell down badly, hit her head. She was knocked out, but didn't seem too bad. No mobile phones in those days. Lisa ran along the front to a phone box and called an ambulance. Andrea never regained consciousness and was pronounced dead at the hospital."

"Carina wasn't there?"

"She was meant to be with them, but cried off at the last minute. She was utterly distraught, even blamed herself saying if she'd been there it wouldn't have happened."

"Why not?"

"Said she would have looked after Andrea."

"Odd thing to say, a veiled criticism of Lisa."

"Ah, but there's more. Although the three were always together, they were not equal relationships."

"Two's company, three's a crowd?"

"Carina was the centre of attention then just as she is... was...now. Andrea and Lisa were rivals for her affection."

"How serious was this rivalry?"

Vince shrugs with a knowing smile.

"Depends who you listen to, but some imply Lisa's actions weren't entirely innocent."

"Meaning it wasn't an accident?"

"She may or may not have meant to kill Andrea, but let's say she wasn't well disposed towards her."

"Things got out of hand, harsh words, pushing and shoving, Andrea goes down and..."

"Something like that."

For several nights Kelly has been sharing the shelter closest to the ice cream kiosk with a girl called Terri, but tonight she's alone. The moon is high and bright, the sea calm and she's been watching the beach for over an hour. The promenade is deserted. The pub across the road, next to Edward Hall 'The Sandbar,' is busiest during the day and doesn't stay open after eleven. It's turned out the last of its drinkers and the gentle lapping of the waves is undisturbed by either passing cars or late night strollers, sober or otherwise. Further along the front, 'The Warren' stays open longer, but that too has disgorged most of its customers. All is quiet and she's enjoyed having the sea and sand to herself.

Out here even when there's no moon, it's never completely dark. The lines of coloured lights, strung along the promenade, twinkle and swing all night, but that doesn't bother Kelly, she finds them reassuring like a child's nightlight, someone is close even if she can't see or hear them. It's getting chilly. She arranges her bedding and snuggles down, but the silence is troubling. She lies awake for some time, listening, the silence heightening distant sounds. The light wind on the water as well as the waves, the odd gulls and other birds, all raised to an unnatural volume. Even under the hood of the sleeping bag her ears are sharpened and acutely hear things usually drowned out by people, cars, trains and dogs.

She leans up and stares across the estuary. She can see the vague outline of the sandy Denzer promontory and the lights of towns further down the coast. Even the sky isn't wholly black, but a constantly merging and splitting pattern of greys. The more she looks the lighter everything seems to become. Just as the sky is more grey than black, the front's greyness gives way to yellowing blue on the promenade and dull redness between the trees. The changing light fascinates her just as it does when it's successfully captured in paintings. Jose's pictures are treasure chests of frozen movements and memories, crammed with savoury splendours for rapid defrosting. Those with discerning eyes can thaw out such marvels and bring them back to life. No one can escape from Jose's pictures. A few brush strokes and they're locked in forever. Even the dead can live again and maybe tell their stories.

She shudders. It's getting cold. She nestles into the sleeping bag again, though still looks up at the sky. Suddenly it seems even quieter. She turns the edge of the sleeping bag to expose an ear and listens carefully. She can just hear the waves, but they seem fainter as if the tide has suddenly ebbed rapidly. It can't be. She turns the edge up again. Now she hears nothing. The eeriness is unnerving. She turns the edge down again and wills herself to hear a car, a gull...anything... but...nothing. She lies absolutely still, staring towards the sea stretched in an awful expectancy, every fibre of being telling her *something* is about to happen. The moments pass. There's a dull ringing in her ears, suffocating what little sound there might be. Probably caused by straining too much to hear nothing!

Then she hears it. Faint at first as if someone has brushed against the edge of the other side of the shelter. Then more like a scraping though still soft like a mouse. No mice live in shelters on the front. Now she pulls the sleeping bag further up, ostrich like, blanketing out the sound. It gets louder. It could be a dog or a cat sidling along the shelter. She lifts down the sleeping bag and cocks her ear. Someone is there!

She looks round, but sees no one. Then she hears it again. A dull movement as if someone has sat on the bench behind and is sliding along. It gets closer. She's reluctant to raise her head, fearful of being seen through the glass. Instead she eases her legs up and out the sleeping bag. The sliding continues and then stops as if someone has got up. Where have they gone, to the end of the shelter where they can turn and get to this side? It could be one of the others, even Terri returning, so why is she afraid? Then why have they not spoken out and why are they on the landward, colder side of the shelter? No one who knows the front would do that.

She's out the sleeping bag now, but ignores the slight chill of the air. The sliding, scraping, swishing come again. She looks towards the end of the shelter, but there's no one, though as she turns back she senses the after image of a shadow through the glass. Did she see it or imagine it? Should she look back and make sure? She freezes and listens. Nothing except the low moan of the breeze and the gentle undulating murmur of the waves. But she's not alone. The sound of that slithering sliding leaves a trace in its unseen passage. Someone is here. Someone who means her harm.

She slinks her legs to the floor and eases a little further along the bench. This makes her own slight scraping sound, which seems incredibly loud, making her freeze again. Then she turns back at the end of the shelter. She blinks several times in the dim light, but is still unsure whether there's a shadow through the glass. She levers herself and leans down to put on her shoes. She's not sure what to do, but knows being shoeless will be unwise. Then as she leans up, forgetting her own shadow she'll cast at the glass, a figure emerges at the end of the shelter. Well wrapped and hooded it stands for a few moments, motionless, menacing, silhouetted in deep blackness against the promenade lights behind. Kelly stares back, unable to move, mesmerised by the dreadful immensity that envelopes everything like the sun suddenly, demonically eclipsed. In its own shadow she sees no face, increasing the terrifying spectre like vision.

Then as it moves Kelly's stupefaction is broken and she jumps up from the bench. The figure immediately leaps forward and outstretched arms lunge at her. She turns quickly, but slips and is grabbed from behind. A hand is thrust at her throat and for a moment she struggles as its grip tightens. Then she rams her elbow into the attacker and breaks free. Even then she's almost caught again before she gets away, running towards the ice cream kiosk and the Plaza. At this time there'll be no one at either place, but she flees for the protectiveness of a building rather than the exposed danger of the open promenade.

She reaches the ice cream kiosk. Her pursuer is close and gaining. She runs on, passing the darkened Plaza and comes to the corner of Emberton road. From here she could run up to Cliff Road and the town, houses, cars, people, but instead she heads forward, keeping to the edge of the promenade towards the Estuary café. Beyond is the open front, the wide parkland of the Meadows behind the roadside beach huts. It'll be darker, lonelier, more vulnerable, yet also offering opportunities to escape into the sand and the dunes.

She reaches the lifeboat station and turns onto the beach, running behind the café and along the sand. As her feet dig into the soft sand she has to expend much more energy and immediately slows as if she's suddenly tramping through treacle. She looks back towards the road. She sees no one, but there's so little light a stealthy intruder would be easily missed. She gets to the firmer sand where her feet get a grip and she runs more quickly, but the dunes obscure the lights from the road and clouds hide the moon. Sea and sand enclose. She can hear the water and see the lights across the estuary, but is otherwise blind while the lapping waves mantle all other sound. She stops and listens, but hears nothing except the whispering wind and the breaking sea. The indistinct outline of the dunes assumes a disabling grimness, hiding from her what lies beyond. She's marooned in the muffled and shrouded night! She shudders in terror. Coming here was unbelievably stupid! She can't stand still! She must move on!

She trips along the sand, not too fast, still unsure which direction to take. Then she picks up her steps and in her anxiety to be away gets too close to the waves and paddles in the water. She runs back out and stops again. She looks towards the dunes and is sure she saw someone. With her back to the sea her pursuer waits to cut off her only exit. Only one option. She must go further and find a way to the road unseen.

Terror and hopelessness can tap unknown strength and energy. She can think only of flight. Even fear is lost for a time in the frenzy of escape. She runs along the beach without direction, running, running anywhere to get away. Her dull pounding feet pummel the sand with increasing speed, hammering through every part of her. She reaches softer sand. Now she slows and tires as she struggles to keep up speed, but she must reach the dunes and get away. Then she hears someone else's feet on the sand. She's not escaped and her terror returns!

She has to hide and runs up to the dunes. She'll be safe in the grass and sand. No one will find her there. It's hard going. She slips and grabs the sand with her hands and is almost crawling at times. At the top of the dunes she stops and looks across the beach and back along the promenade. Her attacker must come from one of these directions and she's relieved to see no one. A stiff breeze builds up from the sea, lifting stray wisps of sand into her face. She sits down, feeling safe behind the tall grass. She's unwilling to move. There's an illusory security about her sandy shelter. She should remain alert, but the alluring peace of the beach at night returns.

She loves these moments, detached in an instant of time from everything immediate as if it's only her and the universe. She could be anywhere, everywhere and nowhere. If only it could be captured beyond fleeting minutes or seconds. Just as Jose's pictures. Look within, not at them and such instances burst from the paint prison of the past to live again. But you must be there, inside, part of the picture yourself. Otherwise the magic won't work. You too must be held in that instance of time. You must be in the picture. Now she's back on that night at the exhibition, staring at *Restful Haven*, drinking the scene in all its liquid dynamism, not locked in statuesque rigidity. Just as you look at an action photograph and remember the moments before and the moments after the shutter opened, so too she sees and hears everything condensed and concentrated on the paper. She's with the people at the church, listening to them, feeling the sun on her face, touching the bark of the trees, smelling the flowers...she is in the picture. Then she is *Waiting for the Tide* and *Sea and Sand*. Not inanimate two dimensional objects, but actual places with living people. And she's there on that day...even though she knows she might really have been somewhere else...but wasn't she at the front on that day like all days so she might have been there...she was there...she is there. And Carina was there...at the church...at the pub...on the front... and she's here now...on the beach walking towards her.

But this is no vision, extruded from dreams and memories, this is real, this is now! There really is someone on the beach and heading towards her! Kelly gets up, rubs her eyes, shaking off the vestiges of subconsciousness and stares intently to make sure. The figure comes closer. Has it seen her? How long has she been dreaming, a minute, five minutes, ten minutes? How long has it been watching her? She looks around. The best escape is the road. She turns, but immediately falls down as she crashes into a hillock of tall grass. She gets up and staggers on, but the sand is deep and soft and she sinks as much as she moves forward. She looks down at the beach again. The figure is closer, but can't have seen her for it moves too slowly. She tries again, but once more slips and falls. She crawls along the sand, afraid to stand up in case she's seen.

She stops and waits. If she stays still long enough it will give up and go away. But it doesn't for she hears the thud of footsteps and even heavy breathing of someone clambering up the dunes. It's getting closer! She can't stay and be found. Rather than a safe haven the dunes are a trap. She'll have to make a break for the beach. She braces herself, knowing she can't delay once she's visible. She stands up and runs down and out towards the open beach away from the figure, but she's immediately seen and the pursuit resumes. She struggles in the soft sand, but must make headway. She can hear her attacker, battering the sand with sinister thuds that are getting closer. She could make for the firmer sand, but that way only leads to the sea and no escape. She lifts her legs higher and further in an effort to counteract the clawing pull of the soft sand. But it gets closer, her lungs are breaking, her heart pounding yet she's not getting clear! She reaches the end of the first line of dunes and can see the road and possible escape on her left. She must keep it in sight. Her face drops as she runs. The beach seems to rise higher and higher, any moment gulping her into an abyss of sand or holding her to be captured by her pursuer. She looks across the estuary, the distant shore, then to the sky, anywhere open, airy, away from the sand's devouring mouth!

Between the two lines of dunes is the safest for bathing where volleyball nets are strung between high stout posts. The nets have been removed for the autumn, but the posts remain. In her desperation to get back to the esplanade, Kelly has forgotten them and in the worsening light cannot see them. She looks between the road and the sea, avoiding the beach below or to her front, imagining the sand will consume her. The pounding behind increases. All she can think about is getting to the road before she's attacked. She thumps into one of the posts and sinks down, half stunned, her shoulder and arm cracking with pain. As she turns on the ground, someone comes up and grabs her.

From the 'Warren' Jose walks along the front turning towards the town centre at the road running alongside the Excelsior Hotel. She hurries. She finds recent memories of the place disturbing and it's later than she intended. Tanya thrashed her at Badminton and then they'd retired to the pub for a 'quick drink,' the quickness becoming distinctly elasticated as the evening wore on till it was eleven before they realised. She's had a good time. They talked about everything and everyone, though Jose gave only the briefest explanation of recent events. She avoided any discussion of Carina Fennell, though painting was on her mind.

"I should start again. I've done nothing since the exhibition and those pictures were done a couple of weeks before – that was nearly a month now."

"You've been busy with other things," Tanya said diplomatically.

She reaches the park, closed and ominously dark. This far from the front there's no brightness from the lights along the promenade. One street lamp out, another shrouded by a tree. She quickens up towards Cliff Road though finds it uncomfortable. She's not drunk a lot, but enough to slow her down. Then she hears footsteps. She looks round, but sees no one. She carries on, a little faster, but it's as if the pavement echoes her steps a second later. She stops, listens again, but doesn't look round. She hears the footsteps distinctly. They stop. She walks on. She hears them again. Someone is following her!

She reaches the roundabout, but instead of going towards Cliff Road, she panics and walks back into town, immediately realising her mistake, but fearful of turning back. That will take her straight to her pursuer! She walks faster, almost skipping along. The street is oddly dark, none of the shops displaying any lights. The footsteps get louder, nearer! She runs to the corner and glances back up the hill. At first she sees no one, then notices a shadow by one of the shop fronts. She turns the corner and steps quickly up Seymour Street.

It was a mistake coming this way. She'll have to double back and make her way to the flat round the back of the hotels. She pounds the pavement, gets a little breathless and feels a slight pain in her side. She reaches the church, pauses and listens carefully. A car approaches, wiping out all other sounds. She glances back down the street, but sees nothing. She mustn't lose valuable time. The car passes. She crosses the road and walks up Church Street, listening all the time. She hears nothing until she gets to the church's west end, where she hovers and looks back. The street is very dark, what little light masked by the church and trees. She can't see anyone, but...yes,...faint...definitely footsteps.

She looks into the church grounds. Suddenly she wants to go in as memories return of that day weeks ago when she stood here with her paints. *Restful Haven*, where is it now, who has it? She even takes a couple of steps before realising the foolishness of retreating into an enclosed area with no means of escape. Then she hears the footsteps again and walks quickly to the corner and up the street. It's dark and narrow with only the back entrances to the houses and hotels of Cliff Road. On the other side is a high wall and trees at the south west end of the church grounds. She breaks into a desperate run, soon reaching the end of the alley, leading onto Cliff Road itself. A few steps and she'll be home! She glances back, feeling sure she catches a glimpse of someone in the gloom. She must be quick!

She runs along the alley, hitting the wall in her impetuousness, turning sharply at the far end and racing the short distance to the steps up to the front door of her block. She leaps up the stairs, fumbling for her key as she catches her breath, then scrabbles it, scraping the door before finally locating the lock. She runs inside and sinks into the chair, relieved and exhausted. She stays only a few moments before getting up. No matter how much she had in the pub she needs one more to steady her nerves and pours a generous portion of martini, downing it in one gulp, then goes over to the window.

The clouds have cleared, the moon casting a welcoming beam onto the glistening sea. As her eyes adjust to the darkness she makes out the distant shore and the lights along the coast. Then she hears a sound of movement from the direction of the entrance lobby as if the front door is catching. She's sure she shut it. She wouldn't have come in without closing the door. Then it comes again as if the door has opened. Then a slight click followed by a dull thud as the door closes. Someone is in the flat! How could she be so foolish to leave the door open! She's trapped! She looks out the window. She's on the second floor and it's a long way down. There's a drain pipe. It looks substantial. From the balcony, she could lean across, grab it and scale down. It's a fair distance from the balcony. What if she misses and falls?

She moves to open the window, only to stop, the noise will alert any intruder, while if she stays silent maybe they won't know she's here. Don't be ridiculous, why else would they come...but then a burglar...someone who's been watching the place, saw her go out earlier, thinks she's still out...yes if she keeps quiet she'll be alright. She stays still and listens. She hears nothing and on an impulse turns the light out. Then she hears it again. Someone is moving in the hall towards the lounge door. She edges to the fireplace. She's sure there's a poker there though she never uses it. Isn't that the chosen weapon to tackle a burglar? She gets down on the floor and rummages in the hearth, her hands flailing around without success. If only she hadn't turned the light out! She strikes something hard and metallic, but as she grasps it something else falls over producing a distinct clatter. No chance of concealing her presence now! She can stand it no longer. If they're going to get her, they might as well get on with it!

"Come out and show yourself!" she shouts into the gloom.

The door opens. Two figures are silhouetted against the light from the hall. They stand for a moment, hovering silently. Jose grips the poker and stands up.

"What do you want?" she says defiantly, though conscious of a slight tremble in her voice.

Then one turns the lounge light on.

"Vince!" Jose says.

He steps forward. The other person hangs back, half hidden behind him and at first Jose doesn't recognise her.

"Can we come in?" he says.

"Looks like you already are. Did you pick the lock?"

"The door was unlocked," he says, looking with some alarm at the poker, which Jose still grasps.

"But why are you here and why not ring the bell?"

"I was worried about you. I wanted to make sure you were alright."

"Why shouldn't I be?"

"Because of something that happened earlier, I thought you would be the next..."

"Next?"

"Yes, you see..."

"And who's this?" she says, motioning to the trembling figure, still half hiding behind him.

Vince steps aside and pulls Kelly forward. She stands with her head down, hands limply at her side and shaking slightly.

"She's had a hell of a shock," he says.

"She's not the only one," Jose says, then motions to Kelly, "come and sit down. It's bad enough him standing around like a scarecrow, I don't need two of you doing it!"

Kelly hesitates, then Jose stretches out her arm and tugs at her jumper. Kelly lifts her head, curls her mouth in response to Jose's smile and shuffles into the chair opposite. Vince remains standing.

"You seem shaken yourself," Vince says, "You've not had any other visitors?"

"I've only just got in."

"Were you followed?"

"How did you know that?"

"I feared so, but they didn't get here?"

"No...not as far as I know...when I heard you outside I thought...why didn't you ring the bell?"

"Because I didn't want to draw attention. If someone was here I wanted to surprise them."

"You certainly surprised me!"

Kelly pulls her legs up from the floor to that near foetal position she adopts in part fear, part reassurance. Jose grabs her knee, simultaneously patting it and gently pulling her legs down.

"And what has happened to you?" she says.

Kelly looks dolefully at Jose, allowing her legs to reach the floor and relaxes slightly, but can't speak.

"I found her on the beach," Vince says, "slumped at the bottom of one of the volleyball posts, crying, shaking and cold. She'd been running along the sand, but she couldn't tell me what was wrong. She just kept pointing back towards the lifeboat station. I was kneeling down beside her so not easily seen. Then I saw someone running towards us. 'Who is this?' I asked her. She didn't reply. I waited to see if the person would go away, but it hadn't seen me and kept coming. Kelly got worse and started whimpering, saying she had to get away. She was exhausted and couldn't keep running. I told her she would be alright. Then I stood up to face whoever it was. It stopped and turned. I ran up and it ran back along the beach. I chased for a long way, but it got away. I was also afraid for Kelly and had to get back to her."

"You say 'it,' was it a man a woman?"

"Impossible to tell in the dark. Kelly didn't know either. She told me the rest on the way here."

Vince explains how Kelly had been attacked at the shelter, had run away and got trapped in the dunes before her final dash along the beach.

"She's in no state to stay outside tonight. Besides I had to check on you. I figured as Kelly's attacker had got away, you could be the next target."

Jose shudders and tells of being followed from the front. The timing is consistent. It could be the same person.

"Kelly can stay here tonight," Jose says, taking her hand, "She's still cold, I think she should go to bed immediately."

Kelly nods slowly, unconcerned at being spoken about in the third person.

"Come," Jose says, pulling her up and leading her into the spare bedroom.

Jose gets her into bed and she's asleep within minutes.

"That girl's utterly worn out," she says on returning to the lounge, "She's had an awful shock."

"So have you."

"Not nearly as bad," Jose shrugs, then angrily at what she sees as weakness, "I only wish now I'd faced him!"

"That may not have been wise," he says doubtfully, "Was it a man?"

"Can't be sure in the dark. If it's the same person who attacked Kelly, could it also be the burglar at Edward Hall, who you saw tonight and also that night?"

"Yes."

"Is it Harry Willard?"

"It could be."

"You're not sure?"

"It was much the same as tonight. It's difficult to be sure in the dark."

"What were you doing on the beach anyway?"

"Couldn't sleep, went for a walk."

"Lucky you did for Kelly. Something must have been on your mind."

"I was thinking about Harry. We have to find him."

"He bought *The Rocks*. He could have hidden it."

"Why would he do that?"

"He tried to hide *Sea and Sand*."

"Either way he's connected to that fourth picture. If he's not hidden it he has it with him. If we find him we find *The Rocks*."

"Why did he try to hide *Sea and Sand*?"

"To keep it safe, he suspected someone was after him."

"Someone who knew he had the picture."

"That's why we have to find it before they do."

"Maybe he wanted to hide it because it incriminates him."

"*Sea and Sand* doesn't seem to..."

"But it does show Carina and we don't know what could be in *The Rocks*."

Vince is reasonably sure they're probably safe from the attacker until morning, but he insists on staying in the flat overnight. Jose is concerned for his comfort.

"I've spent many years in much less pleasant surroundings," he says, curling up on the settee with a blanket.

But after she's left him alone, he lies awake for a long time, staring at the erratic moonlight, drifting and flitting between the clouds. The figure on the beach and at Edward Hall keeps coming to mind and he remembers seeing Dominic at the 'Warren.' Did he really see him or is he fabricating images after the event as Jose paints in birds and people, moving trees, making minor alterations to improve her compositions? But she doesn't change things, at least not with those four pictures. For some it seems they are only too embarrassingly, even disastrously accurate. What about Harry, scurrying around hotel corridors late at night, disappearing as quickly the next morning and now possibly stalking women along the beach and dark streets? He has to be found and quick.

He wakes early and for a few moments is disoriented. He's usually woken by a bird on the roof of the van or the eastern sun striking the curtains. Insulated by tiles, felt, timber frames and stout walls he hears only the distant call of the gulls, not the tippy tappy scratching of closer feathered friends, while the windows face south giving only an obscured light. For a while he lays, adjusting to the surroundings, then gets up and goes to the window. It's a bright, clear morning and he can see far down the coast. He goes out on the balcony and takes in the crisp air as he watches the early risers on the beach, walking dogs or just enjoying the stillness. It's a perfect day for ambling and watching, but that cannot be. There's work to be done and they need to start soon.

He doesn't notice Kelly slipping into the room. She goes over to the table where *Waiting for the Tide* and *Sea and Sand* are lying. She sits down, stares at the pictures, caresses the edges of the frames with her fingers, then lightly draws the tips of her forefingers across them in turn. Her eyes, wide and dilated are expressionless except as she touches the pictures it seems they move slightly as if she interprets some tactile meaning. Vince turns and seeing her, steps back into the room quietly. She's unaware as he stands utterly still and doesn't move. Only her face registers slight movements in response to the pictures, her eyebrows twisting, her nostrils enlarging slightly and her eyes alternately widening and contracting. He's desperate to ask what she sees or feels, but afraid to speak in case he breaks the spell, destroying any chance of interpretation. The door opens and Jose comes in. Kelly looks up and seeing first her and then Vince, sits back abruptly as a child, caught in the pantry tries to look innocent. Jose glances at her, then at Vince. He puts his finger to his lip.

"What have you seen?" he says softly to Kelly.

"I was just...nothing...just looking at the pictures," she says.

"Yes, I know. What do you see?"

She puts her hands forwards on the table as if to push the pictures away, thereby distancing herself, denying any involvement.

"I was just..." she says to Jose, again as if she's done something wrong and is pleading her innocence, "...just wanting to look... again...look again..."

"That's fine," Jose says, "They are there to be looked at, to give pleasure, tell me what you see in them."

Reassured, Kelly leans over and studies *Waiting for the Tide*. She gets very close and turns her head a couple of times, taking in the picture from different angles, almost as if she's trying to get inside it. She looks up, points to a particular spot and turns to Vince.

"You were right, he's there, I can see him."

"Who do you see?" he says.

"That guy you said, the one who was hanging around Plaza Hall. I saw him there and he is here at the pub."

"Dominic Mathers?"

"Is that his name?"

"You are sure?" Jose says.

Kelly nods, then turns to *Sea and Sand*. She stares at it for a long time, then says, "It's her, I saw her again last night."

"Who? Jose says.

"Carina."

"You saw Carina last night?" Vince says.

"When I was on the dunes...trying to get away...I thought about the pictures (she turns to them again, gently stroking the edges of the frames)...I was...there...at the pub and at the clock tower...it was so...peaceful...I was there in the pictures and she was there too...in the pictures with me..."

Jose and Vince exchange knowing glances.

"Yes, of course you were," Vince says, going over and putting his arm on her shoulder.

Kelly leans down again, her head cocked to one side, her face almost touching the painting. Vince goes over to Jose.

"The shock," he says, "she needs time."

"Don't dismiss everything," Jose says, "She's seen Dominic, just as you did and she's sure about Carina in both paintings."

In the kitchen after breakfast Jose and Vince discuss their next moves. They have to find Harry and with luck, *The Rocks*. Vince has a plan, but it means scouring the town and Kelly is nervous.

"Don't want to go out. Don't want to be seen. Anyway, it's not real out there," she says and then glances towards the lounge, "It's only real in the pictures."

“You’ve got to stay in touch with reality,” Vince says, pointing to the window, “Gotta be aware and you can only do that out there.”

Kelly gets up and goes to the door. Vince is about to stop her, but Jose puts her hand on his shoulder and holds him back.

“Leave her.”

”She’s retreating into a fantasy,” he says after Kelly leaves the room, “she’s only seeing reality in the pictures. She’s got to remain aware.”

“It depends how awareness is expressed. What may appear artificial representation may be more real than the apparent reality of mere appearance.”

“She’s afraid of her own appearance, you said so yourself.”

“No, she’s afraid of how she *thinks* other people judge or interpret her appearance.”

“Not like the Carina Fennell she sees.”

“It seems Carina’s reality was *only* an appearance. What we see or rather what we think we see may not be reality just as sometimes what we think is illusion, such as in a painting, may be the closest thing to what really is.”

“Or what really happened?”

“Okay, think of it like that with Kelly.”

He replenishes his coffee cup noisily.

“We have to get out. She’s better not being with us.”

Jose’s unsure whether he means Kelly staying behind is to her advantage or to theirs.

“But she can’t stay here alone,” she says.

Fortunately Tanya has the morning off and is willing to help out, though her normally lively mood is somewhat deflated when she sees Kelly sitting at the table, staring vacantly with occasional glances at the paintings. In her bouncy way Tanya tries to engage her, even slightly successful if morose monosyllabic acknowledgement can be counted as conversation. Then Jose and Vince get ready to leave. Jose is still apprehensive about Kelly, not helped by Tanya’s look of abandoned concern. Vince says the sooner they start the sooner they can return, while Jose’s direction not to open the door to anyone only increases Tanya's mounting distress. It's not clear which she's more afraid of, admitting a stranger or remaining alone with Kelly.

First they stop at the Excelsior. It's possible Harry left a forwarding address. It's a long shot and they're unsuccessful.

"He might still be around," Jose says, "We ought to check the other hotels in town."

"No need," Vince says, "I've already checked."

"Don't tell me...contacts?"

He nods knowingly.

"But I don't know people in all the B and Bs."

"What if he's using a false name?"

"I've thought of that," he says producing a photograph.

Jose studies it carefully. A couple of dozen people are grouped around a table in a large room.

"This looks like the Plaza."

"Taken the day they all arrived in town."

"How did you get it...no don't tell me..."

"A contact in the Plaza restaurant, one of the waitresses. A technician asked her to take it. He developed it that night and next day gave her this copy. I think he had ulterior motives. Dominic is in it – which is why I'm sure it's him I saw outside the Warren. Notice the older guy on the left. I asked if she knew who he was and she's pretty sure it's Harry. So all we have to do is show this around and see if anyone's seen him."

The prospect of tramping around every guest house and B and B in Darrasea fills Jose with dread. She follows wearily, but after a couple of unsuccessful hours Vince calls it off and decides to try the restaurants and cafes.

"An even longer shot," Jose says.

After an hour displaying the photograph, consuming enormous quantities of tea and coffee and staring into blank, uncomprehending faces, they give up. Vince wants to try one last possibility, but Jose is anxious to get back to the flat and only agrees after ringing Tanya, who reassures her they've had no visitors. It's a quiet time at the railway station and there's no queue. At first the booking clerk stares incredulously at Vince's proffered photograph.

"Do you know how many people come through here in a day," she says, "I'm here to sell them tickets, not look at their faces."

"Have a good look," Vince says patiently and then, realising what may be even more significant than the face, "perhaps he bought an unusual ticket?"

She stares at the photograph again and Vince's thumb stuck under Harry's face.

"He might have been going out the area," he says.

"Most people only want a ticket to Darraton," she says grumpily.

"Don't suppose you get many further afield?"

"I got one the other day," she says with a little rising enthusiasm, "Got a ticket for London. Come to think of it...(she stares at the photograph again) ...could have been him... yes, could have been him."

"So he got the train for Darraton, to change for London?"

"Not then, said he'd be back later. I told him the ticket was only valid for the day and the last train to get him there left at 1600."

"Did he come back?"

"Couldn't say. I go off at two."

They return to the flat. Jose is still anxious about Kelly, but Vince is more concerned with the whereabouts of Harry.

"He could be in London," he says on the way.

"It's a big place," she says, seeing the chances of finding him rapidly diminishing.

Tanya and Kelly are at the table. Tanya is very concerned for the practicalities of Kelly's life.

"But what if you want a bath?"

Still looking at the pictures, Kelly appears not to be listening.

"Everything alright?" Jose says.

"It's been an...interesting morning," Tanya says.

Vince has been thinking about Kelly's obsession with the paintings. Having 'seen' Dominic, what about others?

"Do you see anyone else in the paintings," he says, putting the photograph on the table and pointing to Harry, "like this man?"

Kelly looks at the likeness and studies *Sea and Sand*.

"Is he there?" Vince persists, forgetting his earlier scepticism for Kelly's 'fantastic' visions.

She hesitates. He points again to Harry in the photograph.

"Do you see him?"

She indicates a vague figure near the clock tower.

"It could be...I can't be sure...but it could be him...(her eyes flicker across the picture and rest on another figure in white)...there she is...I said Carina Fennell..."

"But what about the man?" Vince demands.

"I see...but...it could be (she moves her forefinger across the surface)...I can feel him...someone...it could be him..."

"Harry, the man in the photograph?"

"...I feel...he's left there now...I see him moving..."

"Oh not again," Jose groans to herself.

"...he's going away...walking along the promenade...he's heading...for the beach huts."

Tanya stares open mouthed at Kelly. Vince turns away and joins Jose near the door.

"We have to leave for London."

He speaks quietly, but Kelly overhears him.

"No, you can't go! You have to stay in Darrasea!"

Kelly eyes narrow, burning, desperate rather than indignant.

"It's understandable you're afraid..." Jose begins.

"I'm not afraid...not for myself!"

She gets up from the table, walks to the window, looks out, then turns to face them.

"You want to find your fourth painting...(they look incredulously)...yes I hear what you say...I know where it is...I have felt it."

"You saw Harry," Vince says, "you saw him walking away from the clock tower with the painting?"

Kelly shakes her head.

"Don't be stupid, Vince," Jose says, "I'd not even painted it then!"

"I've felt where your painting is," Kelly says.

"We have to get to London and find Harry," Vince says.

"No! You should stay here and find the painting!" Kelly screams, "Carina is there!"

Jose and Vince look at her unbelievingly.

"Listen to her," Tanya says quietly, "What if she's right?"

"Where should we look?" Jose says.

"Beach hut, it's in one of the beach huts," Kelly says.

"The one you go to with Elsie and Margaret?" Vince says.

Kelly shakes her head.

"Other one, behind, away."

"What other one, behind what?"

"Behind, away...not used."

"What does she mean?"Jose says.

Vince shakes his head.

"She means the abandoned huts behind the promenade," Tanya says.

Vince is puzzled.

"Didn't know there were any."

"That's because you've not lived here long enough," Tanya says and then whispers something to Kelly, who nods back to her, "They are set back from the road, not been used for years. There was a plan to develop the Meadows area by the cricket ground and the amusements. They were meant to come down to make way, but it never came off. They're the ones Kelly means."

"You can't go!" Kelly shouts.

Jose takes Vince aside.

"I don't like her in this state. It won't delay us long."

Kelly 'feels' something in *The Rocks*, but continues to be vague about the beach hut. Fortunately with her local knowledge and rapport with Kelly, Tanya can interpret this 'feeling' to identify the location. Their tramp along the front is wary and defensive. Tanya leads the way, closely followed by Jose and Kelly, with Vince bringing up the rear, constantly looking around for hostile strangers. Elsie and Margaret are outside their beach hut and the intrepid band stops for a few minutes.

"You're very drawn, dear," Elsie says to Kelly, "looking very peaky."

Kelly unconvincingly mumbles that she's 'alright,'

"If I didn't know better I'd say you needed more fresh air," Margaret says, laughing.

"We have to go," Vince says, "got to find a friend."

"Might see you later, dear." Elsie says.

"Needs a good meal, I expect," Margaret says when they're out of earshot.

"Always looks like she needs filling up," Elsie agrees.

They come to the end of the first line of beach huts and Tanya turns from the road to the long green expanse, running parallel to the front known as the Meadows. Its openness is reassuring. There's no bush, fence or wall for unwelcome intruders to lurk. Beyond the cricket ground is a line of a half dozen wooden buildings, set near the sloping back gardens of the properties on the hill.

"Is this the place?" Tanya checks with Kelly, who nods with a dismal "s'pose so."

Kelly can't say which of the huts contain the picture. She's never been here before and Vince is very sceptical, but as Jose points out, how else would she know the place existed at all. Tanya tries the doors. Some are stiff, but can be pushed open. Two are jammed. Vince has brought a large gas spanner from his camper and while the others spy out, uses this to easily force them open. They work their way through each of the derelict huts in turn. It's amazing how much clutter has been left by the former tenants, old chairs, tables, shelving, pots and pans, newspapers, even an old radio. Even more surprising is the lack of vandalism. Until their own entry, the huts seem to have been virgin territory, untouched by the rippers, breakers and daubers.

"Odd place to hide a painting," Vince says dubiously.

"A very good place," Tanya says, "Who would think of looking here?"

"But would Harry have known about it?"

"There's a lot we don't know about Harry," Jose says, "this reminds me of that storeroom in the hotel."

She pokes her foot through the jumble on the floor of one hut, expecting a familiarly slender frame to fall away from the mess. It's not to be and they move on to the next. Kelly stays outside, staring towards the sea, unconcerned by the search, expecting the painting to quickly materialise. A second hut reveals a hoard of fascinating old magazines, that Jose has to snatch away from Vince who becomes quite engrossed, but no painting. In the third Vince finds a 'useful' box of candles, but nothing else. The fourth has a stockpile of empty biscuit tins and the fifth an old kettle. At first the sixth looks promising. Beneath another hoard of old newspapers, Tanya lifts what appear to be pictures, wrapped in cloth. The packages are of the right size and shape. The cloth is snagged on the corner and Jose has to pull it away. As it falls, Tanya lifts up two pictures, their faces turned towards each other. The door is only partly open and in the dim light Jose can't tell if either of the frames are hers. Tanya turns both pictures round. They are prints, a Victorian view of the moors and an Edwardian beach scene, which could be Darrasea. They stare at them for a few moments.

"Not yours," Vince says, "a waste of time."

"Not mine," Jose says with disappointment.

"I felt *something*," Kelly says, when they come out, empty handed.

"Well it wasn't the picture," Vince says grumpily.

Now even more anxious to resume their quest for Harry he leads the way along the footpath behind the cricket ground and the amusements. It's a quicker route to Cliff Road than returning to the front. They walk in silence. Having gradually moved from outright disbelief to cautious acceptance of what Kelly 'saw' and 'felt,' now he and Jose's doubts and misgivings return. Both feel foolish. In his haste Vince has forgotten the development at the old swimming pool site has finally begun and the footpath has been closed at Emberton road. Too late and within a hundred metres of Cliff Road they come to a barrier stretched across the footpath.

"So much for your short cut," Jose says, "now we'll have to walk all the way back around the cricket ground."

The others turn back, but Vince hesitates, then walks to the fence at the edge of the construction site. A JCB is parked at the rear of the old building, some rubble has been cleared and piled at the far end, but otherwise there's been no activity except for the beginnings of a large hole. No one is around, the contractors having probably moved on to another job for the day. Vince walks along and finds a loose section in the fence. Around the new hole there's a cleared path, parallel to the fence, leading around to the opposite end where the footpath is also closed off. If there's a similar loose section on the other side they can slip through the site and avoid the long walk round. He turns to call the others, then stops. He ought to first check they can get through. He steps around the fence and walks towards the large hole. It s about two metres deep and must have been dug some days ago for he can see where loose rubble has fallen back.

As he gets nearer he realises he may have underestimated the ease of passage, for the gap between the hole and the fence narrows. Maybe this isn't such a good idea. He slows and treads carefully. It's too narrow. They won't get through. He's about to rejoin the others when he sees something in the bottom of the hole. He's not sure, so stops and crouches down. He's not mistaken. A body of a man lies crumpled in the bottom of the hole and it looks like Harry Willard.

8

JOSE waits for Vince at the police station. Unlike him she has little to tell them. Where had she been, what was she doing? She stayed outside the site fence until the police arrived and made Vince do the same. She wasn't tempted to venture inside. Seeing one dead body at the front was enough, she'd no desire to look at another. So it was an opportunity for her to *ask* questions rather than answer them. Stover has been remarkably cooperative. As Vince says, she has this amazing ability, sometimes in the most hostile or inappropriate circumstances to make people talk. Even the police it seems.

Harry Willard had been a suspect particularly because of his previous connection with Darrasea. Inevitably that steers the conversation onto Carina's own past. The unfortunate girl who was killed has a mother. Jose gets a name. Then she asks about Lisa Weldon. Their enquiries are 'ongoing,' which she takes to mean they don't know where she is. She probes a little, but he won't say anymore. Then she asks about the others, Dominic and so forth. Stover suddenly draws the line. The spell is over. He's said too much already and clams up.

She can't understand the delay. Vince isn't like her. He'll not want to talk. What could he possibly be saying? He emerges after an hour with his opinion of the police considerably lower than when he entered the interview room.

"Wanted to know what I was doing at the pool site, as if that was important. How long had I been there? Did I know it was private property and I was trespassing?"

"What did you say?"

"I said he was an arsehole. He couldn't be serious and should be out catching whoever did it. This was a bloody murder, not some boundary dispute."

"Might have helped if you'd not called him an arsehole."

"Asked me if I knew Harry Willard."

"So it is him?"

"Said I'd never met the man, but I knew who he was. How did I know? What connection did I have to Carina Fennell and her programme? Oh yes, I said, I was a special adviser on fashion and I saw her every week. Then he got angry and told me it was a murder enquiry. Exactly I said, so why was he wasting his time grilling me? Wouldn't believe I'd just stumbled onto the site and seen the body in the hole. Said everybody knew the footpath was closed, so what was I doing there? I said I wasn't everybody and I didn't know nothing."

"Do they know who might have done it?"

"They were asking me that! Did I know if he had any enemies, any reason anyone would want to do him harm. How do I know?"

"Do you know?"

"The only thing I can think of is your picture, the second one he bought, *The Rocks*."

"You didn't tell them that?"

"What and be kept overnight? No I didn't!"

"Does his murderer have the picture?"

"They were certainly after it. They may have it by now even if they didn't get it from him immediately."

Jose considers his meaning and shudders.

"He was killed because of my picture?"

"For what the picture says."

"What does it say?"

"We'll know that when we find it."

"If we find it."

"The killer either has to find the picture or silence anyone who understands what it means. They go after Harry to get to the picture. There's a struggle. It may have been forced out of him where the picture is. Then he's superfluous, dangerous even, so he's murdered. Alternatively, Harry has figured out its meaning. That makes him even more dangerous than the picture itself, so he's killed because of what he knows."

"Murdered because of his interpretation of my painting?"

"Could be."

"Which makes anyone else vulnerable who might also have interpreted it."

"They'd have to see it first."

They reach the corner of Cliff Road. Jose stops, shudders and pulls her coat tighter around her shoulders.

"So is it so wise for us to find it?"

Vince looks at her and grimaces.

"We have no choice."

"That's assuming it's there to be found. After all, if Harry..."

"It's there," he says and then in response to her questioning eyes, "I just know it is. The murderer hasn't got it. We have to find it and very soon. We have to get to it first!"

"But the murderer may believe you don't need the picture to draw the right conclusions. Anyone with particular gifts... they've already tried to get to me...and to Kelly. God, Kelly, we have to get back!"

They left Kelly with Tanya and up to now Jose has given no thought to her safety. When Vince discovered Harry's body, she'd not thought of the implications for themselves, but now the full realisation hits her like a bat in the face. Who attacked Harry could also attack them! If Vince is right and the murderer doesn't have the picture he or she won't feel secure and will want to eliminate anyone liable to get there first. They've already tried to attack them three times. First at Staneman Cross near Yaverton, but they got *Waiting for the Tide* from Dominic and also recovered *Sea and Sand* from Harry. If the murderer has *Restful Haven*, it means they are leading the race to recover the pictures by two to one. Then Kelly was attacked and Jose was followed. Now with Harry dead they're in the race to get *The Rocks* and someone has every incentive to kill them!

Jose runs up Cliff Road. The familiar, comforting street suddenly transformed into an area of shadows and places of concealment, peopled by strangers with sinister intentions.

"Have you sketched many portraits in the Warren?" Vince says suddenly.

Still locked in her dispiriting thoughts, Jose doesn't answer at first. He repeats the question.

"It comes in dribs and drabs," she says absently.

"Do you sell them all?"

She has to pull her mind away from imaginary shades and perilous corners. Then almost laughs at his optimism in her talents.

"It's not that lucrative."

"What happens to the ones you don't sell, do you just throw them away?"

"Not all, in fact I've not sorted them out for months. There are a lot in the spare bedroom."

"I'd like to have a look."

She's surprised he's interested.

"Okay, I'll get them out later."

"Not too later. Kelly should look through them too."

She bounds up the stairs to the flat and bobs her head round the lounge door. Tanya is at the window. She goes into the kitchen and then the bedrooms. Vince is at the top of the stairs.

"She's not here," she says, then goes back to the lounge.

Tanya stands fidgeting with her fingers.

"I was only gone a few minutes – just to get some milk from the corner shop so I..."

"She's gone, you let her go? Where is she?"

"I don't know."

Stover is perusing the initial post mortem findings.

"Could have been an accident," he mumbles, "on the other hand...injuries consistent with being pushed. So it's up to us. Did he fall or was he helped on his way?"

"Are we looking at the same suspect as for Carina?" Amanda asks.

"Not long ago we had Harry in the frame himself... Dominic Mathers, Wendy Arbon, even good old Jeremy the out of work television director..."

"If Harry was the innocent accountant ferreting in all their murky activities, maybe he discovered one trying to blackmail Carina. When they were tackled things got nasty and..."

"But why there at the old swimming pool site? Not exactly easy to get to."

"Vince Randall got there. Says he was taking a short cut, so they could've been doing the same."

"Yes, but to get where?"

"He says he was going to Cliff Road from the beach."

"Funny way round, why not walk straight along the front? Odd character, isn't he?"

"Don't you believe him?"

"We'll have to...for now," he snorts derisively, then almost with disappointment as if he'd prefer to pin the crime on them, "...neither he nor the artist appear to have any reason to kill Harry Willard."

"Could it be connected to her paintings? Harry bought two of them?"

"Don't suppose they've turned up?"

"No, Jose Pearsall didn't mention them."

"That's not the same. Willard's sister identified the body. Anything from her?"

"She said it was the first time she'd been to Darrasea for years. Apparently they were regular visitors when they were young. Their parents had a place near Straggle Point. Came down every summer until their early teens."

"So he could have known Carina in those days?"

"Unlikely, he was a few years older. Carina would still have been in primary school when they stopped coming."

"What about the house, do you know it?"

"One of several bungalows round the corner from the old docks. The parents were compensated. It was demolished when the area was converted into a marina and the new housing development. The sister doesn't believe Harry has been back since then."

"But he may have done and he certainly came down early before the programme was to due to be filmed, just as Carina did. So why did he come and what did he find out?"

"Is that the motive, killed for what he knew?"

"Maybe. If we find what he found, we may find the killer."

"So was he lured to that place? Perhaps it had some special relevance, childhood memories of swimming."

"If so it had to be someone who could share those memories, someone who also spent time in Darrasea when they were young."

"You're thinking of Lisa Weldon?"

"Could be something locked up with those young girls. Andrea Curran's mother still lives in town, doesn't she and we have the address?"

"Yes, the one you mentioned to Jose Pearsall."

"I did?"

They start at the slipway and head east along the beach. Tanya keeps blaming herself as she runs after Jose and Vince. They ignore her. This is no time for recriminations and she could hardly have held Kelly down by force. She can't have got far, Jose thinks, but what if she went into town? Every time they stop she looks round nervously. If they were followed from the police station they could have been followed down here. Then at least Kelly would be alone and safe, but if they weren't followed...someone was concentrating on her, followed her from the flat and now she's gone!

"We'll soon find her," Vince says, seemingly unconcerned.

He's either very good at covering up his misgivings or has reason to be confident. He knows just about everybody on the beach and every time they stop to consult a 'contact' there are brief waving of hands towards the other end of the breach and knowing nodding of heads. The apparent efficiency has an almost military air. Jose wouldn't be surprised if Vince has been in the army, a background as a professional soldier is no less likely than anything else. They pass the ice cream kiosk, the clock tower, the 'Sandbar' and reach the lifeboat station. Jose begins to lose hope while Tanya still hammers herself mercilessly for being responsible, but Vince presses on, not yet exhausting his extensive range of beach eyes and beach ears.

Then she sees the familiar long purple jumper wandering along the beach in the distance. Vince sees her too and starts to run. Jose calls, but Kelly doesn't hear. Then Kelly starts to run and the search becomes a race as Vince and Jose chase after her. Vince streaks ahead, despite the clawing softness of the sand and Jose struggles to keep up. Then she loses sight of them both as they round the corner of the sand dunes. She forces herself to catch up and with a sudden spurt sees them again. Vince has almost caught up with Kelly. He must have called for she stops and waits. Then they walk together to the edge of Venture Rocks. It's as if Kelly is drawn and Jose wonders if they were her intended destination all along. When she gets to them Kelly is looking round and fidgeting with her fingers as if she would like to clamber on the rocks. It's very close to where Carina's body was found, not a place Jose wants to stay.

"Why did you come here?" she says to Kelly.

"Needed to get out."

"That's not normally your problem."

Vince walks away and stands with his back to them, staring towards the rocks. Jose repeats the question, this time to him. He doesn't answer, just grunts as if agreeing. She says it again.

"What?" he says, "Oh yes, she needed to come up here. I'm glad she did."

"You didn't say that when we rushed out the flat in a panic..."

"No, no, that's right, but I see it now."

"See what?"

"Stover mentioned Mrs. Curran's address...you've got it?"

"Yes, but what..."

"I have it...what Harry knew...what Harry found out."

She writes down the address from memory as he explains quickly.

"Look after Kelly, she'll be alright now."

He runs along the promenade to his camper, then drives away quickly. Jose watches him go as Tanya joins them.

"Things to do," she says in answer to Tanya's puzzled expression.

They walk back to the flat. Tanya offers to stay, but Jose insists.

"You've done enough and anyway you need to get to work."

Tanya still looks guilty and after she's gone Jose realises her remark could have sounded sarcastically critical, which wasn't her intention. As they reach the lifeboat station it becomes overcast and they walk faster, passing the Plaza quickly in case it rains. Within a few minutes the promenade is enveloped by a murky sky while on the other side of the estuary the sun glints through grey clouds and glistens over the water. The hotel windows dazzle and sparkle, their smooth burnished walls searing into the blackness. Jose looks up, then out to the estuary and back again, awestruck by the stark contrast of light and dark. Black sky and white buildings on this side, on the other piercing sunlight shimmering fierily on the sea. She must capture the moment. It will be gone in minutes as the clouds disperse or their leaden heaviness drifts across to smother the sun. She must paint again.

Sheila Curran lives a couple of miles out of town. She and her husband moved here after Andrea's death. Neither could bear staying in the old house. He died a year ago. She stays for the memories and because she feels secure. It's a small house with a large garden. He was a keen gardener. So is she, but it's too much for her and a man comes in once a week to do the heavy work. That way her pottering can keep it going. She sits in the summerhouse porch, some way down the garden and doesn't hear Vince at the front door. He's sure she's in, her small car is parked in the drive, so wanders around the side and onto the rear patio. She sees him and comes down.

Vince can hardly say he's looking for a painting, which might just include an image of Carina Fennell's killer. He'll have to be a little circumspect, but not too much. He says he's trying to find Lisa Weldon, hoping that's near enough, but not too close.

"Are you a friend of hers?" she says, a hint of disapproval.

"Not exactly," he says, picking this up and trying to distance himself from the woman who might have been responsible for her daughter's death. It's fortunate. He's pitched it about right...or almost.

"Strange, I had the police after her," she says, looking at him suspiciously.

"Er...yes...they..."

"Something to do with Carina Fennell. Can't say I'm surprised, that one's capable of anything. So how are you connected to her?"

"Well...you see...yes, it's not really her as such...you may say she's more of a means to an end."

She eyes him curiously.

"Thing is, I'm really here on behalf of a friend. She's an artist, trying to recover a painting. Yes, well, I know this is all a bit of a roundabout way of going about it... (she stares incredulously, her head cocked to the side, her eyes wide and questioning)...but I thought Lisa Weldon might be able to put me in touch with the man who bought the painting..."

"The one that was stolen from the exhibition?"

"No, but it's the same artist."

Vince expects her to be perplexed, but she nods as if she knows what he's going to say next.

"A man called Harry Willard bought a painting called *The Rocks*."

"And your friend, the artist, she wants it back?"

"Yes...she does."

Sheila's face lights up and Vince is amazed as she beams at him expectantly. Then, without another word, she goes into the house. He waits only a minute or so before she returns with a framed picture under her arm. She sits down and turns it towards him.

"Is this it?"

Not having seen Jose's picture before Vince stares at it carefully.

"You'll be doing me a great favour," she says, "now that Mr. Willard is...he won't be coming."

Vince recognises Venture Rocks, notices the signature and the style is like *Waiting for the Tide* and *Sea and Sand.*

"Harry Willard came here?"

"Oh yes, he wanted to talk about Andrea. You know, my daughter? (Vince nods) Said he was a friend of Carina's, he didn't want to rake up painful memories, but there were things he wanted to get straightened out."

"What sort of things?"

"About how she died. I took it he meant about that Lisa Weldon. He was calm and sympathetic, but I knew he was really quite agitated. He asked if I had a photograph. As it happens I have one of the three girls. Do you want to see it?"

Sheila is anxious to talk and they go into the house. She tells Vince everything she told Harry and shows him her photographs including the one of Andrea, Lisa and Carina together. He's afraid she might get upset, but she's surprisingly relaxed, almost jaunty.

"The triplets they called them," she says, "with good reason."

Vince stares at the photograph, transfixed as much as Kelly is when she looks at Jose's paintings. He asks a few more questions, then hesitates.

"You can go on," she says, "I like to talk about her. I even tried to talk to the police, but they were only interested in whether Harry Willard had been here. He was very interested in Andrea and Lisa, in all three of them. Something was troubling him. Of course he'd just lost Carina, but it was more, there was something else. He didn't stay long though, very nervous. Before he left he asked me to take the painting. I felt sorry for him and like a fool agreed. He said he'd be back soon, but of course he never was. It was only later I realised the significance of the painting and I regretted taking it, but then it was too late. It's the only thing that does upset me."

She nods towards the hall where Vince has left the painting.

"I can't bear to look at it now. I like to remember her as she was not as she...I can't keep something in the house as a constant reminder of where she died. I'll be glad to get rid of it."

"My pleasure to help," Vince says rather limply.

He's unsure what else to say and they sit in silence for a few moments then, having forced such thoughts out of her mind she reverts to something close to cheeriness.

"I told the policeman about the woman outside on the day he came."

"When Harry Willard came?"

"She must have been outside all the time. She drove away immediately after he left."

"Who was it?"

"That's what the policeman wanted to know. She was very quick. I didn't get a good enough look at her. He thought it was Lisa. He told me she's gone away. Asked if I'd seen her. She wouldn't come here, I said...and even if she did I wouldn't be responsible. Anyway I told him she may *supposed* to be away, but she was always very good at *appearing* to be places or not...or *appearing* to be doing things or not...or *appearing* to be somebody she's not. Always was an odd one Lisa, lived in her own private world, could never figure her out even when she was young. They used to meet up in Henbury Woods."

"They?"

"Her and Carina...and sometimes Andrea...secret place they had when they were kids, though Andrea could never understand all that...made up stuff...it was all her, Lisa. I've never been up there since, but I could tell you where it was. I told the police. Said they'd have a look, see if she was up there, but they've not been back so I suppose they couldn't find her."

Jose returns from the front, determined not to let the pied vision of sun, sea and sky disappear like quickly fading dreams when waking up. Black clouds banished and darkened skies cleared, promenade and beach are filled with folk in the glorious sunshine. Kelly has to get out and sits on the balcony, silently immersed in the sea, the hills, the Denzer promontory and the sand, imbibing the afternoon contentedly.

Jose gets out her paints and brushes. It won't be easy. The first three efforts end up as screwed up balls of papers with cries of 'rubbish' as the colours run uncontrollably. Her fourth is more successful, but this too has to be abandoned when she picks out the windows on the hotel badly. She also has trouble with the perspective. The scene demands a subtle curving of the building away from the road without losing the glittering effect of the sun. Then there's the sky, dark, but not quite black, yet deep enough to pull out the contrast with the building. Without it, the whiteness will be flawed and the gleaming effect jeopardised. She tries a fifth time. Somehow she must capture that instant contrasting splendour of radiance and darkness.

She already has a title, *Equal and Opposite*. Light and dark, day and night, the glory of one dependant on the magnificence of the other, but she has to get the perspective right. The eye must hold the contrast and at the same time be drawn into the receding promenade and the distant meeting of sky and sand. She cracks on as the divergence she felt on the front returns. Beneath the black sky above the hotels a glinting brilliance is reflected in the water, then the eye returns to the luminous glitter of the same sun in the walls and windows. Conflicting light within darkness. Struggling darkness in the light. What you see, what you think you see, all enhanced by its opposite. Appearance transforms everything into something else, equal and opposite.

Now she's happy with the composition. It's going to work. She mixes the colours for the sky, very dark, but not quite black, enough to contrast. Tricky but possible, don't mess it up Josephine! She works quickly, pleased with the emerging starkness, wondering what Kelly will make of it. Her new critic interprets so much, seeing Dominic at the 'Warren' and Carina there and at the clock tower. She did see her at the clock tower, didn't she? The woman in red, that had to be Carina.

Kelly comes in, sits on the settee, looks across and asks what Jose is doing. Jose is still engrossed and doesn't look up.

"Just fiddling around," she says, but her attention is not on the picture even though it is coming along well.

Her mind hovers irritatingly near the clock tower. In *Sea and Sand* Jose saw a figure in red and assumed it was the same figure Kelly identified as Carina, but was it? What did Kelly actually say? She and Vince were so excited, did they listen properly?

"You're painting again?" Kelly says, coming to the table.

"I wanted to get down what we saw at the front when it suddenly went very black, the sun on the water, the sky and the whiteness of the hotels..."

"I know, it was great."

Kelly stares intently just as she did at *Sea and Sand*. What did she say? Maybe Jose should get it out for her to see again. Kelly watches her painting and studies the picture.

"I'm being drawn into the centre at the end of the prom and the beach."

"It's called the vanishing point," Jose says, pointing to the spot, "it deliberately draws the eye, everything..."

"...disappears into it."

"Yes, that's right, everything disappears into the vanishing point."

Now Jose remembers. Kelly didn't see a woman in red at the clock tower, what was it she saw?

The bell rings. Kelly starts nervously. It rings again, three times.

"It's okay," Jose says, "it's Vince."

Jose meets him at the door.

"I've just been to see..." he begins, but Jose yanks him into the spare bedroom.

He stands at the door, mystified.

"Just wait there," she says, pulling at the pictures stacked against the wall, adding ominously, "Don't go into the other room, not yet."

He stares in bewilderment as she takes *Sea and Sand* and lays it on the bed.

"Just look at this," she says, beckoning him over, "what do you see?"

"Well, I see the clock tower and the promenade and..."

"No, no, no, the people! What people do you see?"

Vince peers down, screwing his eyes.

"I see a family, two children, an older man, two women and..."

"There, there!" Jose points to the figure in red.

"Yes I see him."

"Him? Him! It's a man."

"Yes, it's a man."

"And here, what is this?"

"A woman, she's in white."

"And that's the woman Kelly said was Carina."

"I can't tell who it is."

"No, neither can I, but *she* said it was Carina."

"Okay, but I don't..."

Jose leaves him staring at the painting while she trips to the lounge and leads a startled Kelly back with her.

"I just want you to look at this picture again," she says, "that figure there, in white, who is it?"

Vince steps back as Kelly looks at the picture carefully. She needs only a few seconds to confirm her earlier interpretation.

"It's Carina Fennell, she's..."

Jose sends her back and then talks to Vince, who has watched this interchange with growing uneasiness.

"See what I mean?" Jose says.

He looks at her blankly.

"Vince! For an intelligent man you can be incredibly obtuse. There's a gap of a couple of hours between the two paintings – I was having my lunch in the 'Warren.' Kelly says she saw Carina outside the 'Warren' dressed in red, but later she identifies a woman dressed in white as Carina. When she was found on the beach she was wearing a red suit."

"So she's changed clothes."

She sighs loudly.

"There's more. You asked her yourself about that figure and she was pretty sure it coming *towards* you, that is from the direction of Venture Rocks."

While Vince studies it again Jose pulls out *Waiting for the Tide* and lays it on the bed.

"Definitely a woman in red there," he says glancing across before turning back to *Sea and Sand*, " the figure in red is definitely a man, even you said..."

"Yes, yes, I know I did. I was too impetuous. Red man, white woman, red woman – it's all about seeing what you want to see. Now do you understand?"

"I'm beginning to."

"We have to talk to Kelly."

He stops her at the door.

"Yes, we do, but there's something she needs to see first."

He steps back and retrieves the painting of *The Rocks* he's left in the hall, then brings it in and places it on the bed beside the others. Jose looks at it in silence for a few moments.

"Where did you get it?" she says, still staring intently at the painting.

Vince explains his visit to Sheila Curran.

"We have to show it to Kelly," she says.

"Yes we do, but there's something else too. I've been up to Henbury Woods."

Stover goes over the mass of information the team has collected on Carina Fennell's financial and programme making activities. There can be no doubt now of major irregularities and the significant questions they throw up. Who knew and of those who had the most to lose by it being divulged? Did they feel threatened by Carina knowing and who was in the best position to stop her? As soon as he reaches a tentative conclusion, putting one of the suspects more clearly in the frame, another emerges to unseat him or her! It should be easier now Harry Willard is no longer around – unless we have two separate murderers. If Harry killed Carina to silence her exposing his financial fiddling (though as yet there's not enough to conclusively prove that he was) who killed him and why? Amanda has not been successful in tracking down Lisa Weldon, but she has a lead on Dominic Mathers. He may be back in town. A further talk with him could be revealing...

The phone rings and the caller surprises him.

"Jose Pearsall?"

"I want to talk to you about how Carina Fennell's body was identified."

Sun, sea, sand and sky – the coming together of fire, water, earth and air always fascinates Vince. After returning from Henbury Woods he parked the camper and wandered along the beach, seduced by their eternal wonder, for a short time unwilling to go up to the flat. Further discoveries are too much like that old life, grubbing around in the struggle to make a great deal out of very little, wearily competing, always leading to a debilitating emptiness. Here he can reflect on the motion of the four elements...he stopped and looked around...all those grubby issues are not distinct, but part of the same revolving process. Suddenly he realised what they know, what they have and how all these issues can be brought to a head. Now he was ready and went quickly up to Jose's flat.

Jose puts the phone down and returns to the balcony where Vince still sits looking down at the front.

"As I thought. Wendy Arbon identified the body."

Vince nods and outlines his plan.

"Alright," she says, "but Kelly needs to see the sketch first. I suppose she's not said anything yet?"

Vince shakes his head. Kelly has been studying *The Rocks* for over an hour. Jose is anxious to talk to her, but Vince cautions patience.

"With time she's sure to see something."

"They're only rocks," Jose whispers as if she speaks in a large empty church.

"She's been right about other things."

"She didn't lead us to the picture at the beach huts."

"She led us to Harry."

Jose shivers.

"So she doesn't always get it exactly right, just vague feelings."

"Wait and see."

Desperate not to disturb whatever 'communications' might come to Kelly, they stay on the balcony. Out of earshot and out of sight, they speak quietly, almost conspiratorially, even cupping their hands away from the door, though with their voices carried by the wind away from the building there's no possibility she'll hear them. Jose adds her modifications to Vince's plan. Even then she can hardly believe the conclusions they've reached.

"Why did Carina come to Darrasea early before they started making the programme?" she says, "To escape from something or somebody?"

Vince shakes his head.

"That's what I thought at first, but not now. What if she wasn't escaping at all, but came to find somebody?"

Kelly calls out, but they can't distinguish the words. They get up and go into the lounge, where she still sits with the painting in front of her.

"I see them," she says as they come to the table, "Look, there!"

They lean across and peer at the painting.

"It's a good view of the rocks," Vince says

"But only the rocks," Jose says, "I don't see anyone."

"They are there!" Kelly screeches, stabbing the painting at a point near its centre."

"How many?" Vince says.

"Three. Three girls."

"You're sure, three young girls?"

"Yes."

"Okay," he says, looking at Jose, "It's alright."

"But I don't see..." Jose says as Vince pulls her away from the table.

"It's enough she sees them. Now, have you got those sketches?"

Jose goes to the bedroom and rummages through the collection of sketches she's made at the 'Warren' over the last few months. She takes her time and Kelly leaves the table to sit beside Vince.

"I do see them," she says almost apologetically, "But you don't see anyone?"

"No, I don't and neither does Jose, but don't worry about it. I believe you and if you see them, that's all that matters. And are they...I mean...do you see them...more than..."

"You mean do I see them moving?"

"Yes."

"Sometimes, but only their bodies or their arms swaying, they are standing still."

"And can you recognise one of them, is it..."

"It could be Carina Fennell."

"But you're not sure?"

"It's near where they found her, isn't it. Am I seeing her being murdered...is that what it is...God it's so scary, tell me is that what it is...is it?"

"None of them move around?"

"No."

"Then it's alright...but one of them could be Carina?"

"Yes."

Kelly stares at him, her wide eyes puzzled and fearful. He pats her hand and smiles. She's slightly reassured. Jose comes in with some of the sketches and sifts through them, eventually picking out one, which she examines and then turns towards Kelly.

"I think this is the one, it should..."

Kelly's sudden intake of breath stops her short.

"You recognise her?" Jose says.

Kelly nods.

"That face...I've seen somebody like that..."

"Don't say anything! She has to be sure." Jose says to Vince, then turning to Kelly, "Who do you think this is?"

Kelly stares for a few moments, concentrating intently to make absolutely certain. Then she nods with slow deliberation.

"It's very much like her...like in the painting of the rocks... I think it's Carina Fennell."

Jose goes back to the bedroom and returns with *Restful Haven*, the picture stolen from the art exhibition, in which Kelly had first 'seen' Carina. Kelly stares at it, wondrously tracing her fingers across the images of the church and the trees.

"Do you still see her?" Jose says.

"Yes, yes, she's still there, see..."

Kelly points to what seems a small splash of red beside one of the trees, hardly recognisable as a person, let alone a particular individual. Yet even that Jose can't remember seeing before, though she must have painted it. Kelly sees it as Carina, so Jose must accept that Carina had been there in the morning at the church.

"Where did you get it?" Kelly says.

"Vince got it."

Kelly seems satisfied, though Jose feels she ought to reply to the unasked question.

"He found it at Henbury Woods."

Kelly nods as if this is what she's known all along, requiring no further explanation. She continues to cradle the painting avidly as if meeting up with a long lost friend. Jose indicates to Vince and they retire back to the balcony.

"How *did* you find *Restful Haven*?" she says.

"I told you at Henbury Woods."

"But where did you know where to look?"

"Sheila Curran told me when she talked about the girls original hideout."

"It's amazing it was still there, but what about the police if they'd been there before?"

"Some things don't change and anyway it looked like the hideout had been recently remade. It's no doubt where she's been. The police were looking for Lisa Weldon, not the painting. They'd be soon gone when they didn't find her, but I had a feeling the painting would be there. All I had to do was look a bit more carefully. So now we have everything we need. You've told Stover?"

"Yes."

"Then the trap is ready to set. What about the newspaper?"

"I'll ring them now. There's much to be done. First you have to get back to Henbury Woods. I'll talk to Kelly."

"Will she cooperate?"

"We're sunk if she doesn't."

"The continuing story of Jose Pearsall's painting 'Restful Haven', stolen from Edward Hall shows no sign of abating.

The mystery woman, who said she saw Carina Fennell in the picture has contacted Mrs Pearsall, saying she has 'recovered' the missing picture. "I got this strange phone call from someone calling herself Kelly," said Mrs. Pearsall, "She wouldn't say whether she'd stolen my picture and rang off when I said I wanted it back. I was sure this was no hoax and she really had my picture. I'm determined to get it back, but I've made it as easy as I can for the girl to return it without any acrimony. I know where she hangs out, but as she can't be contacted in the normal way I left a letter with a mutual acquaintance with details where she can leave it in a neutral place. I'm not sure what game she's playing because she's since phoned to say she's lost the details. I've repeated them to her, but I'm wondering if she's really serious. If she doesn't turn up with the painting I shall be forced to take further action."

Tanya's in the 'Warren,' waiting for Jose and is a little early. She skims through the rest of the Darrasea Advertiser, but finds nothing to grab her attention. That's not a reflection on the rest of the news, for she's too excited with Jose's statement to concentrate on anything else. With some amusement she wonders what readers will make of Jose's 'further action.'

"An interesting story."

Tanya puts the paper down. Wendy Arbon is sitting opposite.

"Intriguing too. Is Jose confident Kelly will be there?"

Tanya hesitates, looking quizzically, before recognising her.

"Oh yes, she'll be there."

"It's just that in the paper Jose seems doubtful...and there seems to be some confusion about how they will meet."

"Not really, but it's best not everybody knows the details."

"That's quite understandable, you don't want the whole town turning up."

"Oh, that wouldn't happen, it's not very well known and at that time of night..."

"...that time?"

"Nine o' clock."

"So not everybody would know how to get there?"

"The old abandoned beach huts behind the Meadows – it's a lonely place...and at that time..."

"Yes...of course."

They talk about topical issues of local politics and after exchanging a few pleasantries Wendy leaves. Tanya tells Jose when she arrives.

"I think she went away quite satisfied, probably thought she'd wheedled it out of me quite well."

"I'm sure she did," Jose says with a titter, "just as much as you wanted her too."

Despite her bustling assurance, Jose had only been half confident of Vince's plan when she approached the newspaper. Not only were there many things to go wrong, one of the key players was not yet completely on board. Since running away from the flat, Kelly's anxieties returned. She kept talking about her mysterious pursuer on the beach and wouldn't go out on her own again. She was happiest with Jose's paintings, staring and examining them for hours. They seemed to give back some of the security she'd lost. Jose had to tell her of the plan. She tried to skirt round Kelly's part, but had to say something.

"Of course, you won't be on your own, there'll always be somebody with..."

Kelly said nothing. Jose found that more alarming than if she'd thrown a wobbler. When she came back from the newspaper she sat down with Kelly again, schooling her in her role. Kelly was nervous, constantly having to be reassured she 'wouldn't be alone' and only gradually accepting her involvement. Then she suddenly refused to take part.

"We can't do it without you," Jose said.

The process had to start again and time was running out, but by the time Vince returned Kelly had settled again. Jose went to meet Tanya and Vince stayed with Kelly, nursing concerns of his own.

Henbury Common and Woods were deserted when he arrived. He'd felt exposed and nervous, doing what he had to do as quickly as possible. He was like a schoolboy with a writhing stomach, on some mischievous prank, any moment afraid he would be discovered. He was sure he wasn't alone. Yet every time he looked around he saw no one, until he got back to the car and caught sight of a man in his wing mirror. Then, when he looked round he'd gone. Vince drove away quickly.

By eight thirty everybody is in place. Vince cleared out one of the derelict beach huts in the morning so it's now reasonably habitable. Kelly sits just inside the open door. Leaning against the outside wall, neatly wrapped in brown paper, is a thin rectangular parcel. Vince and Jose are concealed in the hedgerows behind the huts. If all their assumptions are correct, all the arrangements carried out efficiently and the bait has been taken, the object of the operation should soon approach. As they wait Jose goes over in her mind all the preparations, the newspaper, the interpretation of the paintings, Vince's visit to Henbury Woods, above all what she said to Stover and what he's told her. Have they forgotten anything, have they done everything properly, what can go wrong?

The sun is low though there's still enough light. They will be able to see, won't they? She wants to say something to Vince, hear him agree with her, reassure her, but she's afraid to speak. They can't afford to alert anyone to their presence now. What if someone else comes along, an innocent stranger exercising his dog away from the usual haunts, what if he gets caught up at the crucial moment, disturbing their quarry, what then? They've not allowed for this, what can they do to make sure no one comes along? She glances each way, seeing nothing but the trees, the grass, the hedges, the flowers. She listens. All is quiet. Or is it, she hears disparate unrecognisable sounds. Birds, the wind, the grass, footsteps, breathing? Is she imagining things? She looks at Vince. He doesn't stir. She looks to the back of the beach huts. She can't see Kelly! Vince said if they see Kelly anyone else will see them. She needs to talk to him again. She looks one way and then the other and then each way again. She sees something...a shadow and then hears something...the whispering of the wind. There's a persistent dull sound like footsteps...heavy...a rhythmic thudding...what is it...only the beating of her own heart!

Here, behind the front they can't see the sea. It unnerves her. Now she knows how reassuring it is and how she misses it. Like embarking on a dangerous journey without an old friend. She'd feel much safer in the open, on the beach or even in the dunes, but in such a conspicuous place they'd never attract their quarry. Another sound...from the front of the hut...then a movement, a glancing shadow. It's Kelly. What's she doing!

She looks around, then towards them. She'll give them away! Vince waves and pushes his hand towards her. She shrugs, then goes back inside. Vince turns to Jose and sighs. Then, over his shoulder she sees the figure walking stealthily in a zig zag fashion at the side rather than on the path beside the cricket ground. Someone who doesn't want to be seen. Vince pulls back and crouches down, motioning Jose to do the same. Has Kelly seen him, will she hold her nerve at this crucial time?

The figure reaches the end of the path. As it turns towards the huts they can see it's a man. Vince turns to Jose with a silent reminder to be ready. Then, as they both recognise Dominic Mathers, Vince grimaces and edges forward slightly. Only a few metres from the hut, Dominic stops. They can't see Kelly so don't know if she has seen him too. She's made no sound. That's probably good. It means she's keeping calm.

"You have the painting," Dominic calls, then steps forward.

Kelly doesn't reply. Dominic moves quickly and in a few strides he's out of view.

"Damn!" Vince cries and lunges forward, through the undergrowth, into the open. Jose follows.

They hear Kelly cry "Leave it!" as they run round either side of the hut. Dominic has picked up the parcel. Kelly has stood up and is tugging at the other end.

"Where are the others?" he says.

"There are no others and you can put that down," Vince says.

Dominic turns to him.

"You took the other painting from my sister, the one at the pub."

"Your sister stole it from me!" Jose shouts, pulling the parcel from behind him.

Dominic turns to her, but he's too late. Jose has the parcel and hands it back to Kelly.

"What's so important about the painting at the pub?" Vince says, "Afraid it'll show you there on the day Carina died?"

"What if it does?"

"Didn't want Carina to know you were in town?"

"Could be, it's nothing to do with you. In any case..."

"Carina is dead?"

"No...of course...but then, well..."

"Doesn't mean you're off the hook. In fact it could be even more sinister – like you were around on the day she was killed?"

Dominic backs away.

"No, no, I didn't..."

"Why not, you had every reason...?"

"Shut up Vince!" Jose cuts in as she hears more footsteps tripping along the path.

Vince looks round, but sees no one. The footsteps have stopped. He turns back to Dominic aggressively, but speaks softly.

"How did you know Kelly was here?"

"Because I told him."

While they've argued Wendy Arbon has stepped up.

"It had to be him!" she shouts, pointing to Dominic, "snivelling, conniving shit!"

"You said they'd have *my* picture. All that guff in the paper, you said it was just dross, they'd be doing a deal and exchange my picture for this one."

Dominic points to Jose and the parcel Kelly holds.

"Where is it? Where's the other one, where's my picture?"

"It's not your picture," Jose says.

"It was you all along," Wendy shouts, "You killed Carina."

Dominic moves closer to Kelly, who steps back nervously into the hut, still clutching the parcel.

"Get away from her," Vince says, coming between them.

Wendy comes across and starts berating Dominic again. Frightened and confused, Kelly edges to the side of the hut and slips out, still clutching the parcel. Jose doesn't notice her as she also turns on Wendy.

"You identified the body," Dominic says.

"Yes, you did," Jose says, wagging her finger, "You may have a lot to answer for."

Wendy steps back from both her and Dominic. Vince looks at his watch apprehensively. It's almost nine o' clock.

"What the hell do you mean?" Wendy says.

"Get her out of here," Vince says.

"Who else did you tell?" Jose says.

"I don't know what you're talking about."

"Jose!" Vince calls, tapping his watch, "Get her away!"

Suddenly Jose realises, but she's unsure what to do. Dominic, who's never stopped looking at the parcel, suddenly sidles past her and tries to grab it. Kelly cries out and steps away sharply. Vince sees it, but can't get round Wendy.

"Quick!" he shouts to Jose, but Wendy pushes in front of her.

Dominic lunges again. Kelly grabs the parcel and putting it tightly under her arm runs onto the path, then very fast across the Meadows towards the road. Jose turns, but bumps into Wendy. Vince also tries to get to her, but only succeeds in knocking Dominic into the hut and falling himself. By the time he gets up, Kelly has already reached the road. Jose has Wendy by the collar, but is looking away from her bewilderingly towards the road. Dominic starts to get up. Vince pushes him back down with his foot.

"Leave her," he says to Jose, "Come on, before it's too late!"

He grips Jose's arm and snatches her away from Wendy, then runs into the Meadows, pulling her after him. They race together towards the road, though by now Kelly has reached the other side and is sprinting along the promenade towards the sand dunes. They have to wait at the road for the traffic to clear, all the time scanning the dunes for any sign of Kelly.

"Damn! Damn! Damn!" Vince shrieks as they wait, "It's all going wrong!"

"I can see her. Look!"

Kelly's head bobs up and down as she scampers across the top of the dunes. The road clears. They run across and along the promenade, though as they reach the dunes Kelly has disappeared again. Vince leaps over the wall and clambers up the steep sides of the dunes, slipping and slithering as he desperately claws at the grass. He slips again, but Jose is behind and pushes him back up. Gradually they scrabble up together and stand slightly breathless at the top of the dunes. The beach is deserted. They scan it desperately, then see Kelly running on the hard sand near the sea towards Venture rocks.

"Come on," Vince says, "We'll catch her quicker along the road."

He scrambles to the end of the dunes, then slides down, vaults the wall again and runs along the promenade. Jose follows a little slower, so she can keep watching Kelly and make sure she doesn't change direction. Once she's sure she runs down to join Vince, not noticing the other figure running along the beach. Keeping to the road while Kelly labours on the sand, Vince shortens the distance between them. Always holding Kelly in her sight, Jose is not far behind, afraid they might lose her as the jumble of rocks comes into view. Kelly scrambles over the first rocks, at first picking her feet carefully, which slows her down, then as she tries to go faster, she falls down. Jose calls, but Kelly doesn't hear.

"What's she doing?" she says to Vince as she catches up, "Why doesn't she come back to the road, we've blown it now anyway."

"We'll have to go down and fetch her," he says.

Then Jose sees the woman reaching the rocks and making for Kelly.

"My God! It's her. Vince, it's her!"

They run towards the rocks. It's hard going. Once beyond the sand and shingle, it's impossible to move quickly without snagging their shoes in the crevices or sliding on the smooth stones. Kelly turns to her pursuer, horrified and baffled.

"It's you," she says, "You are in the picture at the rocks. No one else sees you, but I do and I know."

"How can you know?" the woman says.

"I just *know*."

"You weren't there. It's so long ago..."

"I don't have to be. The picture doesn't lie. I see what was. I see the three girls. You were there. You killed her!"

Jose and Vince are close enough now to see them both clearly. The woman also sees them. She suddenly grabs Kelly from behind, takes a knife from her pocket and holds it at her throat.

"Don't come any closer!" she shouts.

They stop instinctively.

"Stop, stop, wait for me."

Wendy is clambering along the rocks towards them. Jose turns, but Vince only glances back before moving on.

"It wasn't me," Wendy shouts, "I didn't tell her. I don't even know her, I wouldn't tell her what Tanya told me."

"Of course it wasn't you," Jose says, "but you do know her – know her much more than the body you failed to recognise in the mortuary. She didn't get here because of what anybody told her. The papers have had a running commentary on everything since we first found the body. We knew she'd read the latest instalment and we knew she'd been hiding in Henbury Woods. So we only had to leave the details for her to find. Vince went back to the hideout and left an old purse. I stuffed it with items, apparently belonging to Kelly to make it look like she'd been up there. All innocuous stuff except for a letter I'd sent to Kelly indicating the time and place of the meeting. Of course, the letter was never sent, it was never meant to be, anymore than we had any of those daft telephone conversations reported in the paper. It was all to set the scene and it worked...only too damned well!"

Wendy looks towards Kelly and the woman, startled, but blank and mystified.

"Don't you see yet?" Jose says, "Look at her!"

With her eyes Wendy recognises the woman, but her mind refuses to believe. Putting her hands to her face, she calls.

"Carina!"

"Yes, Carina."

"But I..."

"Identified her as the body. You recognised what you thought was Carina. The face was so bashed and battered it was easy to see what you thought it was, especially if it was a face very much like Carina's. A face you didn't know, but Carina did, for they called them the triplets."

"Carina," Wendy mumbles, "she's alive, but then who..."

"The other girl, the one who took the blame, Lisa Weldon."

"But Carina, what did..."

"...is what we were hoping to prove, but we've messed it up or rather you and Dominic have. We had to get her here and we knew Kelly would draw her. Telling you was just insurance, in case Carina didn't figure it out. Besides I wondered if you'd been involved all along, feeding her information..."

"I had no idea. What have I done, identifying Carina when it was..."

Vince has got close to Kelly and Carina.

"Don't come any nearer," Carina shouts, gripping Kelly even tighter.

"Leave her," he says, "it's all over now anyway."

"Is it? Then I've got nothing to lose."

"Don't be stupid."

"I thought if I could get the picture, the one she saw me in...but I was in them all, wasn't I? Is that how you knew?"

"Not at first, but the pictures don't lie."

"I should have destroyed the damned picture."

"It was that red suit of yours. Kelly saw you in it at the church and the pub, but in the picture painted at the clock tower a couple of hours later Kelly saw you in white. That was after you'd discarded the red suit. In that two hours you killed Lisa and exchanged clothes with her. When Jose painted you at the clock tower you were on your way back."

Carina stares at him intently. The clear bright eyes, the soft pinky complexion, the gentle curve of the lips, the subtly appealing blend of beauty and kindly warmth – he can see the magnetic, haunting allure that drew them all – Dominic, Harry, her millions of fans. Yet lurking beneath the attractive exterior is an unsettled, even frightened girl, still encumbered by the trauma of her past.

"Clever," Carina says, "very clever, but you couldn't have been sure it was me."

"Putting together what Kelly knew with what I knew made me sure," Jose says, coming up beside Vince, "I remembered a face that seemed like yours. At first I thought I'd really seen you before, especially when we learned about your background in the town. Had I sketched you along with dozens of others? Did you come back one day and slip into the 'Warren?' It nagged me, but I couldn't believe it really had been you. I had to be sure. I got out the sketches I'd never sold and there it was, staring back at me, not you, but like you. I showed it to Kelly. It had the same effect on her. It was like you, but she wasn't sure, it could be...but it may not be. So it had to be someone like you. The police were looking for Lisa Weldon, your old schoolfriend, who mysteriously disappeared. Was it her, was there some dreadful secret you shared that had come back?"

"There was a secret, wasn't there?" Vince says, "the secret of what really happened to the third of the trio, Andrea Cullen. Tell us about when you were young girls and the imaginary world you lived in."

Carina's eyes, up to now for all their attractiveness, hard and tense, relax slightly, becoming wistful, though pained.

"We played out future lives in our imaginary worlds and for Andrea...she never really shared our fantasies or our dreams, but for me and Lisa they were as real as the sandcastles on the beach."

"But sandcastles get washed by the tide or blown away by the wind," Jose says.

"So it was for Lisa. She never made it, only I got away and became a success. I think she always resented that."

"But what happened that day at the rocks all those years ago?" Vince says, "You were there weren't you?"

"Yes, if course I was there," she says angrily, the tension returning to her face, "That bloody fool Andrea, she wouldn't be quiet. Her and Lisa were always jealous of each other. I don't know what it was about. They'd been rowing about something trivial. I'd had enough. Andrea had been mewing for ages in that pathetic whine of hers. I kept telling her to shut up. She wouldn't. I pushed her. She slipped and fell onto the rocks, banging her head. I was glad, you know, I was really glad, even when Lisa said she might be dead. Then I came to. I panicked. I screamed. Lisa had to calm me down. 'It'll be alright,' she said, 'it's an accident, they'll understand. Leave it to me.' I ran away. Later I heard she'd said she'd been alone with Andrea. She was so worried about me she took all the blame.'

'After that it was easy to let things go on, say nothing, allow people to make assumptions, not speak up when your friend is being vilified. I was a coward. I couldn't face it. Suddenly I was the victim, almost like Andrea. I learnt the lesson that silence and the right look can carry you a long way. I've been doing it ever since. But I had to leave. I couldn't stay. Lisa left too. I thought she'd died years ago, but she came back. I never did. We never saw each other again, not until..."

"...you decided to make one of your programmes here?"

"It crossed my mind not to do it, but then I thought 'what the hell, it's a long time?' Then she rang me. 'You're not coming to Darrasea.' 'Why not?' I said. 'You can't, you have no right, you forfeited your origins years ago.' That's what she said. 'Forfeited your origins."

Carina repeats the phrase several times, gradually quieter, slower.

"I refused of course. She rang off. I thought no more of it, but she rang again. Still I refused. She was being ridiculous. But she resented me, you see. None of the dreams of her childhood had materialised, hers was a life of bitter disappointment and every time she heard of me it reminded her of our young days and how we'd dreamed and talked and laughed and...but it wasn't for her. She could take it as long as she didn't see me, but my coming back to Darrasea was too much. It was as if I was transgressing hallowed ground."

She laughs, but then stops abruptly.

"I had to come down and sort it out. I couldn't find her at first. She was like a lot of people in this town, everywhere and nowhere, constantly flitting about, never in one place very long. Then we met up, walked along the front. I tried to reason with her, but she wouldn't have it. I had to leave, get away and never come back. 'What about the programme?' I said. 'You can sort that out,' she said, 'you can sort out anything the way you twist people round your little finger.' I was walking away. It was pointless going on.'

'I'll tell everybody,' she said, 'They'll all know and it'll ruin you. Where will the great and gorgeous Carina Fennell be then? Your success isn't real, it's based on lies, you're still living out those big ideas when you were a girl, but there's one big lie."

"Isn't that true?" Jose says.

Carina looks into the distance, above and beyond Jose, just as her mind isn't with her, but pursues another, separate course.

"All my success was artificial, nothing was real and it had never brought me happiness. 'You stopped being happy that day on these rocks.' She'd tell. She had nothing to lose. 'No one would believe you,' I said. She just laughed, 'Try me.' I snapped, picked up a stone and hit her. I kept hitting. It was good. I kept hitting and hitting and it felt better and better... battering the past, hammering out everything she said. Her face...it was...so then I changed clothes and..."

She looks back at them, her eyes empty, not cold, dejected as if she's trying to hold onto something, but doesn't know what it is.

"Did you steal *Restful Haven* because of what Kelly saw?" Jose says.

"I had to, I didn't know what it might lead to."

"And you had to get rid of Harry for the same reason?"

"He always knew too much, ferreting about when he shouldn't have done. It was bad enough this girl seeing me in that picture, then when I knew he'd bought two more pictures..."

"All the pictures gave you away and not just you. Dominic was afraid too."

Carina laughs.

"One of many, he was pathetic."

Vince moves a little closer.

"Let Kelly go, it's over. We don't want another Harry."

Carina's eyes start suddenly, her lips stiffen and she grips Kelly tightly again, the knife ominously close to her neck.

"No! You are all like her, like Lisa."

The knife is pressed even closer. Vince and Jose freeze, powerless. Wendy screams. Then Carina is knocked sideways as Stover dives and wrenches Kelly away from her. Amanda follows, pushing Carina away, then trying to grab her, but she's too quick and leaps over the rocks out of her grasp. Yet with so much speed, she loses her balance and totters precariously on other rocks. Amanda tries to follow, but gets her foot caught in the gap and has to step back to regain her balance. Meanwhile Stover has got Kelly off the rocks where she joins Vince and Jose.

"Where did you come from?" Jose says.

"From the end of the prom. Action rather than words."

"Was I right?" she says.

"Yes, we've checked the dental records as you suggested. It is the body of Lisa Weldon."

"Maybe you should have done that earlier."

"We had a positive identification," he says, glancing at Wendy, "You shouldn't have started this on your own."

"You wouldn't you have believed us," Vince says, then grudgingly, "But I'm glad you're here."

"That's down to you," Stover says, "I was suspicious. The piece in the newspaper didn't ring true. Then Jose rang and we checked. I had a hunch you'd be up to something. We've been watching you for some time. When you went up to Henbury Woods I wondered if we'd missed something the first time. I found the purse and the letter you'd so carefully left."

"So it was *you* I saw."

"I put the purse and letter back. We had the time and place."

"We never saw you," Vince says ruefully.

"We kept well out of sight, which was when we saw Carina."

Amanda tries once more to get to Carina, but stops again as she slips and slides on the rocks. Stover calls to her.

"Keep still and wait for back up," then mutters, "We'll get her."

Behind Carina is a sheer drop to the sand and he's afraid if they attempt to reach her, she may panic and fall over the edge.

"I could go down, around these rocks and get onto the beach the way you came," Vince says and starts to move.

Stove stops him.

"She's not going anywhere."

But Carina has seen Vince move. Whether that decides her or whether she has already made up her mind they will never know.

"Lisa was right," she says, "I left my real life behind and exchanged it for a false one of glitter and coloured cardboard, but it's the only one I know. I can't go back and I can't go forward. I've made my life and I can't make any other."

Then she turns and jumps over the edge. By the time they slither and crawl over the rocks, she's picked herself up on the soft sand below and is running towards the sea. Vince, Stover, Amanda and Jose scramble down, but they're too slow and she's already paddling into the water. She doesn't look back and keeps going in, the water soon reaching her waist.

"It's not safe for swimming here," Vince says as they run down the beach, "the current is strong."

Carina keeps walking. The sun is almost at the horizon and sends long streaks of gold across the water, sea and sky coalescing in a glittering ball. The others reach the water. Blinded by the dazzling rays they can hardly see her, but their eyes are drawn to the point where sea, sky and sun meet. The water reaches her neck as the sun sinks faster. As it slides below the horizon, she vanishes.

Cross Cut

ISBN 978-0-9557928-0-9

"All darkness now. Silence, then the sounds again, scratching, voices. Someone is close, very close as if they're breaking through to him..."

Where is Bernard Weston? Is he dead or alive? How is his disappearance connected to the campaign to reopen the brooding and abandoned Cross Cut canal?

For Detective Chief Inspector Jenner a routine missing person enquiry quickly turns into something more sinister with the present dislocated against the turbulent background of 1840s Nottingham. Trusting his instincts as much to reason and logic and teaming up with Ettie Rodway with her psychic insight, he's forced to adopt unconventional methods. Combining their skills of intuition and deduction produces a powerful partnership, but this is stretched to breaking point as they try to avert disaster.

Looming ominously throughout this tense thriller is the foreboding atmosphere of the canal with its shrouded secrets and the fearful power of its tunnel to reach across time.

Can Jenner trust his gut feelings and take a path he's reluctant to go down? How much can Ettie risk her own safety to help him? Can they unravel the crime only in the present or must they step into the past?

Cross Cut is historical novel meets thriller, ricocheting through time, keeping the reader guessing to the end with its dark alleys, riots, foreboding tunnels and caves, gaslit docksides, terrifying train journeys and nerve racing pursuits across town and country, vividly recreating the desperate world of the past.

Out of Time

ISBN 978-0-9557928-1-6

"...a tall angular figure appears, dressed all in black with sharp penetrating eyes, a long nose and short black hair ... she flies around the whole circle, accompanied by the ear splitting clamour of the birds and the whoosh of her black cloak, pointing her finger in menacing jabs..."

International financier Sarah Layman wants to discuss a 'mystery' with freelance journalist Carla Diemer, which has nothing to do with finance. Carla arrives to find Sarah dead and is immediately embroiled in a murder investigation led by the dogged Chief Inspector Jenner.

Carla links up with psychic investigator Ettie Rodway, who has also been approached by Sarah. Joining them is a maverick historian, obsessed with a lost Anglo Saxon Chronicle and Carla's dubiously motivated father. Their perilous search of revenge, discovery and intrigue spans 1200 years, from the perilous wetlands of eastern England to the shrouded hills of the west and even to America, pitting them against forces of power, greed and deception.

From the 9th century they must find a ring, a sword, a brooch and a belt, which can solve the mystery, but also unlock immense unpredictable powers, sweeping them into the swirling currents of a distant age where fearsome warriors fight out their bloody inter family feud. Confronted by ruthless adversaries intent on the same discovery further deaths follow, the hunters become the hunted and they realise the Chronicle is much more than an obscure historical document.

A riveting quest, combining mystery, thriller, detection, historical drama and the interplay of past and present, Out of Time unravels against this tense atmosphere, penetrating to the heart of origins and identities in which friend and foe are difficult to disentangle. Once the past's magical powers are invoked, all the pieces have to be fitted together against a frightful deadline in which Time could itself be the ultimate victim.

...only those that dream can return from the far journey...

Wake Us Tomorrow

ISBN 978-0-9557928-3-0

...Never have so many reached so high, then fallen so low in so short a time...

June 1381. The fate of the nation is in the balance. The peasant army occupies London and confronts the king in Smithfield, threatening to bring down the whole edifice of medieval society...except this is not the 14th century, but now and the Great Revolt is suddenly brought back to life on the streets of the capital.

A year later psychic Ettie Rodway gets a call from Warren Grover, convinced he has made contact with Grindcobb, 14th century local leader in St. Albans.

Meanwhile film director Chris Pleasant's project to bring the terrible story to the screen is running into trouble, disturbed by peculiar interruptions and appearances on the set, while screenwriter Charley Kennet demands the inclusion of additional scenes to take in the St. Albans events.

Ettie agrees to meet Warren, but finding him murdered determines to mount her own enquiry, overlapping with Chief Inspector Jenner's own investigation. But Warren's death is only the beginning as events in past and present frighteningly come together. The demolition of a 14th century house unleashes unpredictable forces and a mysterious 'falling man' is constantly seen in the area.

...Back in 1981 on the exact 600th anniversary Warren staged a dramatisation of the local Revolt and the victim of a further murder is also linked to that re-enactment. While unravelling this they are beset by a renegade outlaw from 1381, as the pivotal anniversary of the Revolt's climax draws near. The mysteries of the present can only be solved within the frightful events of 600 years ago and the film changes from pretence to a dreadful re-run of the real past.

...we will always be with you...for we only sleep, but if you forget what we have done our sleep will be forever. Truly remember and wake us tomorrow into those truer, freer days...

Rivenland

ISBN 978-0-9557928-4-7

...England in 1645 is a country riven by three years of civil war...

Captain Matthew Fletcher is seriously wounded the previous year and teeters between life and death. He spends the winter in London and by the spring has recovered, but permanently disabled he cannot return to active service in the Parliamentary army. Instead he reluctantly accepts an assignment to assist local magnate Joseph Manning to investigate strange disturbances in his village of Harringstead.

He arrives to find Manning's steward murdered and the local minister convinced it is the work of witches, while the village is ripped apart by land disputes and family feuds. Needing to find one of Manning's servants and his daughter's secret lover, Matthew is pulled back to war torn London, full of rumour, conspiracy and peculiar religious sects. Assisted by his streetwise ex corporal, Ezra he delves into its seedy and desperate underworld, is driven into the hands of the desperate 'clubmen' and has to confront disturbing reminders of his own past.

Tensions reach fever pitch in Harringstead, his assistant goes missing and Matthew must think again whether one of the 'witches' conceals dangerous secrets. Following another murder Matthew is accused of being a Royalist spy, relentlessly pursued across town and country and seized by his old enemy from the army.

Set against the shattering conflict of the civil war *Rivenland* is a tense story of detection, intrigue and mystery.